GERONIMO

JOSEPH BRUCHAC

SCHOLASTIC PRESS • NEW YORK

ACKNOWLEDGMENTS

My interest in Geronimo's life, an epic tale that has been told and mistold many times, began over forty years ago when I first read his as-told-to story. My understanding was deepened not just by the years of research that followed, but also by Apache people who helped me see the old man's journey of resistance and survival in more human terms.

Swift Eagle (Pueblo/Apache) was the first to patiently try to explain things to the very eager and innocent young man I was then. Michael Lacapa (White Mountain Apache) taught me more in one day on his reservation than I could have learned in a decade on my own.

Harry Mithlo (Chiricahua), direct descendant of Fun, read my manuscript several times and offered generous advice. He may not know how honored I felt when he said my tale rang true to stories passed down in his family.

Michael Darrow (Chiricahua), Fort Sill Apache historian, advised me not to use the word "warriors" to refer to Geronimo and those others who fought so passionately for life and land because it is not a word or concept in Chiricahua language. You'll also not find "renegades" or "raiders" in my text as I've tried to echo the Chiricahua language in the words of my narrator.

I also must thank the places. Place your feet where things happened and your perspective changes. You feel the spirits of those places—some uplifting, some heavy as a weight that will never leave your shoulders. I still have on my shelf a red stone from the old parade ground of Fort Apache and I will never forget the way those ancient shadows flow down at sunset in the Dragoon Mountains or how the Atlantic looks at dawn through the battlements of that Florida fort, or the stone eagle that stands above Geronimo's grave at Fort Sill.

This is a novel, but little in it is fiction. With the exception of my main character and his parents, the people and events can be found in the written and oral histories of the period. My narrator is, however, based on several real Chiricahua boys who survived and grew to manhood in the Apache prisoner-of-war camps of Florida, Alabama, and Oklahoma. Because I've relied on primary sources (including newspaper accounts and the stories still being shared by those Chiricahuas whose ancestors lived these things), I have not always agreed with a number of well-known "facts" about Geronimo, including some in the famous as-told-to autobiography that is not completely Geronimo's "own story." I hope—not for my own sake but to honor those who lived this story of courage and betrayal, honor, and sacrifice—that I have done well in my telling. Geronimo's story parallels not just what happened to other native people in the past, but also the world in which we live today. It is, as in Geronimo's time, a world in which we need to recognize our friends while respecting those whose cultures differ from our own.

To all those who have
fought for their country.

CONTENTS

One day Badger came up to his friend Coyote with a bag.

"What is in that bag?" Coyote asked. "Can I help you carry it?"

"I will let you carry this bag," Badger said. "I have to go do something. But do not open it while I am gone."

Coyote took the bag while Badger went off to do something. "If I am not supposed to open this bag," Coyote said, "then I should look inside it so that I can know what it is I am not supposed to look at."

So Coyote opened the bag. As soon as he did so, it got darker. Inside that bag were many other bags. Coyote began to open them, one by one. Each time he opened another bag, it got even darker. Finally he had opened all the bags and let out all the darkness. It was so dark even Coyote could not see.

That is how darkness came into the world. It was because of Coyote.

GERONIMO'S ANGER

FORT SILL, 1908

Geronimo, they say to you,

You! You!

They call you again and again.

CHIRICAHUA APACHE SONG

WHERE IS IT?" he growled, holding out one hand that was clenched as if it held a knife. "Where?"

He seemed to grow taller and more menacing with each step. There was anger in Geronimo's eyes as he stalked toward me.

There had been a time when few who saw such anger survived it. Even now, more than twenty years after his last surrender, the whisper of his name in Sonora or Chihuahua could bring fear to the hearts of the Mexicans who had been his bitterest enemies. That is what my friend Al Capron told me. He had traveled to Mexico before he was posted to Fort Sill.

Mothers in Old Mexico, Al said, had only to softly mention his name. "If you do not do as I say, Geronimo the Apache will get you." Then even the stubbornest child would behave.

"Who has tried to deceive me?" he growled as he came even closer. "They may have taken me from my land. They may have tried to kill me, but they could not."

He held up his right hand to show how his third finger was bent back from being struck by a bullet. Then he thumped his palm against his chest, his shoulder, his thigh, touching places where bullets and knives had pierced his flesh in the past, where scars showed how hard it was to kill Geronimo. There were more than fifty of those old healed places to be seen, though not as many as the wounds that would never heal, those not in his flesh, but in his long memory.

"They may have killed my family, but I have survived all their tricks. My power has been too great for them. Ha! They may try to deceive me, but they will not succeed. Instead I will dance *haskegojital*, the angriness dance. I will go and take death from the enemy. Is it here behind my pillow?" He bent to squint under his bed and then into another corner of the room.

Finally he stopped looking and stood there, his hands hanging loosely, a sad look on his face.

"Where is it?" he said. His voice was no longer angry. It was that of an old man whose eight decades of hard life were beginning to grow too heavy for his shoulders to hold.

"Grandfather," I said, "what are you looking for?"

"My hat," he said. "Someone has taken it."

There was so much despair in the tone of his voice. It was as if after having so much taken from him in the past, this one small loss was what the *Pendalick-o-yis*, the White Eyes, call the straw that broke the camel's back.

I didn't say anything. I simply flicked my eyes up and then politely looked away.

"Oh," he said, his voice growing small.

He raised both his hands to the top of his head to feel the favorite hat that had been there all along. Then he sat down on his bed.

"*Ke-yahhh*. I'm nothing but an old fool," he whispered.

"No, Grandfather," I said. "That will never be true. No one will ever say that the Clever One was a fool. They will tell stories about you as long as the winds blow through the canyons and men have memories. And the land will not forget you, either."

My grandfather smiled up at me. He patted the bed next to him.

"Sit down, Willie," he said. "You are so tall now. It is hard to believe I once called you Little Foot. Your legs are so long that it hurts an old man's neck to look all that way up at you."

I sat by him, and he put his hand on my shoulder. Even though he was old and small now, I felt the great power still within him. He had fought so long and so hard, not just for revenge, but for our people and our land. For the last twenty years, his weapons had been words, but they had been no less pointed. Not only that, he had sung for so many, used the powers he was given to heal so many who were sick in body or in spirit.

I found myself wondering again what it would be like when he was no longer with us. Even my grandfather could not carry the weight of so many bitter harvests forever. My own life was much shorter than his, but I had already seen too much pain, too much difficulty, too many heartbreaking losses. So had all of our Apache people in this place of exile. The day would come when Ussen, the Life Giver, would finally call Geronimo to ride the ghost pony to the Happy Place.

I knew well that even among our own people, there were those who did not approve of some of the things my grandfather had done. There were those who felt his decisions had sometimes been too hasty and that his actions had brought misfortune. There were even some Apaches who hated Geronimo and whispered evil things about him. Far too many of those who had loved him the best were no longer among the living. What did that mean?

I pushed away the thought of my grandfather passing from us. Who remained who had resisted for as long as he did? Who would be left who could truly remember what my grandfather remembered? Who would we be when Geronimo was gone?

"Your memories will keep you strong," Geronimo said.

Just as he had done so many times in the past, he had heard my thoughts. He squeezed my shoulder as if I were still that little boy being forced toward the train by armed soldiers and not the tallest of all the Apache men here at Fort Sill.

"You will remember, grandson. You will remember it all."

Remember. That is what I now do. I tell the story as best I can. With each line of my tale I will place a kernel of corn on the ground. Then, when I am done, that corn will be there for you to pick up. Eat it and this story may stay with you as it has stayed with me. Do not fall asleep, or the story may be broken, as were our lives.

Listen.

A CRADLEBOARD CEREMONY

APACHERIA, 1873

GERONIMO'S FACE IS MY FIRST MEMORY.
Geronimo, my grandfather.

I have been blessed with a good memory. In my mind I sometimes even see things from the time before I had words to describe my experiences. My older relatives joke about my being able to remember conversations between my father and my mother before I was born. Such as this one:

"You should not ride that horse. It is not good for a woman to ride a horse when she is expecting a child. It is bad for your health."

"Hunh. I am worried about the health of my feet. My feet are hurting. Also, I am already on this horse's back."

Perhaps I do not remember that conversation from the exact time it happened. Maybe I only know it from stories. After all, many others in our small band overheard that talk between my parents on the trail to our next camp. My mother and father loved each other very much. Quarreling in loud voices so that everyone could hear was part of their love for each other. They enjoyed those arguments, which my mother always seemed to win. Notice that I say "seemed." For example, she rode the horse all that day until they made camp for the night. The story ends, though, with the conversation they had the next morning.

"My wife, wake up. I have made breakfast for us."

"My husband, what is that I smell cooking?"

"Horse meat."

That is the story as it was told. I heard it more than once when I was a very small child. So, indeed, that remembrance, it may only be a memory of the story told, not the event as it happened. But I know my memory of Geronimo's face is true.

It was summer, the time when all things are ripe. My birth was hard. The woman who knew the right ceremonies could not convince me to come out. So they called for Geronimo. As a medicine man, he knew many things. He was called upon to help in all kinds of circumstances. Most men are uncomfortable being close to a woman giving birth. Perhaps it is that they are embarrassed because there are always so many women around at such a time. Or maybe they are fearful of being made sick by the flow of blood from a woman's body.

Geronimo, though, was not most men. He did not fear such things. Perhaps the only thing that truly made him fearful was the thought of losing his freedom. That fear made him run many times, sometimes without considering what would happen to himself or others as a result.

Geronimo crouched beside my mother where she rested upon her knees. Her hands grasped the oak post that had been set in the ground before her. Her face gleamed with sweat as she breathed deeply.

Geronimo took black paint from his bag, drew a cross upon his hand, and began to sing one of his chants. As he sang, he placed his hand upon my mother's arms and her shoulders. He touched her chest, her sides, and then her stomach.

"Stubborn One," he said. "Be born now."

And, just like that, I was.

I am fairly sure that the year of my birth was 1873. I am absolutely certain of the place. It was Ojo Caliente, the place of the warm springs, in what is now the state of New Mexico. It was during those last few years of peace that my people spent there before we were taken from our beloved homeland. We identified with that place so much that when the *Pendalick-o-yis*, the White Eyes, referred to us in English, they called us Warm Springs Apaches.

Our own name for ourselves was Chihenne, Red Paint People. We were the easternmost of the three Chiricahua bands. To the west, in what became known as Arizona, were the Chokonen. Furthest south, down into Old Mexico, where their lives were always at risk, lived the Chiricahuas we called Deindai, or Nednai, the Enemy People. Geronimo was born among that southernmost band, but because of marriage and other circumstances, he had come to live with us Warm Springs People. When he lived with us he was happy. For a time.

The exact place where I was born is at the edge of a small valley. There a stream of sweet water still flows. There is a large red rock there with an indentation in it like the palm of a hand. I know that place as well as I know my own hand. It is important to know the place you were born. Then you can always return there.

Many years later, when I regained my freedom, that little valley was one of the places I visited. It was no longer Apache land, but I found the fruit tree in which my umbilical cord had been placed. That tree was growing straight and tall. I thanked it for protecting my life all of those years. Then I took off the White Eyes clothes that had hidden the fact that I was an Apache. I sat on the exact place where my mother had given birth. I laid myself down on that good earth and rolled to each of the four directions. That was what my parents did each time they brought me back to my birthplace when I was a child so that we could check the health of my tree. They placed me on the ground and rolled me to each of the sacred directions, ending with the east. That is how it was first done at my cradleboard ceremony, four days after my birth.

Of course, Geronimo was the medicine man asked to perform that ceremony. My father went to Geronimo's wickiup, an oval hut covered with deer hides, shortly after I was born. Geronimo was sitting out front by himself, rubbing a deerskin with yellow ocher. His wife, Chee-hash-kish, was off with their little daughter Dohn-say gathering grass to make baskets. Chapo, Geronimo's son, was down by the creek with a group of other boys, hunting rabbits.

My father sat down by Geronimo, picked up a stick, and began to scrape its tip on the earth in front of him. He did this as if he were just scratching the ground without any real pupose, but as he did so he drew the shape of a cross. Such a shape indicates a boy. If he had drawn a circle or a half-moon, it would have stood for a girl.

"We need you to help us again," my father said. Then he waited.

Even though he always enjoyed doing such things, Geronimo sat there as if trying to make up his mind. That is the way we do things. When you jump into something too fast, it may be that you are not yet fully prepared and things may not go well. Being deliberate is a great virtue. Finally, Geronimo made a sound deep in his throat, yawned, and nodded.

"*Ha-ah*," Geronimo said. "Yes. I will do it. *Enjuh*. Good. But first you must give me four things. One of them must be a gun. One must be a string of white beads. You decide what the other two things will be."

As my father walked away he felt pleased. Geronimo could have asked for any four things he wanted. He could have asked for something as hard to find as a roan horse with a white blaze on its chest or as costly as a pile of cloth blankets. A gun and a string of white beads would be easy. My father's cousin had just told him he would give him a gun to offer to Geronimo, and my father had recently obtained a string of fine white beads from a Navajo trader — although he had not yet told anyone else about that, not even my mother.

My father stopped walking. *How had Geronimo known to ask for those things?* He turned and looked back toward Geronimo's wickiup. The medicine man was no longer there. My father knew that if he looked into the wickiup it would prove to be empty. It was as if Geronimo had vanished into the air itself. My father shook his head and then laughed.

The next day, he returned to Geronimo's wickiup bringing four gifts. Those gifts were a gun, a string of white beads, a pile of blankets, and a roan horse with a white blaze on its chest.

As is our custom, the actual ceremony was done four days after I was born. But the days before required much preparation. During that time, Geronimo busied himself with songs and prayers. He gathered the materials to make my cradleboard, singing and praying as he did so. Those songs and prayers were to thank the plants and to help me have a long and healthy life.

For the frame around the cradleboard he chose oak. Because I was a boy, he gathered sotol stalks to make the crosspieces of the backboard. Red-barked dogwood stalks were readied to shape the canopy that would shield my face from the sun and the wind. The buckskin that was stretched over the frame of my cradleboard, from a deer Geronimo himself had killed two seasons ago, was colored with yellow ocher. In the skin over the canopy, he cut the shape of a small cross. That would let in the light of the four directions to touch my face.

On the sides of my cradleboard he fastened special talismans for my help and protection. Those included a piece of wood he'd taken from an ash tree struck by lightning, and bags of pollen. Onto the frame he tied the right paw of a male badger. Badger is a great man. He will not back down from anyone or anything, even a grizzly bear or a human being armed with weapons.

On the morning of the ceremony, my cradleboard completed, all of our relatives and neighbors gathered. Singing and chanting, Geronimo took pollen from his pouch and used it to mark four dots on my face. Then, holding me in one arm and my cradleboard in the other as he faced the sunrise way, he turned and sang.

Hayaade-go. From the south.

O'i-ah'biyaahyu. From the west.

Hadaazhi. From the north.

Ch'igona'ai hanadahye. From the east.

The downward direction, sunrise direction, sunset direction, upward direction, and then the sunrise way again. At each of those four sacred directions he held up my cradleboard. Then, the ceremony done, Geronimo placed me in my cradleboard.

"Grandson," he said in a soft voice, "you will live long."

I remember his face looking down at me as he did that. He was not just looking at me, but looking into me. He was seeing my life unfold. He was offering his power as a protection for my life. That is what I remember. That is what I will never forget.

Because he was the first to place me in my cradleboard's protective embrace, a special relationship was created between us that day. Even though we were not relatives by blood, he was now my grandfather. I would always have the right to call him that.

Geronimo, my grandfather.

THE TRAIN PLATFORM

FORT BOWIE, ARIZONA, SEPTEMBER 8, 1886

Nobody ever captured Geronimo. I know. I was with him.

Anyway, who can capture the wind?

JASPER KANSEAH, NEPHEW OF GERONIMO

INDEH

M Y LEG IRONS RATTLED as I shuffled forward on the platform. Even though the soldiers barked out their commands like yapping dogs, urging us to go forward more quickly, I dragged my feet. I didn't know much English yet. Much of what the soldiers said around us was a mystery to me. But since those soldiers had been with us since Skeleton Canyon, I had been listening a lot. So I had learned a few words. Some of them, I later found out, were words that it is not polite to speak, even though the White Eyes soldiers say them often. Others were words I had already learned to resent:

Stand up. We all understood what that meant, for we would be yanked to our feet if we did not obey quickly enough.

Move. That had become familiar, too, as familiar as a rifle barrel jammed into my back.

Prisoners. That one had been taught me by the chains that clanked on our hands and feet.

Although my grandfather, Geronimo, and most of the others were already on board those two cars designated for us prisoners, I was trying to hold back. Trains never brought anything good to Apaches. I had seen trains before, but never this close. The way this one had appeared, getting larger and larger, making more and more noise, made it even more fearful. It looked like a giant worm on fire, a hungry monster roaring toward us on those long steel bars that the White Eyes used to cut our land into sections like pieces of meat. That train was terrible to behold.

I learned later that some of the old people in the larger group of pathetic captives sent out two days before us from this same station actually made prayers toward the train. They took pollen from their pouches and offered it — as if that long machine were a spirit being. But we did not show the fear we felt. Geronimo and Fun, Perico and Naiche, and Chapo and the other grown men stood up straight. So did my aunt Lozen, the fighting sister of Victorio. My elders kept their faces calm as the train approached. Small as I was, I tried to do the same. Even the green parrot on Perico's shoulders, for he never traveled any-where without one of his beloved birds, did not flap its wings in alarm.

It is important to show courage in the face of danger. That was what my mother and father always said. Even though I would never again hear their voices except in my memory, that thought gave me the strength to stand up straight, even though I was the smallest boy on that platform.

White Eyes soldiers were all around us on the platform, not just those of Captain Lawton, who'd been assigned to accompany us on the train and had been with us since my grandfather and Chief Naiche agreed to the terms of surrender. Other soldiers from Fort Bowie were at the depot, white men and black white men. Many of them hadn't even been assigned to be there. They just wanted to watch our departure and catch one last glimpse of Geronimo. Although we were surrounded by White Eyes soldiers, if it hadn't been for those leg irons I would have tried again to escape from them. There's no shame in running.

Geronimo had taught me that.

"A good fighter must also be a good runner," he explained one evening as we sat watching the sun set over the Sierra Madre. "Fight, run, hide, fight again." Then he laughed that short, hard laugh of his. "We did not run from our enemies just to escape them," he said.

I had nodded, knowing what he meant. Those foolish enough to pursue what seemed to be one or two terrified Indians might find themselves led into an ambush as Apache fighters suddenly appeared all around them — as if springing up out of the earth. Years later in

Alabama, one of my teachers would read us a Greek story from *Bullfinch's Mythology*. In that story, the hero sowed the ground with dragon's teeth. Then soldiers grew up out of the ground.

Those soldiers must have been Apaches, I thought.

We Apaches have always been good at escaping. Even after our surrender, we all could have slipped away at almost any time. The White Eyes soldiers with us found that out. Two nights before we reached Fort Bowie, eight of our small party made a run for it in the night. It did not include our leaders. Geronimo and Naiche, Fun, and Perico had been taken in ahead of us to Fort Bowie. The rest of us were at our camp in the hills, waiting to be escorted in.

We were nervous already, but it was worse without our leaders. Then, late at night, a White Eyes soldier came riding his horse into our camp. It was just a foolish White Eyes officer, coming to check on us. He did not realize that we Apaches might assume — as had happened so often in the past — that we'd been betrayed.

"*Nanlyeeg!*" someone shouted. "Run."

I did not have to hear that more than once. I ran. I did not intend to act like one of the foolish people of our old stories. Just like the others who fled into the darkness, I was certain it was a night raid to kill every Indian.

Of the eight who ran, I was the only one who was caught. Those who got away, three men, three women, and a boy older than me, found some horses and reached the safety of the mountains. I will not mention their names. The White Eyes officers declared that those who escaped were all killed by Mexicans. I do not think that is so. They may be living to this day, surviving as free Apaches in the Sierra Madre. It is better for the White Eyes soldiers to continue listing them as dead. Apaches who die on paper are not likely to be hunted.

Why was I caught? Although I was thirteen years old, I was very small for my age. My legs were so short, I could not keep up with the others. When I realized that, I decided to do my best to help the others get away.

"*Daku!*" I yelled at the soldiers who were pursuing us. "Right here!"

Then I threw the fist-sized rock I'd found. It hit one of the soldiers in the chest and knocked him off his horse. That got their attention.

I made it hard for those soldiers to catch me. My legs might have been short, but I was agile. I was able to duck and dodge around, even when they had surrounded me. Then I struggled like a wildcat. By making it so difficult for them to take me, I gave the others more time. It took four soldiers to finally pin me down. That was when they put the leg irons on me.

I was still wearing those leg irons as they pushed me toward the train. They would not take them off until the last moment. They were tired of having to chase me.

As I stood there, staring at the door of the train, a puppy came up to me and thrust its nose against my palm. I knew it was an Apache dog. There were dozens of them, dogs of all shapes and sizes, hanging around the depot. Some of them were resting in the shadow below the platform. Whenever a White Eyes soldier approached them they would either growl or run away. When that big party of Apaches, all of the Chiricahuas from the reservation, had been brought here two days ago, their dogs had come with them. They had run along behind the wagons all the way from Fort Apache to the railhead at Holbrook. Those people had carried as many of their possessions as they could. They brought their saddles, great bundles of clothing, baskets, and jugs. One man even brought along one of our one-stringed Apache fiddles, the wood that sings. They had been allowed to load the baggage they brought with them onto the freight car on that train. But they were not allowed to bring their dogs. Some of those dogs ran along behind the train until their feet bled and they could run no further. Then, limping, they made their way back here to wait for their people to return. None of them would ever live long enough to see that day.

A soldier with a growth of hair on his lip that looked like a yellow caterpillar knelt down by me on the platform. He held up one long bony finger, drawing my attention away from the puppy that was licking my hand. He shook his finger back and forth in front of my eyes. Then he unlocked my leg irons. He handed them back to a man behind him. Leg irons were clearly worth more than an Apache boy. I was being sent away, but they were keeping those leg irons.

However, now that I was free of those chains, my feet would not listen to me.

Move, I said to them inside my head.

But my feet rebelled. They stuck to the wood of the platform. They acted as if they were trying to grow roots. The Apache puppy whimpered and patted at my knees with its paws.

One of the soldiers finally lost patience with me. It was not Caterpillar Lip, but another skinny soldier with hair like yellow dried grass. He kicked the puppy aside. It yelped and scrambled away as Skinny Yellow Hair grabbed me up by my shirt and lifted me — as if I, too, was a puppy taken by the scruff of its neck. Then he tossed me up the stairs.

I landed hard, but managed to struggle quickly to my feet. My chest felt as if it was being gripped by the hand of a giant. It was hard for me to breathe. It wasn't just that I'd never been in a train before. I was so uncertain of what those White Eyes intended to do to us.

I knew that they were sending us on a very long journey. My aunt Lozen had foreseen this. We were going further than we could see from the highest mountaintop. We were almost going further than Lozen's sight could reach in one of her visions. That was her power, to be able to see people and places far beyond normal sight. So many times when our enemies tried to surprise us, Lozen saw them first and saved us.

I remember how she did this. I stood close to her and watched and listened on the day when she helped us decide which trail to take through the mountains above the Mexican town of Fronteras. Even now, I have only to close my eyes to see her and hear her words again. When I do so, I can smell the mountain sage and feel the small warm breeze that came to touch our faces as she sang.

"Wise Woman, use your power to help us," Geronimo asked.

Lozen stood up tall, proud to be of use to the people. She stretched her arms out to either side, like an eagle taking flight, and began to chant to Ussen, the Life Giver, who was here before the world was created. As she chanted, tears came from her eyes. Palms held up, she turned slowly in a circle.

Over all in this world
Ussen has power.
Sometimes he shares it
With those on this earth.
This power he has given me
For the benefit of my people.
This power is good.

It is good, as he is good.
This power I may use
For the good of my people.

When she stopped, the palms of her hands were as red as if they had been held close to a fire.

"Huh," she said, pointing ahead of her with her lips. "The foolish Mexicans think they are going to catch us in an ambush at the end of that canyon. We will go around them."

Even though it was our custom for women to marry and not scout around, Lozen's great power meant she could choose another way. The way she followed was that of one who rode back into camp with the men, her rifle held high above her head. She was truly the equal of any man in battle, as respected as her great brother, Victorio. Had she been there by his side when he was finally ambushed by the Mexican troops and the Tarahumara Indians, she might have been able to save his life, even though Victorio and his band were tired and outnumbered four to one and had almost no ammunition.

Strong and brave as she was, Lozen could be as kind to a child as any Apache mother. Perhaps it was because she never had children of her own. She did not mind when I leaned against her on cold nights as we sat around the fire in the mountains of Old Mexico. Sometimes she would answer my questions. Usually her answers made me feel better.

However, the answer she gave me at Fort Bowie, just before the arrival of that Florida-bound train, worried me. Lozen was standing, looking off into the distance. Her head was tilted in a way that made me suspect her power was showing her something and she was paying close attention to it.

I clanked up to her in my leg irons.

"What do you see?" I asked.

She looked down at me for a moment. "I see," she said at last, "that I am going too far away. I will never see my home again."

ON THE TRAIN

SEPTEMBER 8, 1886

Those Chiricahua scouts under Chiefs Chatto, Noche, and others did most excellent service and were of more value in hunting down and compelling the surrender of the renegades than all other troops engaged in operations against them combined.

GENERAL GEORGE CROOK

GENERAL GEORGE CROOK, HIS AUTOBIOGRAPHY

"MOVE," SAID A WHITE EYES voice behind me. Even though I was now being pushed into the train car by a soldier with a gun, I moved slowly through the narrow door. It led into a long room. There were windows on both sides, but even though it was as hot inside that room as a mountain lion's breath, those windows were tightly closed. On both sides of the long room were many benches bolted to the floor.

"Sit," the soldier behind me grunted.

I sat and the soldier moved on. He did not chain me or the other children and women who had been placed in this car. That gave me some hope. If we discovered that the White Eyes did plan to do us harm — as had happened to Apaches so many times in the past, even when we came in under a flag of truce and were promised good treatment — then perhaps some of us could break out through those windows and escape before they killed us all.

As I sat there, I thought of what Lozen had just said on the platform. Her sad words made me wonder if I, too, would never again see my home. I did not know yet just how many long years I would have to wonder about that.

I tried to think of something else. But, as often happens when you are in a difficult spot, my mind turned to yet another troubling thought. Had the White Eyes prepared well enough for so long a journey? In our many years of fighting their invasions of our land, we Apaches had learned that the White Eyes do not always do a good job of planning ahead. When they pursued us, they almost always ended up short of supplies. Even when they did bring enough provisions, they often lost track of their pack trains — sometimes with our help.

It had been that way only a few days ago when we agreed to go to Skeleton Canyon with Lieutenant Gatewood, whom we Chiricahuas all called Nantan Bay-chen-daysen — Chief Longnose.

Chief Naiche asked Geronimo to speak for us.

"Now that we have surrendered," Geronimo said, "we would like you to feed us. We are hungry."

Nantan Longnose looked embarrassed. "I have no food," he said. "We lost our mule train with our provisions several days ago."

Geronimo began to laugh. "Then we will have to feed you," he said.

And that was what we did. All the way in until we reached Skeleton Canyon, where General Miles was waiting, we shared our meager food with Nantan Longnose and the two White Eyes officers with him. Poor Nantan Longnose. He was almost as skinny as a skeleton himself. If it wasn't for us Apache prisoners, he would have starved. We all thought that was funny.

Those White Eyes soldiers were always so out of place in our mountains and canyons. None of them could find their way unless they had an Indian to guide them. If it were not for the Apache scouts who agreed to help the army, they never would have captured us.

Our journey into exile was not without Apache scouts. But those scouts were not guides. They were prisoners, held in the same way as those men who had kept fighting to remain free. On this very train were Martine and Kayitah, who had led the army to my grandfather's favorite place in Mexico, a place that no white man ever found on his own.

The army had invited Martine and Kayitah to the depot. They said they wanted them there to help while their Chiricahua relatives were loaded onto the train.

"Come," they were told, "you were the ones who led us to their hiding place in Mexico. We could not have gotten their surrender without you."

So Kayitah and Martine came. Perhaps they expected they would finally be paid the big reward they'd been promised for taking the White Eyes to the favorite place Chief Naiche and Geronimo had chosen to camp. They had been promised seventy thousand dollars. Instead, they were given a different reward. Just before the Southern Pacific train pulled out, a signal was given. Martine and Kayitah were each grabbed by two soldiers, stripped of their knives and guns, and forced onto the train with the very people they had been guarding only a minute before. Later on I would discover that every other Chiricahua Apache scout was rounded up and shipped. They had been the allies of the White Eyes, but they were treated just like those of us they called hostiles and renegades.

Hostiles and renegades. I do not like to hear those words applied to those of us who resisted the Whites Eyes and the Mexicans. I like to know the true meaning of words. Words have great power when you understand them. One of the books I grew to love the best when I was sent to school is that book of words called a dictionary. A *hostile*, it told me, is an enemy stranger. Who were the strangers who came to Apache lands and behaved as enemies?

A *renegade*, I learned, is a deserter, one who goes against his people or their beliefs. It also means one who breaks an oath. That word also fit the White Eyes well. But maybe it could also have been used to describe at least one Apache — Chatto.

Chatto had gotten his name, which means Flat Nose, from being kicked in the face by a horse. Although he once had fought the White Eyes and Mexicans as fiercely as any other Chiricahua man, when he changed sides and became a scout, he could no longer be trusted. He began to stick his wide nose into everyone's business, trying to make himself more important. He became a spy for Lieutenant Davis, who we called Chief Fat Boy, Nantan Enchau. Chatto was seen sneaking into Fat Boy's tent at night along with Mickey Free to tell the *nantan* lies about Geronimo and others. Chatto had always been jealous of Naiche and Geronimo. He hoped to take their places. When Geronimo broke out from Fort Apache in May 1885, Chatto even tried to lay claim to the field of alfalfa that Geronimo had been tending all that spring.

While we were being hunted in Mexico, Chatto was at a big meeting in Washington. He met the secretary of war and the one at Washington himself, President Cleveland. They gave him a big medal. Chatto was sure that those important white men would heed his requests to be allowed to stay in his homeland. He even asked them to give him more land and better water. As the train left Washington, he was puffed up with pride. He thought he was coming back home to be honored by our people, to be their greatest chief. But Chatto would never see Arizona again, either. Just like all the other Apache scouts, his final destination turned out to be far from his home. His train was stopped at Emporia, Kansas. White soldiers took his weapons and sent him to Fort Leavenworth. There he was arrested and put onto a prison train to Florida, still wearing his worthless medal.

Even as an old man at Fort Sill, Chatto still wore that medal. He showed it to anyone who would listen to him. I saw it far too many times. On one side of that medal, which was as big as a plate, was a picture of a white man and an Indian shaking hands. On the other side, surrounded by billowing clouds, was written a word that Chatto could not read at the time it was placed around his neck. *PEACE*.

My grandfather never forgave Chatto. Even as old men in Oklahoma, Geronimo and Chatto avoided each other. My grandfather often said that Chatto was a bad man, one whose tongue was forked like that of a snake. At first, being young and foolish, I took some pleasure from the fact that those Apaches who had led the army to us were being exiled from our land, too. Later on, when we were all prisoners together, my heart could not stay hard toward those men who had served the U.S. Army, and their innocent families who were sent into exile with them. I no longer saw Chatto as a bad man. He was just another Apache who made the mistake of believing the promises made him by dishonest white men. In his heart, I think, Chatto, too, wanted to do the best for our people.

But that September day in 1886, as our prison train pulled out of Fort Bowie, I was too angry and frightened to have any space in my thoughts for sympathy. The little room lurched as if it had been struck by something heavy. I almost fell out of my seat. I looked out the window. Everything — the buildings, the poles, even the small trees — was moving backward. It made me feel sick and dizzy, even after I realized that it was our little room that was going forward.

The sound of the train's iron wheels rattling and clanking on the tracks turned into a steady roar, like the sound of a giant animal's growling breath, as we picked up speed. Soon the Fort Bowie station was left far behind. We were now going much faster than a man could go on horseback, at least as fast as a bird flies. As the feeling of dizziness left me, I began to wonder if we would run into something and all be killed. Disturbing as it was, it was also exciting, as terrible and thrilling as riding on the back of a whirlwind. I could not stop looking out the window. On and on we went, leaving more and more of our land behind.

I do not know how much time passed before I noticed that the day was ending, the sky growing dark. The train was climbing a grade. Would we be going over high mountains where early snow might slow our passage? Then, going back to my earlier thoughts, I began to worry about something else. Something frightening.

Kanseah, who was a little older than me and two hands taller, had been placed in the seat behind me. He had been given more responsibilities than I had around our camp. I was proud of the way Geronimo had been using me as a lookout, but Kanseah was closer to becoming a man.

Since our train journey began, neither of us had spoken. There'd been too much to look at and wonder about. We also didn't want to attract the attention of the soldiers who stood at either end of the train car. Now, however, the question that had come into my mind was so troubling that I had to speak it. I turned to look back at Kanseah.

"Brother," I said, "what will the White Eyes do if they run out of food?"

He motioned for me to be quiet. Then he dropped down from his seat, crawled beneath the bench I was on, and slid up to join me. I moved over so that I would remain next to the window.

We looked around, moving only our eyes, not our heads. The guard soldiers had not noticed Kanseah change his seat — or if they did, it hadn't troubled them. Kanseah leaned close.

"Remember the story of the White Eyes wagon train that got caught in the deep snows?" he asked in a low voice.

I nodded. I knew the story well. Even though it happened forty winters ago and far to the north of our lands, it had passed from campfire to campfire among the Indian nations.

"Yes," I said, keeping my voice as soft as his.

It was well that we talked so quietly. Some of the white soldiers could become upset if they saw one Apache prisoner talking to another. They were certain that we were either plotting escape or saying something uncomplimentary about them.

They were usually right. Fortunately, most white soldiers have the ears of men not used to small sounds. They live in a world of loud noises. The rumbling of wheels and the rattling of their wagons, the harsh voices of men who cannot speak without bellowing like a wounded bull surround them all the time. When it does get quiet, it makes them uncomfortable. They have to fill up that silence with loud, nervous talk and laughter like the braying of mules.

Even when White Eyes try to be quiet, it is hard for them. When we were in our mountains it was almost amusing to hear groups of clumsy soldiers trying to creep up on us through the brush, making more noise than a three-legged cow. But because they were coming to kill us, it was not all that funny.

When I answered yes to Kanseah's question, I hoped that would end it. I hoped he would not tell me the story again. But I knew in my heart that he would tell it to me whether I wanted to hear it or not. He would tell it to me not to frighten me, but to remind me what kind of people our captors were. He would tell it to prepare me for the worst that might happen, to strengthen my spirit. That which we expect we can prepare for, even if it is a monster. And sometimes even a small Apache boy may surprise the monster that comes for him, especially when that monster does not know the Apache boy has a sharp knife hidden in his boot.

Kanseah put his mouth close to my ear.

"This is the story of what happened to that wagon train," he said. "Listen."

I listened.

THE WAGON TRAIN

SEPTEMBER 8, 1886

In my talks with the Indians they showed no resentment of the way they had been treated in the past; only wonderment at the why of it. Why had they been shifted from reservation to reservation; told to farm and had their crops destroyed; assured that the government would ration them, then left to half starve; there in the hot malarial bottoms of the Gila and San Carlos, when they were mountain people? These and other questions I could not answer. And above all they wondered if they would now be allowed to live at peace.

LIEUTENANT BRITTON DAVIS

THE TRUTH ABOUT GERONIMO

BEFORE WE APACHES heard the story of the lost wagon train, we knew that we could not trust most White Eyes. We'd learned that white traders would often cheat us. We'd discovered that no matter how hard we tried to live our lives peacefully and be allies with them, most of those new people would still mistrust us — even though they began each conflict. The minds of the White Eyes seemed as tangled as a badly knotted rope. Their ways of seeing the world were twisted. Yet some of our own people who agreed to work for them became almost as bad as the White Eyes.

We Apaches value the truth. We teach our children from their youngest years that true talk is a great virtue. But the way of speaking falsely seemed to be one of the first lessons taught by the White Eyes to their people. Some of us came to believe that every white man was a liar. There were a few we could trust. I think Mr. Wratten was the best. In some ways, he almost became an Apache. Nantan Longnose and Fat Boy spoke straight. They tried to keep their words, even though they were sometimes misled by bad advice. General Crook, who we called Nantan Lupan, Fox in Tan Clothing, was tough and dangerous, but whenever he promised something, he kept his word.

If Nantan Lupan said we would be fed, we were fed. If he said he intended to kill us, he would try hard to do that. In 1883, when Crook met with Chief Naiche and Geronimo, Loco, Nana, Kayahtenny, Bonito, and Chatto in the Sierra Madre, he did not tell them to surrender. I know this to be so, for I sat just outside the circle of leaders who gathered, and I heard his words.

"I did not come to take captives," Nantan Lupan said. There was a stern look on his face and steel in his voice. "Mexican troops will soon join me. It is our intention that in a few days all of you will be killed and in the ground. I advise you to take a few days to talk things over and then try to fight your way out, if you can."

Those straight words impressed me. They impressed our leaders, too. Even Nana, the oldest of them all and the one who had fought the longest, saw the wisdom of ending their war. They talked it over and chose Geronimo as our spokesman to negotiate a surrender.

It is good to have an enemy that you can trust. That is what my father taught me. He also told me it is much worse to have an enemy who pretends to be a friend, puts one arm around your shoulder and uses his other arm to thrust a knife into your side. I saw the truth of my father's words that day. I think it was because Nantan Lupan told the truth that the White Eyes leaders sent him away. It was a sad day for us when they replaced Nantan Lupan with General Miles.

Nantan Miles spoke sweet words — like fruit that smells good before you bite into it and find out that the center is rotten. He was the biggest liar of all. That is what Geronimo often said. Considering the promise that Miles made to him and Chief Naiche, I think so also. What Miles drew in the sand on the day of our final surrender meant no more than dust in the wind.

That White Eyes were liars was bad enough. But when we Apaches heard the story of the wagon train, we realized they were even worse than liars. They were also cannibals.

"Listen," Kanseah whispered to me on the train. "Forty harvests ago a White Eyes wagon train set out toward the west. They had Indians, not Apaches but two mountain Indians — Snakes, I think — guiding them. They started out too late in the year, close to the time when snow fills the mountain passes. The Snake scouts told them they should turn back, but the white man who had agreed to lead the wagon train was a greedy fool. He refused to listen.

"Before long they were high in the mountains. Then the snow did fall. It rose over the top of the wagon wheels. Those foolish White Eyes tried to turn back, but their animals could not pull the wagons in the deep snow. They were stuck. Days passed. The supplies of food began running out. The Snake scouts hunted as best they could in the snow. They brought back deer for the White Eyes. But they could not bring back enough. Those white people grew more hungry. They grew so hungry that they killed and ate the animals that pulled their wagons.

"The Snake scouts grew nervous now but did not want to desert these helpless people. They had given their word. But then one day the white men looked at the Indians with hungry eyes. Hungry eyes.

"Those Indians tried to run away, but the deep snow slowed them. The white men caught them, killed them, and ate them. But the White Eyes were still hungry. Winter was not yet half over. So those white people started eating their own dead. They cut the flesh from the bodies of their own relatives and cooked it and ate it. But they were still hungry. So they killed those too weak to resist and ate them."

Kanseah paused in his story. The train was slowing as it went around a great bend, making a terrible screeching noise. I had heard the tale before, but never in such detail. My cousin Kanseah was a good storyteller. Too good. I felt as if I was inside the belly of a giant snake. My head throbbed, and my heart thudded almost as loudly in my chest as the clacking of the train. It seemed my head and heart were racing to see which would be the first to explode.

Only the thought that I must behave as one who was becoming a man kept me from crying out. I reached my hand down to my soft boot to feel the reassuring hardness of the bone hilt of my little knife. Outside the window it was dark. All I could see were shadows whipping backward as the train once more picked up speed.

"How did it end?" I whispered to Kanseah.

"The snow finally left the mountain passes. Other white men went looking for the lost wagon train. By the time they found them, only half were left. They had cut strips of meat from the bodies of the dead and had them hung up to dry like deer jerky."

I shook my head, feeling sick. "What happened to those who survived? Those who ate other people? Were they killed? Were they sent into exile?"

"Huh," Kanseah said. "As far as I know they just went on their way. Maybe, though, they told their rescuers they could not leave until they had packed up their good dried meat."

It was a grim joke. I did not laugh.

Kanseah slipped down to the floor, crawled back beneath my bench, and resumed his seat behind me. I heard him stretch out and then begin sleeping as I sat awake, thinking and thinking.

It was not just the wagon train story that made us think the White Eyes ate people. Something we saw at Turkey Creek convinced me and many other Chiricahuas that White Eyes were man eaters.

It was August of 1881. It was the day when White Eyes soldiers killed Noche-del-Klinne, the White Mountain Apache prophet, for no good reason. While the fighting between the army and the White Mountain Apaches was still going on, Lozen rode into our camp. She was leading a string of army pack mules that she had managed to drive off during the confusion. We were all pleased at the success of her raid. There was ammunition and food and clothes in the packs. I looked at those fat mules with pleasure. Good eating. We were given more rations at Turkey Creek than we'd had at San Carlos, but there never was enough food. During those years at Fort Apache I was always hungry. My rib bones stuck out.

Geronimo and Juh began to open the packs to divide the supplies while others led the first of the mules off to butcher it. We children hung around close. There might be sugar or crackers in those packs, and we knew if that was so, then Geronimo would give those good-tasting things to us little ones.

Suddenly Juh jumped back as if a rattlesnake had struck at him.

"*Ch-ch-chidin bi-bitzi*," he stammered, staring at the cans that had fallen out onto the ground from the unlaced pack. "Ghost meat!"

I stared at what was painted on those cans. We'd seen canned food before. We knew how the White Eyes marked the cans with pictures to show what kind of food was kept inside. The pictures might show peaches or beans or the head of a cow. These cans, though, were different.

"Ah!" I gasped. I raised my hands in front of my face and stumbled backward just as Juh had.

The pictures on those cans were not of fruit or animals or vegetables. Each had a drawing of a red man with horns on his head. Those cans were full of human meat! I had to close my eyes and turn away. I was sick in my stomach.

No one wanted to come close to such evil. Finally Geronimo dug a hole and used a long forked stick to shove those cans into it. We all breathed easier when the earth had been piled over them and we could no longer see those containers of ghost meat.

Later, when I was in Florida, I learned that we had been wrong. Those cans did not really hold human meat. That picture meant a food called deviled ham was packed inside. Deviled ham is made from the meat of pigs, not men. At the time, though, those cans convinced me that the White Eyes were as bad as Hungry Giant.

No, that is wrong. Those Whites Eyes seemed even worse. At least Hungry Giant did not eat his own kind.

HUNGRY GIANT

SEPTEMBER 8, 1886

Thus did the son of Ussen conquer the enemy of mankind. He lived long and taught good and the use of good things to the Apaches, all of whom are descended from Him. He told them to live at peace with their neighbors. They were not to fight unless attacked, but, if attacked, He bade them to protect themselves. He told them that if an enemy laid down his arms his life was to be spared.

JAMES KAYWAYKLA

IN THE DAYS OF VICTORIO, RECOLLECTIONS

OF A WARM SPRINGS APACHE

WHEN I TRAVELED on the train for the first time, it was not the right season for telling stories. Because our stories are so sacred, they are only told in the wintertime. Stories are very sacred things, even the funny ones about Coyote. We would go at night to the wickiup of one of my uncles to hear them. Those Coyote tales always made us boys laugh, but there was a serious side to them. Our elders used those stories to point out to us when we had done something foolish. They would shoot those stories at us like arrows so that their lessons could enter us and help to straighten our path.

To tell a story such as the one about Hungry Giant out of season might attract the attention of the lightning or the snakes or the wasps that lay quiet when the snow was on the earth. It was not winter when we started out on my first train journey. It was When the Leaves Begin to Turn. September. The storytelling season, When the Hawks Begin to Scream by Day and by Night, was still two full moons away.

Yet as I sat inside the belly of the great clattering snake that was our train, the story of Hungry Giant came to me. It would not leave. It spoke itself inside my head, spoke in the voice of Geronimo, whose storytelling we boys loved so much. Geronimo never missed a chance to give Chiricahua children the lessons they needed to survive.

Perhaps, I thought, *it is that I need to listen in my head to this story now. Perhaps my grandfather knows my fear, even though he is in the other train car and cannot see me. Perhaps he is sending this story to me.*

I closed my eyes and relaxed, ready to let that story speak itself.

As soon as I did so, I was no longer on the prison train. I was back in Geronimo's brush wickiup there in our winter camp. I was in that favorite place of his hidden in the mountains deep in Mexico. It was so far south that we were close to the place where mountains and desert turn into jungle.

The fire was burning in the center of the lodge, but the warmth that came to me from his story was greater than that from the flames.

I could no longer hear the train or feel the strange texture of the hard seat under me. I was sitting on a soft deerskin spread on the gentle earth. There was no rattling and clanking of iron wheels and steel tracks. All I heard were the sounds of the night around our wickiup, the cracking of the dry oak branches in our fire, and the voice of Geronimo, as powerful as a healing chant.

Ah, the way Geronimo could tell a story! When he spoke of things that were sacred and powerful or things that were dangerous, his voice grew lower and came almost in a whisper from the back of his throat. Other times his voice became loud, especially when something funny happened — such as the shooting contest between Hungry Giant and Child of Water, which happened at the place where there are four small hills with piles of white flint that are the giant's bones.

His storytelling was a map of our beloved land. Whenever he came to a place, he did not just say a name the way white people do when they talk about such places as Deming or Fort Apache. Instead, as is our Apache way, his words were so descriptive that you could see the place as clearly as a picture.

Let me help you try to understand that. The name that the White Eyes gave to the place where they took us in Florida was the Castillo de San Marcos. If that place had been named by an Apache, it might have been called Place with Stone Walls All Around Us Beside Big Water That Tastes Like Tears Where Land Is Flat and Evil Insects Bite Us and All Get Sick and Die.

"*A'ko'go*," Geronimo said, starting his story. "Then it happened. Yehyeh, Hungry Giant, was one of the first beings on earth. *Djindi*, so they say.

"This was back long ago, not long after the time of creation, so they say. But he was not like Child of Water, who was one of the two children of White Painted Woman. Yehyeh was a monster, big and slow-witted and hungry. He wore a coat made of four layers of stone so no weapon could harm him. He carried a knife and a big bag and he hunted the human beings and he ate them. So they say.

"Also, whenever Child of Water's older brother went hunting and killed a deer and cooked its meat to eat, Yehyeh would come and take that deer meat away from him. Then Child of Water's older brother would just sit down and cry.

"Hungry Giant also loved to eat little children. So whenever he came to the home of White Painted Woman, she would hide Child of Water.

"'I heard a ba-by cry-ing,' Yehyeh would say in his big, slow, stupid voice. 'Give him to me so I can eat him.'

"'There is no baby here,' White Painted Woman would say. 'I am lonely, and so I am just imitating the sound of a baby crying to keep myself company.' Then she would cry like a baby, and Hungry Giant would be fooled and he would go away.

"Finally, Child of Water became old enough to do something.

He saw how hard it was for his family because of Hungry Giant. He asked his brother to make him a bow and arrow. So his older brother made him a little bow. He made arrows out of grama grass and tipped them with thunder flint.

"'Now,' Child of Water said, 'I will go and kill Yehyeh.'

"*Djindi*. So they say.

"Then Child of Water and his older brother went out hunting. They killed a deer and made a fire. Sure enough, as soon as their food was cooked, along came Hungry Giant.

"'That deer meat is for me,' Yehyeh said.

"'No, it is not,' Child of Water said. 'You are not going to make our meat into big piles of excrement anymore.'

"Hungry Giant laughed at Child of Water. Child of Water was so small and he was so big. 'What po-wer do you have?' Hungry Giant said. 'What will you fight me with?'

"'I will fight you with my bow and arrows,' Child of Water said, holding them up.

"Hungry Giant took the bow and arrows from the hands of Child of Water, used them to wipe his butt and then threw them far away. But Child of Water was not discouraged. He just went and got his bow and arrows and came back. 'What will you fight me with?' he said to Yehyeh.

"'Those are my ar-rows,' Hungry Giant said, indicating four big pine logs. They were as long and straight as the poles that the White Eyes string their talking wires on. Child of Water took off his loincloth and rubbed it along each of those big arrows.

"That displeased Hungry Giant very much. 'Who are you?' Hungry Giant said. He was really angry now.

"'I am Child of Water, and I have come to kill all the monsters. Now it is time for us to have our contest,' Child of Water said. 'Let us shoot arrows at each other.'

"'*En-juh!*' Yehyeh said. 'That is good. I am rea-dy to kill you now, so I will go first.'

"'*Enjuh*,' Child of Water said. 'You shoot your arrows at me, and then it will be my turn.' He went and stood so that he was facing the direction of the sunrise.

"Yehyeh lifted up his bow that was made from a huge pine tree. He shot his first arrow. There was a rumble of thunder as it sped through the air. But Child of Water told that arrow to strike the earth in front of him, and it did. Yehyeh fired his second arrow. Child of Water told it to pass over him. The third arrow was fired.

"'Let it strike to one side of me,' Child of Water said, and it did. Then Yehyeh released the final giant arrow from his bow.

"'Let it strike to the other side of me,' said Child of Water. And so it did.

"'Now it is my turn,' Child of Water said.

"He shot his first arrow, and even though Hungry Giant told that arrow to miss him, it struck Yehyeh right in the chest and shattered his first stone coat. Child of Water shot his second arrow.

"'Let that ar-row miss me,' Hungry Giant rumbled. There was fear in his voice as he said it. But Yehyeh's power was less than that of Child of Water. That arrow hit him, too, and shattered his second coat of stone.

"The same thing happened when Child of Water shot his third arrow. That third stone coat fell away, and now Child of Water could see the giant's heart, throbbing in its chest. He fired his final arrow and it killed Hungry Giant. Yehyeh fell to the earth, where his bones scattered over those four hills covered with piles of white flint stone. Child of Water had destroyed the first of the great monsters that troubled the people.

"*Djindi.* So they say." This was how Geronimo's voice ended the story.

"Little Foot," Geronimo said. "Are you sleeping? Wake up and add some wood to our fire."

I opened my eyes. There was no fire in front of me. The mountain camp was gone, and so was my grandfather. I was on the train. Yet I no longer felt as if I were in the belly of a monster. Fear no longer held me by the throat. I no longer felt sick with anxiety.

Hearing that story in my mind had given me courage, almost as much courage as I used to get from knowing that even after most of us had surrendered to the White Eyes, Geronimo was still free. His freedom had been like a fire on a distant mountaintop. Perhaps other Apaches could not reach that spot, but knowing that fire was there gave us something to look to, even in the darkest night.

No bullet could ever kill Geronimo. I knew that as well as I knew that no one could ever capture him. It had seemed to those of us who admired and loved him that Geronimo would never be defeated, no matter how great the odds were against him. It did not matter that he was no longer young. Even those Apaches who were angry at Geronimo and thought his resistance was foolish and just causing trouble for everyone admitted that my grandfather still had his power. To me, Geronimo was like Child of Water himself, using his power to fight those who sought to take our lives and drive us from our land. As long as he was free, I still had hope.

But Geronimo was no longer free. Geronimo, my grandfather, was on this train with me, sitting in the car ahead of us. However, even though it was true that his body was held captive, I realized no one could chain his spirit. The story of the Hungry Giant reminded me of that. I was still an orphan and a captive, but it gave back hope to my own life.

GRAY LIZARD'S ESCAPE

SEPTEMBER 9, 1886

I do not recall how many nights we spent on that train, but it seemed a very long time. Each time it stopped we expected to be taken off and killed; but we didn't care much. That was to happen soon, anyway, and at times I thought the sooner the better. An Apache does not want to die, but he does not fear death as White Eyes seem to, perhaps because he really believes in a Happy Place.

DAKLUGIE

INDEH

KE-YAH. I HOPE I NEVER AGAIN have to take a journey like that long one we took on the White Eyes train. Though I was a boy who could easily ride a horse for days without becoming sore, traveling that way in the train, always in one place whether awake or asleep, made my limbs as stiff as those of an old man. They only let us out a few times to stretch our legs beside the tracks. After a few days I ached all over. Perhaps it was because I was always tense. I no longer feared that they would eat us. There was enough food. But we still expected at any minute to be beaten or bayoneted or just taken from the train and shot.

Perhaps because I was so young, I was sometimes treated rather kindly by the soldiers. True, they threw me onto the train as if I was a piece of firewood. But at the end of that first day of travel, I was one of the first to whom they handed food. Of course, I did not eat until I looked around and made sure that everyone else had been fed. A man must always think first of others.

When it grew dark, the train did not stop to let us off so that I could put my blankets on the ground to sleep as a human being is meant to do. Instead, it kept on going without stopping. I am sure they feared we might try to escape if they stopped. No one on our train tried to get away, but that was not true of the other groups of exiled Apaches.

I learned later that ours was only one of several trains that set out for Florida. Those prison trains caried every Chiricahua Apache the White Eyes soldiers could find. It did not matter whether they were men who had been fighting the army or gentle people who had always been peaceful and cooperative. It did not even matter if they were Indians who were working for the army and wearing the uniforms of soldier scouts. All that mattered was that they were Chiricahuas. In their rush to gather us all up, the army even included some Apaches from other tribes.

The first train, which carried the largest number of our people to

Florida, had gone out in April, five months before us. On that train, two Indians did try to escape. I will tell their stories, which are tales of great courage, as they were told to me some years later while I was at Fort Marion.

Those two men were Massai and Naisho Libaai. I knew both of them. I had seen them often around Fort Apache. Naisho Libaai was a small, thin man who did not speak much. He was a very watchful person, his eyes always alert, as if he expected to be attacked at any moment. He was known as Gray Lizard to the White Eyes. They thought he was a Chiricahua, but he was not even an Apache. He was a Tonkawa Indian. When Gray Lizard was a small boy, his parents and he had come from their homeland a journey of many days to the southeast of us. They were fleeing the White Eyes. They wanted to join the last Indians who had not been beaten.

Massai was a big man with broad shoulders who was always joking. He was very different from Gray Lizard, but he was Gray Lizard's best friend. They liked each other so much that they decided to be brothers. Whenever I saw them, they were always together. When they were younger they had sometimes joined Geronimo and Naiche's band of fighters. However, when all the Chiricahuas were rounded up, they had been living peacefully at Fort Apache.

Massai and Gray Lizard were on the biggest exile train, the one that took more than 400 of our people to Florida. It was hot and crowded. The people on that train suffered the most.

One of the Indian scouts with them, who knew those two young men had been with Geronimo's band, taunted them.

"They will chop your heads off when you get to Florida," he said.

Massai and Gray Lizard decided they had to escape. They spent three days loosening the nails from the window next to them. One night, when the train was slowing as it went up a hill, they slipped out. None of the White Eyes saw them escape. The big train had been going toward the sunrise for days, so they found themselves in a heavily wooded country that was strange to them. But they knew what to do. They traveled at night when no one could see them, always heading in the direction of the sunset. It took them many weeks, but they found their way, first to the Pecos River and then toward the peaks they saw rising in that sunset direction. At last they saw Mescal Mountain, near the White Eyes' new town of Globe, Arizona, where miners were eating the earth.

Because he was not a Chiricahua, Gray Lizard did not think the army would search for him. So he went to live among the White Mountain Apaches. That is where he lived out his life in peace. But Massai knew he would always be a hunted man. He went high up into the White Mountains in the valley of the Rinconada, where it would be hard for the White Eyes to find him. I have been told that he found a wife and had children. I do not know more of his story. All I know for sure is that he and Gray Lizard were the only Indians who truly escaped the prison trains.

COUNTING WORDS

SEPTEMBER 9, 1886

The indolent and vicious young men and boys were just the material to furnish men for the future; and these people although fed and clothed by the government, had been conspiring against its authority. They had been in communication with the hostiles, and some of them had been plotting an extensive outbreak.

GENERAL NELSON A. MILES

ANNUAL REPORT, U.S. ARMY DEPT. OF ARIZONA, 1886

"UH-ONE," A THICK-NECKED, red-faced soldier said, pointing a chubby finger at me as if it were a pistol. The train rocked, and he grabbed the seat next to him to keep his balance. Then he lifted his hand again. "Uh-too," he continued, aiming at Kanseah as he continued his count.

This counting was a thing that the White Eyes soldiers seemed to love. Three times each day, the White Eyes guards walked up and down the aisles, numbering us one by one as they had done time and again ever since we were brought in to Fort Bowie.

"Uh-threee, uh-fo-werr . . ." Red Face's voice was slow and

deliberate. However, as often as he did it, he was not very good at this counting job. He had to stop and start over several times when he lost track partway through.

I heard those counting words so often that I found by the time our prison train reached Florida I, too, could count pretty well in English. I say "pretty well," because it took me a long time to stop saying "uh" before each number and drawing them out as Red Face always did.

I repeated those counting words in my head as if they were part of a song or a chant. I used them myself, day after day, as the train went deeper into the land of the White Eyes. I counted the telegraph poles, the peaks of mountains, the antelope that ran from the train, the White Eyes' cows that were so stupid they did not even look up as we roared past.

Day followed day. We came to one train station after another, where we were stared at by big groups of White Eyes. Sometimes at those stations we heard the roar of guns as soldiers fired salutes to the White Eyes officers on our train.

The food was not bad. We ate all that we were given. But that caused a problem. Eating so much meant that I had to answer the call of nature. I have told you that they did not stop for us to sleep. It was worse that they did not stop for this. I could not go out into the brush and do things properly, making a hole in the earth and then covering it over — just as the mountain lion does. Having a latrine close to your wickiup or even inside it was a custom of the White Eyes, a custom that I found both disgusting and confusing. Our people are very modest and are taught to not even speak of such things. Even a small child learns that the proper thing to do is simply say, "I am going out," and then go away from camp.

I remember what happened that first day on the train when soldiers began escorting us one at a time to a small room on the train. Caterpillar Lip took me there. There, he told me by signs, I was to take care of my business.

I looked up at the small window. It was high on the wall and not large enough for a person to escape through. Was I supposed to use that window? But it was too high for me. I looked around and saw where someone before me had used the corner of the room. But that, too, did not seem right. I opened the door and looked out. Fortunately, just then Mr. Wratten was passing by. He saw my problem and explained what to do. He lifted up the covering from the small bench inside the room.

"You must make use of this bench with a hole in it. It is not good, but you and all the others must use that same hole. It is the White Eyes way."

I did as Wratten said. It made me feel ashamed and sick to go in there, but I had no choice. I cannot imagine how bad going to that little room must have been for our Chiricahua women.

I learned later that on the exile train that took the biggest group of Chiricahuas it had been worse. All they did was give the Apache prisoners cans or buckets in which to put their bodily waste. There was not even a private room for them to do this. It was something that no Apache had ever been forced to do before. It was sad and embarrassing for everyone.

We Chiricahuas are clean people. Little children are allowed to run around the camp with dirty faces and hands. But when you are old enough to be a hunter, when you begin to apprentice to be a man, that all changes. You must go down to the stream each day at dawn and plunge in over your head. I longed for a cleansing stream, even one chilled by winter.

A hunter does not want to smell strong. If he does, the game animals will scent him from far away. Before we went hunting or scouted about, we would always cleanse ourselves, not just in the running streams, but also in our sweat lodges. We would rub our bodies with purifying sage. We wanted to smell good around camp, too. If you smelled bad, people would make fun of you. We always kept our bodies clean. When a young Apache man was interested in a young woman, he wanted to smell especially good for her. So he would gather mint and make a little bundle of it to tie onto his shirt.

It surprised us that most White Eyes did not seem to know how to keep clean. The White Eyes soldiers who hunted us seldom bathed. We joked that white men could not creep up on us because we could smell them coming.

There was no sage or sweet mint on the train. No streams to bathe or wash our clothing in, no purifying sweat lodges. There was only that awful little room. Before long, I didn't just smell as bad as the dirtiest White Eyes, I smelled worse.

All that kept me from going crazy was my memories. I dove into them often, dove in deep as if they were a cold stream. When that smell was at its worst, I closed my eyes. I went back to the last time we were in one of our favorite places high in the the Sierra Madre. There was snow on the ground. There was ice on the surface of the water. Ah, it was so cold! But we continued to bathe. It made us stronger.

Geronimo appointed himself to make sure we boys bathed properly. Each morning, holding a stick in his right hand, he would lead a line of boys down to the creek. I was always the smallest.

"Build the fire, Little Foot," he would say to me.

I always felt honored that he asked me. It made me feel that I was the best fire maker. I lived for his praise. With my father and my mother gone, killed by the Mexicans, my mother's and father's parents all dead, I considered Geronimo my true grandfather. Like me, he had lost so many of his relatives. Nearly all of them had been murdered or taken away by the Mexicans or the White Eyes. Until I came to Florida and first saw someone die of sickness, I thought being killed by enemies was the only way an Apache could die.

After my fire was burning strongly, Geronimo would nod toward the water.

"Go first. Break the ice for the others," he said, handing me his stick.

Without hesitation, I waded into the stream. I shivered like a dog shaking water from its body. But I did not stop until I had made a big hole in the thin ice and dunked my head. Only then did I come out, hand Geronimo back his stick, and go to the fire to warm myself.

One after another, uh-one, uh-two, uh-three, just like that, every boy was sent with a gesture of Geronimo's stick to plunge into that icy flow and then come back to crouch shivering by the fire. But that was not the end of it. Once we were warm, Geronimo nodded again and pointed at the freezing water with his stick. Back into the water we went.

It was not something that I loved to do. But I was always glad I had done it. When you begin your day that way, it toughens you against the cold. The last time we sat by the fire before putting our clothing back on we absorbed so much warmth from that fire that the cold of the day no longer bothered us. The White Eyes have always been amazed at the way we Indians could go about comfortably in the winter with our legs bare, wearing only half the clothing a white man would wear. I think that our practice of bathing each dawn in that way is one reason why the cold does not bother us so much.

· · ·

We were tested that way by Geronimo because he wished us to grow up strong and tough. I never thought of how old he was when I was a child. To me, Geronimo was like a big old tree or a mountain, rooted and powerful and always there. I realize now that, by my reckoning, he was already more than sixty-five years old when I was a small boy. Yet at a time when most men only think of sitting in their wickiup, he was still out fighting our enemies. He had been fighting that way for more than forty years. That was one reason why no Apache was better known or more feared by the Mexicans and the Americans. His power was so great, both as a healer and as one who knew the medicine to confuse and defeat his enemies. No one living was his equal.

He had fought in more battles than could be counted and been wounded so many times, wounds that would have killed other men. Yet he remained unconquered. No gun could ever kill him. Despite his age, he was still thinking of training the next generation of men who would fight beside him. That is surely one reason why he gave us boys so much attention. But it is also true that Geronimo truly loved children and wanted to protect them. Training us to be strong and tough was part of that protection. The stronger and tougher we were, the more likely we were to escape death from the hands of our enemies.

It was Geronimo who made me my first weapons, a small bow

and little arrows. Uh-one, uh-two, uh-three, uh-four little arrows with blunt points. Normally a father would have done that, but I was an orphan by then.

I treasured that beautifully made little bow. I practiced with it every day. When I shot my first bird, a chubby ring-necked dove, I brought it to Geronimo. He praised me and then told me to make a fire. Together we cooked that bird and ate it. Others feared Geronimo for his fierceness or resented him for his fame, but I knew him as one who loved his family. That is why he always made war on the Mexicans. He never forgot that Mexican soldiers killed his first family, those he loved most in the world. They killed his mother, his wife . . . and his children.

It was always different for my grandfather when he was fighting the Mexicans. When he scouted about into Arizona and New Mexico, it was to take goods, especially ammunition. The Springfield and Enfield rifles we used were from the United States. Mexican bullets would not work in them. But when Geronimo led men into Mexico, it was to take revenge.

I once heard old Nana, who was with us there in the mountains and as fierce as any man a third his age, say something that explained how my grandfather felt.

"For each Apache that falls," Nana said, "we kill ten of them."

He did not say this just because he was thirsty for revenge, but because it was the only way we could fight and hope to win. Our enemies always outnumbered us by more than ten to one. It was Nana's way of reminding us that we had to be ten times as good as those who wanted to wipe us out or make us their slaves.

Sometimes, though, we took captives. We did not do this to sell them as slaves. We did so to add to our numbers and replace those we lost. There were always men among us who had been born as Mexicans but became Apaches. When we took children, it was to raise them as our own. Although it was hard for them at first, those *niños* soon learned to speak our language and know our ways. They discovered that the enemy Apaches they'd been taught to fear were kind to children. They never struck them or shouted at them, but treated them better than had their Mexican parents.

I remember one such captive boy. He told me that his name was Santiago McKinn. That was the first thing he told me, even before he had learned enough of our language to speak of more appropriate things. It is that way with White Eyes. They do not know enough to hide their names or just use them sparingly. They are always telling everyone who they are.

My friend Santiago was half-Mexican and half-white. It was 1885 when we took him from the ranch in New Mexico where his family was living. Because we were the same age, I spent much time with him, teaching him how to speak real language, not that foolish English which sounded to me like baby talk.

"Ant," he would say, pointing with his finger at one of the little red ones moving purposefully across the sand.

"*Dah*," I would have to say. "No. *De'ilch'che'e.*"

"*Dah*," he would repeat. That was one word he quickly understood. Then he would get a look of concentration on his face and try to talk like a real person. "*Duh-duh-hilk-ch-ch . . .*"

It would end up with us both laughing about the way our simple human words could stick in his throat like a bone.

I pulled cactus thorns out of his fingers when he was foolish enough to try to pick the fruit from a prickly pear. I showed him how to tie his headband, how to move so quietly through the brush that we could catch little quail with our hands. If we were not hungry, we would just let them go. Santiago and I laughed as we watched them bobbing and zig-zagging through the saguaros.

When the season of long nights came, Santiago and I sat as close as possible to Geronimo as he told stories by the fire. Chapo, the only one of Geronimo's sons who had lived to adulthood, always sat with our circle of boys when stories were being told. Chapo was a good listener. I tried to copy what he did. He was good at everything he did, whether it was hunting or defending the people or assisting his father in his curing ceremonies. Chapo was a good singer, just like his father. I knew, too, that he was in training to be one of those who carries the Mountain Spirit dancers. When Geronimo painted the dancers, Chapo was always there to help him. So even though he was now a young man, Chapo was always eager to hear his father's tales. Chee-hash-kish, Chapo's mother, was gone. She had been captured by the Mexicans. Like so many other Apaches before her, she was probably turned into a household slave or sent to work in the mines. That is the root of our long struggle with the Mexicans — their practice of stealing our people as if they were cattle. For years, Geronimo tried to find her, but she was never seen again by her family.

Santiago listened well. He never squirmed or poked other boys, or spoke when he should not. So he was never asked to go on one of those errands an Apache storyteller will give to an unattentive child.

"Ah, I do not have that thing which I need. You, go over to the wickiup of Nana and ask him if he has it."

Then the boy would go off to Nana, who would understand why that child had been sent.

"That thing he needs? *Ha-ah*, I know what it is. Let me see, do I have it? *Dah*. You must go over to the far side of the camp to Yahnozhe and ask him for it."

But Yahnozhe, too, would search in vain, then direct the boy to Perico. So it would go until that boy finally realized he was being taught a lesson about paying attention.

One night, when the wind in the mountains came from the winter direction, Santiago began to shiver. He was not yet as used to the cold as an Apache. My grandfather took off his warm cloth shirt.

"I am tired of this shirt," Geronimo said. "Is there anyone who would like to have it?" Then he held it out toward Santiago's little hands.

Santiago was only with us for the space of five full moons, but he was well on his way toward becoming a real human being. He had become tough and strong and finally spoke Chiricahua. He, too, had learned to bathe without hesitation in the cold, cleansing waters of the stream. When he was returned to his original family, he did not want to go. Head down, still wearing that shirt my grandfather gave him, my friend cried as if his heart would break.

I leaned back against the trunk of the old piñon tree beside that beautiful little stream where we had bathed. It was good to be there again. It was not winter, but the time of year when fruits ripen. I didn't remember coming there, but my heart was at peace. Any moment, my friends would find me, but it was good to be alone, to feel the earth beneath me, to hear the sounds of the birds and savor the warm touch of the wind.

Suddenly, the ground lurched beneath me and I was thrown forward. Was it an earthquake? I reached out my hands to keep from falling. But what I grasped was not the branch of a tree or the earth. It was something strangely flat and stiff and hard.

I opened my eyes. I was no longer in the mountains. I no longer smelled the sweet scents of fresh water and the wind through the piñons. Instead, the air was stale and smelled bad. Once again I was surrounded by the rattle and rumble of iron wheels on steel rails. My hands were gripping the seat in front of me. I was still on the prison train. Telegraph poles whipped backward past the window.

"Uh-one, uh-two, uh-three . . ." I began to whisper.

Then I shook my head and stopped. I could count forever and still never reach the end. I closed my eyes, but I could not find my way back into my memories, even in dream.

CUTTING OFF HEADS

SEPTEMBER 9, 1886

The murder of Mangas Coloradas was perhaps the greatest wrong ever done to the Indians.

GERONIMO

MANGAS COLORADAS

THE GUARDS ON OUR TRAIN were careful. Because ours was the train carrying Geronimo, they were especially watchful. Aside from the two train carriages that held us prisoners, there were two other cars filled with forty soldiers, one in front of us and one behind. The soldiers were all from the 16th Infantry, the men who had escorted us in from Skeleton Canyon.

We were not allowed to even touch the latches of our windows. I had managed by now, the second day of our journey, to get from the car that held mostly women and children into the one that held the grown men. I even got close enough to my grandfather for him to nod to me before I was told by a soldier to go to one of the empty seats farther back in the car.

In this car, the guards went around more often from seat to seat, keeping a closer watch. Caterpillar Lip showed me how the back of my seat could be placed down to make it into a bed.

I looked out the window as we went along. The land was now totally strange. But even though I was so much further than I had ever imagined from our homeland, I wished that I was out there on foot or horseback. It might be a journey of many days to go as far as we had gone in one day on this train, yet I was certain I could find my way home. Throughout our journey we had always been making our way more or less to the east, the direction of the sunrise. To find my way back I would only have to follow the train tracks toward the setting sun.

Since most of us could not understand English, we felt nervous when our guards pointed at us. Among our people, it is impolite to point your finger at another person unless you mean that person harm.

One guard in particular, Skinny Yellow Hair, seemed to think it was funny to try to scare us. He was the one who had kicked that puppy, then picked me up like a sack and tossed me onto the train. His eyes were small and mean. Skinny Yellow Hair had discovered a gesture that was easy for us Chiricahuas to understand. He would stare at one of us and then slowly draw his finger across his own throat.

That sent a chill down my spine. Why? Because of what we Apaches remembered.

Perhaps Skinny Yellow Hair did not know how seriously that threat of cutting your throat might be taken. Skinny Yellow Hair was only taunting us. He was not really going to cut off anyone's head. But we all remembered what had happened to Mangas Coloradas.

Mangas Coloradas means "Red Sleeves" in Spanish. That name was given to him because of a favorite red shirt he wore, and it is the name by which both Apaches and white men remember him. We do not speak his Chihenne name. It is improper to call out someone's Apache name after they have died.

Mangas Coloradas was the tallest of all the Mimbreno Apaches, six feet six inches as the White Eyes measure height. His vision was as great as his height. He tried to bring our different Chiricahua Apache bands together, seeking to unify his Chihenne with my own Warm Springs people and the Nednai of Geronimo. He also attempted again and again to find peace with the new white men. But each time Mangas Coloradas trusted them and came in under a flag of truce, he was betrayed.

The first time was in 1851. Prospectors had come into the land of the Mimbrenos to look for gold. Gold is sacred to Ussen, our creator. The Mountain Spirits do not want human beings to dig up the land searching for it. We knew that if they dug for gold, great sorrow would come to us. The Mountain Spirits would send earthquakes to shake the land. Many bad things would happen.

So Mangas Coloradas went to meet with the miners. He offered to guide them further south, into Mexico. There he could show them places where there was gold just sitting on top of the ground. They could pick it up without disturbing the earth. Instead of listening to him, those miners tied him to a tree and beat him with a whip. He was no longer a young man then. He was sixty years old. Still, he was stronger than most other men. In the night, he freed himself and escaped.

That was in 1851 at Pinos Altos. Great scars from that beating remained on Mangas Coloradas's back for the rest of his life. Whipping him that way was worse than killing him. It is the greatest of insults to beat a man as if he were a mule. He had only to show his scars to the other Apache chiefs, such as Cochise, to convince them to join him in a war against all of the White Eyes.

Our war to wipe them out and drive them all away had failed. Even though he had been betrayed and beaten by them, Mangas Coloradas realized we needed to find some way to live in peace with the White Eyes. So in 1863, he agreed once again to come in to Pinos Altos and talk with the army. The White Eyes soldiers had shown him a white flag of peace, but just as before, he was taken prisoner. This time he was handed over to General West. West was a hard-eyed man. He looked up at the tall old chief and then spoke to the soldiers assigned to guard the prisoner.

"You know what to do," General West said. Then he went to his tent.

That night, those white guards began to torture Mangas Coloradas. They heated the long knives fastened to the ends of their rifles in the fire until they were white-hot. They used them to burn his bare feet. Mangas Coloradas lifted himself to one elbow and spoke to them in Spanish.

I am no child to play with this way, he said.

In reply they emptied their rifles into him. They took his scalp. They cut off his head and boiled it in a black pot to clean off the flesh. Then they sent his skull back east.

The story of the death of Mangas Coloradas and how they took his head will never be forgotten by the Apaches. When our spirits travel to the Happy Place, we go in the same form our bodies were in when we died. Until the skull of Mangas Coloradas lies buried with his body, his headless spirit will wander that path forever.

So when Skinny Yellow Hair made his gesture of cutting off heads, a fist formed in my stomach. It was the same feeling I had as a little child whenever Gray One came into the camp to carry away badly behaved children. I was a well-behaved child, but I always ran and hid anyway. On this train, though, there was no place to run, nowhere to hide.

Fun and Perico were in the seat next to mine. Perico had allowed me to hold his parrot. I was stroking its head with one finger and trying to feed it a piece of bread crust, hoping it would not bite me again. Perico and Fun had been playing Mexican monte with a deck of cards when Skinny Yellow Hair came up to them. The mean-eyed soldier leaned close to them, grinned, and drew his bony finger across his throat.

"If Skinny Yellow Hair makes that gesture one more time," Fun said in a soft voice, as he shuffled the cards, "I will take his long knife and make another mouth for him in his throat."

"*Enjuh,*" Perico said, studying the four cards that had been placed faceup in front of him and then tapping the ace of spades. "I will hold him while you do it."

Perhaps they would have done so. Fortunately for Skinny Yellow Hair, there was someone with us in that train car who spoke both English and our language. It was our true friend, Mr. Wratten. As a boy, Mr. Wratten had worked for the trader at Warm Springs. Bit by bit, he had learned about our people. Each thing he learned had been like one rawhide stitch after another drawing together two pieces of leather until they become one piece of clothing. His love for our Chiricahua ways became a garment that would cover Wratten for the rest of his life.

Mr. Wratten had been with Nantan Tan Fox and Nantan Longnose when they sought out Geronimo and Chief Naiche in the mountains and talked them into surrendering. Mr. Wratten never twisted our leaders' words or tried to frighten us as Chatto and Mickey Free did. Only true words, whether in English or Apache, could live in his mouth. Because Mr. Wratten translated the words of Crook and Miles, Chief Naiche and Geronimo believed them and agreed to the surrender. Even years later in Oklahoma, when there were times that my grandfather and Wratten quarreled, my grandfather still trusted him as a translator.

When Nantan Miles said he was shipping the Chiricahuas far away, Mr. Wratten was chosen to go with my grandfather as his translator. But he was more than just a translator of words. Some of our elders, such as Nana, said Wratten must have been born a White Eyes by mistake. His spirit was clearly Chiricahua. He was at home among us.

Mr. Wratten was sitting several seats ahead of Fun and Perico and heard what they said to each other about Skinny Yellow Hair. Wratten looked over at my grandfather. Geronimo gave no outward sign. He just busied himself polishing his new boots with a cloth. But some unspoken message passed between them.

Skinny Yellow Hair was at the end of the car now, with Caterpillar Lip and another guard. Skinny Yellow Hair was laughing and pointing back down the aisle at the men he had just threatened. It seemed he was going to come back and do it again. Caterpillar Lip, the big soldier who had been kind to me, looked unhappy, but did nothing. I wondered why.

Later, I learned about how White Eyes soldiers command each

other. Caterpillar Lip did nothing to stop his foolish comrade because Skinny Yellow Hair outranked him. Among our people, any man can speak up when he thinks his leader is doing wrong. He can even refuse to fight, take his weapons, and go home to his family. It is very different among the White Eyes. Even when your leader is a fool, leading you to your death or ordering you to do something awful, you are never supposed to disobey.

Mr. Wratten stood up. As he passed Fun and Perico, he held out one hand. It was a delicate gesture. It meant that in no way was he giving them orders. He was just asking them to be patient, to wait for a moment. Perico just stared out the window, but Fun nodded his head.

The gesture Mr. Wratten made to Skinny Yellow Hair when he reached the end of the train was not subtle at all. He stabbed one of his long fingers into the man's chest, pushing him backward.

"Listen up," Mr. Wratten said.

The words he then snapped at the man in English were tight and hard. My favorite, which I held in my mind long enough to ask its meaning from Mr. Wratten, was one he repeated often to Skinny Yellow Hair. It meant just what I thought it did. It refers to a part of the body, and it is not a polite word in English. So I will not repeat it. However, it was a good description.

I watched Skinny Yellow Hair's face. At first it grew red, the color of anger. However, as Mr. Wratten spoke, making certain gestures, the red color went out of the guard's face. His face grew more and more pale. He began to look sick. He turned quickly and left the car with his hand over his mouth.

Mr. Wratten nodded to Caterpillar Lip, who saluted him. Then Mr. Wratten turned and came back down the aisle. He paused by Fun and Perico.

"That fool," Mr. Wratten said, "will not bother you again."

"*Ahehe'e*," Fun said. "Thank you. But Shee-kizzen Wratten, what did you tell him that made him grow sick?"

"Hmm," Wratten said. "I think he misunderstood. I simply described to him the way a Chiricahua guts and skins a deer."

"*Enjuh*," Fun said.

"*Ha-ah*," Perico agreed.

That was all they said. But after Mr. Wratten sat down, I noticed how hard it was for both Fun and Perico to hold back the smiles that kept trying to come to their faces. And when Wratten sat down by Geronimo, my grandfather was chuckling.

OPPORTUNITY

SEPTEMBER 9, 1886

Wratten is naturally reserved, and in addition to this has been warned against disclosing anything relating to Geronimo's capture. He informed this writer, however, in positive terms, that Geronimo and his band would be taken to Florida, and none of the Indians would be shot or hanged, and that was understood when Geronimo surrendered. He was asked if Geronimo could have escaped from Captain Lawton's command had he desired to do so. He answered "of course," as if it was mere child's play for an Indian to escape from the United States Army.

UNNAMED CORRESPONDENT

THE NEW YORK TIMES

OCTOBER 2, 1886

B Y THE TIME OUR TRAIN crossed the border into Texas, those White Eyes soldiers no longer seemed so worried about us. They thought they had us well guarded. A soldier with a rifle stood at either end of the car. Other white men were seated throughout the car to keep watch on us. They did not have rifles, though. Perhaps that was because their leaders had feared we Apaches might take their guns away from them and try to fight our way to freedom.

By the third day of our trip most of those guards were beginning to feel they had nothing to worry about. They had also been reassured by their nantan, Captain Lawton, that Geronimo and the other men had given their word not to try to escape. The two White Eyes soldiers in the seats closest to me even dozed off when their nantan was not watching them.

Skinny Yellow Hair was no longer a problem. Mr. Wratten had spoken to Captain Lawton, who had accompanied us as the nantan of the soldiers on our train, about the bad behavior of Skinny Yellow Hair. Perhaps it was not needed after the fright Mr. Wratten had given him, but Skinny Yellow Hair made no more trouble. Of all the White Eyes guards, only Skinny Yellow Hair still looked nervous. That was especially so whenever he had to go through our car and pass by Fun and Perico.

To the other White Eyes soldiers, we fearsome Apaches seemed to be nothing more than a ragged group of pathetic people. The job of guarding us had turned out to be easy. None of us resembled the bloodthirsty monsters of the dime novel stories the soldiers all read.

Although we were not monsters, we were still much more than those soldiers thought we were. Underestimating us was a mistake made often by people who did not truly know the Apaches. When they saw us at the San Carlos Agency or at Fort Apache, they were fooled by our appearance. They did not realize that though we might have been thin and wore dirty, torn clothing, each of us had been trained to be as hard as oak. Every one of us in those days, unless we were sick or very old, could run farther than the strongest horse. We could survive in mountains and deserts that would quickly take the life of one of their fat, well-dressed soldiers. We could not only use the lance and the knife and the bow and arrow, but also firearms. By the time they shipped us from our land, we had become as capable with rifles as the finest of their marksmen.

Geronimo himself often did not appear at first glance to be at all dangerous. It was not until men saw the fierce intelligence in his eyes, realized that his mind was always at work, and heard him speak that they quickly changed their opinion.

Geronimo liked to fool people with his innocent appearance. Many years later a white newspaperman came to Fort Sill to write something about Geronimo. He was disappointed when his bloodthirsty Apache warrior turned out to be a small old man. After talking for a while, the newspaperman began to brag. He had a new gun with him and was proud of his marksmanship. I was standing nearby, but the newspaperman did not even notice me. My grandfather did, though. He turned to me and winked, and I nodded back. This man, I thought, does not know what he is getting himself into.

"If the soldiers who fought Geronimo had owned guns such as this," the newspaperman said, "and shot as well as I do, they would have made short work of you Apaches."

My grandfather smiled at that.

"Let us have a contest," Geronimo said. "I will use my old gun and you will use your new one. There is a nail in that tree way over there. The one who hits closest to it will win the other man's gun."

The thought of winning Geronimo's own gun was too much for the newspaperman to resist, and he quickly agreed to the contest. He took long and careful aim before pulling the trigger. His bullet hit right next to the nail, only a hair's width away from it. But when it was Geronimo's turn, he just squinted, flicked up the barrel of his gun, and fired. Geronimo's bullet drove the nail into the tree. The white newspaperman went home without his new gun and with a story he was too embarrassed to tell anyone.

At each place we stopped between Bowie Station and San Antonio, crowds gathered. Mr. Wratten had explained to me why that was so. Word had spread that we had on board the most famous of all the Apaches.

Everyone wanted to see my grandfather, the fierce Apache whose name was always in the newspapers, the man no gun could kill, the bloodthirsty killer who had evaded capture for years, even when thousands of White Eyes soldiers hunted him. It surprised us. Until our train journey, even Geronimo himself had not realized how well known he was, not just to the army but to all the White Eyes. Now, though, seeing how great his fame had become was giving him ideas.

Soldiers and newspapermen, bankers and laborers, proper housewives and women with painted faces lined the tracks or peered out of nearby windows as we passed. Boys looked down from the branches of trees, where they had climbed up to get a better view. Sometimes the schools along the way let out their classes so that the teachers could escort the children down to join the staring crowd.

I tried to remember my manners and not stare back out the window, but it was hard not to do so. Although we were a show to them, they were just as much a show to us. I had never seen so many White Eyes. Whole populations of towns might be waiting at the rail station when our train pulled in. In fact, it was not just White Eyes who came to see us. I saw Mexicans, other Indians, even Chinese workers thronging the edges of the railbed. Some of them seemed to have been waiting throughout most of the day.

"They are waiting for a memory," Wratten said to me as we passed slowly by yet another great crowd of waving, shouting people. "They want to be able to tell their children they saw Geronimo."

My grandfather kept that restless mind of his busy by making plans. Now, having realized how much of an attraction he had become, his newest scheme had nothing to do with returning home.

At the last station stop before El Paso, the chance came for him to try that new plan out. We'd been allowed out of the train to stretch our legs under the relaxed guard of the soldiers. My grandfather tapped me on the arm.

"*Ka ch'igot'i*," Geronimo said. "There is opportunity here. See?"

My grandfather was looking out of the corner of his eye at one of the White Eyes soldiers who had clearly come to this station stop just to see the famous Apache. That man was staring openly at the cartridge belt my grandfather wore. The belt was, of course, empty of cartridges, but was being worn as a sign of my grandfather's ability as a fighter, and as an object of personal ornamentation.

That new cartridge belt was only one of several that Geronimo had in his considerable baggage. He had purchased it, along with his fine boots and a new alpaca coat, at the Fort Bowie commissary. Going into a fight or hunting, it was customary for our men to wear very little clothing. But on other occasions — especially on a journey — we would wear far more than most White Eyes. Perico, for example, sometimes put on as many as five shirts, one over the other, with a vest and a coat on top of them. The shirts we preferred were like the one my grandfather had on under one of his favorite vests that day. It was a colored calico shirt with long sleeves, buttoned at the neck, but not tucked, worn in what the White Eyes called Chinese style. There was certainly no effort on our part to dress like those Chinese workers we often saw in the towns and around the railroads. We just found it more comfortable and more sensible to wear our shirts that way, loose and long, hanging down to our knees, bloused in at the waist by a cartridge belt like that one my grandfather was wearing. All of our men were fond of not only such cartridge belts, but also necklaces, earrings, bracelets, and rings of all kinds.

Wearing most of the clothes you owned and all your jewelry when you traveled made great sense to me. Not only did you look fine and feel comfortable, you did not tire out your arms and shoulders by carrying a bulky valise as white men did.

"Opportunity, Grandfather?" I said.

"*Ha'ah*," he said. "You will see it." Then he gestured to Mr. Wratten, who was standing close by. "My friend," he said, "come and help me."

Together they walked over to the soldier who'd been eyeing my grandfather's cartridge belt. When they came back, the soldier had the belt and my grandfather was jingling a handful of coins.

"Seven dollars and fifty cents," Geronimo said, counting them one more time before putting them into his pouch. "*Nzhoo*. Good opportunity."

It was only the first of many cartridge belts that Geronimo would sell on our journey, each white buyer delighted to be able to brag that he now owned the very cartridge belt that the most famous Indian in the world had worn into all his battles.

·　　·　　·

However, not everyone knew that our train was carrying Indian prisoners of war. Because of that, one of the funniest things I've ever seen happened after we left the station that Mr. Wratten told me was named El Paso.

We had been traveling all day and it was now dark. Almost everyone on the train was asleep or dozing off. It seemed as if I was the only one still fully awake. I was again in the car with the men, sitting just behind Mr. Wratten, who was sharing a seat with Ahnandia. Except for my grandfather, there was no one Mr. Wratten liked better than Ahnandia. Ahnandia was a young, pleasant man who was always smiling and joking. Only a few years older than Mr. Wratten, Ahnandia was a cousin of Geronimo. Ahnandia's wife, Tahdaste, who was in the other car with the women and children, had served as a messenger for my grandfather more than once, going with Lozen into Mexican towns to trade or disguising herself as a Mexican woman to find out information.

Wratten's friendship with him was a deep one. Ahnandia had saved Mr. Wratten's life back at Turkey Creek. One night, as Wratten was walking back to his home, he sensed someone coming up quickly behind him. Before he could do anything, he heard a loud thump. He turned to see Ahnandia standing over a drunk White Mountain Apache man he had just knocked unconscious. Had it not been for Ahnandia's quick action, that man would have killed Mr. Wratten with the big knife he still held in his hand. Mr. Wratten had spoken to his superiors and written letters trying to get them to spare Ahnandia and his wife from being sent to Florida, but they had ended up on the train with the rest of us.

Both Ahnandia and Tahdaste were determined to do the best they could, even in captivity. While we were held at Fort Bowie, only my grandfather had done better than they did at making things and selling them to the White Eyes soldiers and civilians who came to stare at us. Ahnandia had used part of the money he earned to purchase an elementary reading book. With Mr. Wratten's help, he was making good progress learning to read and speak English. Ahnandia's beloved reading book rested on his chest as he slept, visible in the moonlight that came in through the window. I stared at that reading book. What would it be like to be able to make out words from those strange little black marks on white paper?

Then I heard noises that took my gaze away from Ahnandia's book. A soft thud and then another came from the back of the train, followed by whispered words in English. A creaking sound told me that the back door of our train car was being slowly opened. I turned to look back, keeping my head low as I did so. What I saw shocked me. There, in the doorway, was the face of one of the strangest White Eyes I had yet seen. His beard was brown, covering every bit of his face except for his wide, bloodshot blue eyes. He was certainly not a White Eyes soldier. His clothes were ragged and dirty, and he wore a half-crushed black top hat on his head. A face appeared over his shoulder. That face was as dirty as the first man's, although this second White Eyes had no hair at all aside from a scraggly black circle around his mouth. The two men took one slow step together into the train car that they'd thought was empty. In the half-light their eyes were just taking in the shapes of passengers reclined in sleep, most of them covered by blankets.

I did not know it at the time, but apparently only empty passenger cars were usually taken along this part of the train line late at night. Ours, of course, was not a regularly scheduled train. By now, those two ragged men were halfway down the aisle. They looked more confused with each step, yet they continued on.

I'd thought I was the only one awake in our train car, but I wasn't. Geronimo was aware of all that was happening. Just as the two ragged men reached the seat where he lay, he sat up and looked straight at them.

"*Quien es?*" Geronimo said in Spanish. "Who is this?"

My grandfather's words were softly spoken. However, the light of the moon showed his face to them. Because of all the photos that had appeared in the newspapers, those features of his were well known. Even those two hobos who had hopped onto the wrong train realized that the one confronting them was none other than the fierce and dangerous Apache Indian, Geronimo.

"ARRRRHHHHH!" yelled the first man.

"SAINTS PRESERVE US!" screamed the second one.

As one, they turned and tried to run. But the two tangled their legs together and fell to the floor of the car. By now, everyone in our car was awake. Some, such as Fun and Perico, truly were shouting battle cries. Those were answered by the ululating cries of women and the screams of frightened little ones from the car next to ours that held the rest of our party. Even Perico's bird was shrieking. Skinny Yellow Hair came running into the car, just in time to be bowled over by the two hobos, who had righted themselves and were trying to escape from what must have seemed like the worst nightmare they had ever had. My grandfather watched it all in quiet amusement.

I looked toward Mr. Wratten and Ahnandia. Both of them were bent over with laughter at the sight of our two unexpected visitors still shouting and scrambling to get away from the angry soldiers coming into our car from either end. Skinny Yellow Hair lay stunned in the aisle, the mark of a large footprint across his face where one of the frantic bums had trampled him. My friend Caterpillar Lip was standing at the far end of the car. He was leaning against the wall of the train and holding his sides, as weak with laughter at what he saw as we were.

Finally, the two hobos were caught. The train was stopped so that the two men could be put off. But as Caterpillar Lip walked the two pathetic men past my grandfather, Geronimo held up a hand to stop them. Then he looked toward Mr. Wratten.

"Amigo Wratten," Geronimo said, "these two men who made us all laugh, they look even poorer than Apaches. Tell them to hold out their hands."

When Mr. Wratten translated those words, the two confused hobos nervously extended their right hands toward my grandfather. With great care, he put one of his brass rings into each of their dirty paws, closed their hands, and then patted each of them on their shoulders as if they were children.

The next day, after all of our amusement the night before, my grandfather seemed relaxed. It was just after the sun reached the middle of the sky that our train came to another depot. As always, there were many White Eyes gathered to see us. To my surprise, we were all taken off the train. Then, instead of waiting for us to get back on board, that train left the station. Not only that train left us. The guards who had been with us were replaced by new men. Caterpillar Lip and Skinny Yellow Hair and all the others from the 4th Cavalry were sent back.

I did not mind seeing most of them go, but all of us, including my grandfather and Chief Naiche, were disturbed when we realized that the nantan, Captain Lawton, was also being sent back to Fort Bowie.

"Why are they taking away Nantan Lawton?" Geronimo asked.

"It is the way the army does things," Mr. Wratten explained. "White Eyes who go to war must always stay in the same band unless their leaders assign them to another. His leaders have ordered him to return."

There was nothing we could do. It seemed as if whenever the government gave us a white soldier and we had taught him enough for him to begin to understand us, he would be taken away.

The crowd waiting at the depot did not get a chance to see much of us. There was no opportunity for my grandfather to do any business. We were quickly escorted by a new party of White Eyes soldiers onto another special train that would take us the short distance to Fort Sam Houston. Before we left, I stared hard at the sign that was fastened to the side of the station house. If I had been able to read then as I can now, I would have known where we were. I would have known that those black shapes that crawled like insects across the white board spelled out the name of the place we had arrived.

SUNSET DEPOT
SAN ANTONIO, TEXAS

But even if I had been able to read, I would not have known why we were to be kept so long at our next stop. I would not have known what great danger my grandfather now faced. There were powerful men who planned not just to end Geronimo's journey, but his life.

EVERYBODY HAS TO DIE SOMETIME

SEPTEMBER 10, 1886

I HOPE NOTHING WILL BE DONE WITH GERONIMO
WHICH WILL PREVENT OUR KEEPING HIM AS A
PRISONER OF WAR IF WE CANNOT HANG HIM
WHICH I WOULD MUCH PREFER.

TELEGRAM FROM PRESIDENT GROVER CLEVELAND TO

GENERAL NELSON A. MILES, SEPTEMBER 1886, SENATE

EXECUTIVE DOCUMENT 117, 49TH CONGRESS, SECOND

SESSION, PAGE 2, AUGUST 24, 1886

OUR STOP AT SAN ANTONIO was supposed to be short, just enough for the soldiers who had accompanied us to leave for home and be replaced by new guards. But it turned out to be long. Very long. We waited there for forty-two days.

Why? It was because General Miles still had some honor. When Chief Naiche and Geronimo surrendered to Miles, the general made promises to us. Almost all of them were soon broken. But there was one promise that General Miles refused to break — to treat my grandfather and the others in our little band not as criminals but as prisoners of war. The white father in Washington, President Cleveland, was not pleased about that. He wanted my grandfather to be hung. It was his message, sent over the talking wires, that ordered the train to stop in San Antonio and the Apache prisoners to be taken to Fort Sam Houston.

I imagine the talk that happened then.

The president, a fat man with a mustache as big as a small animal, stands in front of his desk in his round white room.

"We will hang Geronimo now," he says. He makes one hand into a fist and pounds it into the palm of his other hand.

General Miles stands in front of the president. He raises his hand to show he is speaking the truth.

"Geronimo agreed to terms of surrender," Nantan Miles says. "To try him as a common criminal and execute him now would break all of the rules of war. We cannot do this."

Nantan Lupan comes into that round white room with the president.

"The Apaches," Tan Fox says, "are prisoners of war. That is how they must be treated. They must be sent to Florida. We have signed papers promising this."

The round face of the president becomes as red as fire. He turns his back on his two generals and glares at his desk. He knows their words are true, but he is not yet ready to admit it.

So that argument and others like it went on while we waited, waited while those who wanted to kill us and those who wanted to send us on to Florida talked back and forth.

As soon as we arrived at Fort Sam Houston, they escorted us into the fenced-in place where they had their warehouses for the quartermaster. A row of tents had been set up for us to stay in. Those tents even had cots for us. It was so much better than having to sleep each night on a rattling train.

The iron gate that led into the enclosure was guarded by night, but there was plenty of room to walk about in that fenced-in area. During the days the gate was left open. Before long, people from the town, which was only two miles away, began to come in big numbers to see us. They seemed delighted to look at us and also a little fearful. Some of the white men scowled at us and said things that I knew, from the tone of their voices, were not polite. We ignored such comments. Others treated us with such respect that you would have thought we were their relatives. Women handed us bouquets of flowers they had picked and asked permission to come close and pin little ribbons onto our shirts.

General Stanley was the nantan in charge of the fort. He behaved in an equally friendly way to us. He took us all on a tour of San Antonio so that we could see the sights of the town. The most important place was the ruins of a fort where a small band of white men fought a great fight against a big Mexican army. The White Eyes soldier who told us the story of that battle had tears in his eyes as he spoke to us of the brave men who fought there and refused to retreat. It was a good story that we all appreciated. We Apaches all knew how treacherous the Mexicans, who had killed my own parents, could be. It made me wonder yet again why the White Eyes did not just make us their allies so we could fight the Mexicans together.

A few days after that, we were allowed out to watch the regimental band play and march on the parade ground. That was very good. I liked the uniforms they wore. The different sounds those instruments could make were very pleasing. They made my feet want to move along with them.

"What are these songs?" I asked Mr. Wratten.

"They are called marches," he said.

"Someday," I said, "I will learn to make this kind of music."

On yet another day, Nantan Stanley permitted a clothing peddler to come and display his wares to us. We still had plenty of money, both dollars and pesos. That peddler did well. Soon all of the men had new boots on their feet, and the women had fine new dresses.

Nantan Stanley also allowed Chief Naiche and Geronimo to come and talk with him. They asked why they were being kept at Fort Sam instead of being sent on to Florida to join the rest of the

Chiricahuas. With Mr. Wratten's help, they told Nantan Stanley about the promises General Miles made them. He said he had never heard of those promises. That upset Chief Naiche very much. For a time he stopped talking to my grandfather, blaming him for trusting a liar.

One day stretched into another. Aside from watching the constant stream of white visitors, there was little for us Apaches to do. All we could do was sit around Fort Sam Houston, wondering what would happen. Each day was like the one before. We walked about, played cards, ate, slept, and worried. None of us knew about the big debate between the white father and the generals about what to do with Geronimo. However, the feeling began to grow that the army was getting ready to kill us. We were being treated well, but we had been treated this way before. One day the soldiers would be our friends and the next day they would try to wipe us out.

Some men talked of trying to escape. They were only half-serious. A few of us had knives, like the small one I kept hidden in my boot, but those were our only weapons. Well-armed soldiers were all around us.

Our tents were set up together. Mr. Wratten's tent was right in with ours. For some reason the soldiers did not seem to notice or care that Mr. Wratten had his own guns with him. He had pistols, several rifles, a shotgun, and much ammunition.

One day he came to my grandfather's tent to talk with him. Mr. Wratten was worried.

"My friend," Mr. Wratten said, "I am afraid that they are making plans to seize you and hang you."

To Mr. Wratten's surprise, my grandfather was not upset.

"My friend," my grandfather said, his voice as calm as if they were talking about taking a walk together, "I do not fear for myself. They are not going to kill me. I have the promise of Ussen, the Life Giver, that I will live to an old age and have a natural death. Ussen also promised that my sister and Daklugie would not die."

Geronimo paused and then nodded his head thoughtfully.

"But Ussen said no such thing about my men. For them I fear. They are unarmed. If we had weapons we would fight it out as we have in the past. Everybody has to die sometime and regardless of the odds, we would fight. Haven't we done so for years? And in the last three years haven't the odds been five hundred to one?"

Mr. Wratten sat there for a long time nodding his own head after my grandfather finished his speech. He knew how true Geronimo's words were. Throughout the five moons before our surrender we had been hunted hard. There were five thousand American troops looking for us to the north and at least as many Mexicans seeking us in the south. There were only thirty-seven of us then, including women and children. We had fought battle after battle, always greatly outnumbered. But we never lost, and not one of us was killed.

After each battle we left the bodies of at least ten of the enemy on the field behind us. When we needed food, Geronimo got us food. When we needed ammunition or clothing, my grandfather found it for us. Each time our enemies thought we were trapped, my grandfather used his power or we turned to Lozen to see what she could see. Then we would find a way to escape.

I remember one time in particular. This time the White Eyes had us pinned down. It was still dark, and there was a chance we could use that darkness to escape. Soon, though, the sun would rise, and the only route for our escape led across an empty basin with not even a bush to give us cover.

Geronimo began to sing. His power was in that song, a song that asked the dawn to hold back its light so that we might get away. His song held back the dawn. I know this may be hard for one who was not there to believe, but it is true. We escaped in the darkness that went on far beyond the time when the sun should have risen.

It was no idle boast that my grandfather made when he told Mr. Wratten we would be ready to fight if needed, even though we were without weapons and faced such great odds.

Mr. Wratten looked down at the ground and scuffed the red earth with the toe of his boot. Then he spoke words that showed me how closely his spirit was connected to ours.

"If an attack is made on unarmed men," Wratten said, his words as deliberate and slow as the steps of a man climbing a high hill, "I cannot watch it without doing what I can to help. In my tent are some guns and ammunition. Tell your men. If an attack comes, they are to get them. I can't let unarmed men be murdered, even if I have to join them."

Chapo was standing off to his father's side while Wratten spoke. A little smile came to Chapo's face as Wratten finished. Geronimo's expression did not change, but I could tell that what Wratten said had pleased my grandfather very much.

After Wratten left the tent, my grandfather sat for a time looking at the door, which faced the east. Then he pulled out the bundle of things he always kept with him and held them in his lap. Those were the things he used for some of his curing ceremonies. Most white men do not understand that my grandfather was as great a healer as he was a man. If someone was suffering from a sickness sent to him by a dangerous creature such as the bear or the coyote or the snake, if someone was in need of being sung over, Geronimo was the first one they would think of asking for help. Time and again, people would call him by name to come to them and help. He never refused.

No matter where Geronimo went, he always was able to keep his bundle with him. The soldiers would take away the personal possessions of other Apache men, but somehow they always missed that bundle of my grandfather's. It was as if they could not see it. Or perhaps it was like Perico's bird, able to take wing and then return.

I was the only one present and I sat there quietly, being careful not to scratch myself or do anything you are not supposed to do when a ceremony is being done. I had been trained this way by my grandfather to help him. But Geronimo did not open his bundle. He did not take out the bag of pollen or the black tray or the downy eagle feather or the abalone shell. He just sat there, holding that leather-wrapped packet in his hands. I think he was listening to his power. Then he turned and looked at me.

"Our friend Wratten," he said, "is a good person. He has proven his loyalty many times. If we call him by his name, he will answer and stand by us, even if it means fighting against the other White Eyes."

Chapo nodded. "You are right, my father."

Then my grandfather smiled. "But we do not have to worry," he said. "None of us will die here."

Just as my grandfather predicted, the attack never came. A few days later, Wratten came again to my grandfather. Wratten was happy and wore a big grin on his face.

"We are to get back on the train tomorrow," he said. "They are taking us to Florida as they promised."

"Ussen has spoken," Geronimo said.

Many years later, I learned how close a thing it was. It had taken six weeks for a decision to be made while we waited in uncertainty. Not only did many in the government wish to take my grandfather and hang him, they also thought of doing the same with Chief Naiche, Fun and Perico, Yahnozhe, Chapo, and the other grown men. The only two Apache men among us who were not in danger were Martine and Kayitah, the army scouts who had come to us and urged Chief Naiche and my grandfather to surrender. But as soon as they had done their job, the army shipped them off with all the rest of us — even though they were still enlisted in the army and supposed to be drawing pay from the same government that was now sending them into exile.

Neither Chief Naiche nor my grandfather nor any of us treated Martine and Kayitah badly. We knew they were honest and honorable men. Still, they kept at a bit of distance during our journey. You can see that in the photo taken at a rest stop just before we got to San Antonio. There was a photographer who wished to take a picture of the hostiles. My grandfather had been happy to agree. He always liked the idea of having his picture taken. But Kayitah and Martine did not get out onto the embankment to pose with the others. They stayed on the train. All you can see of them in that photo is Martine's head in the window of the train.

When we were all back on the train again I began to think about what Martine and Kayitah had done. My thoughts carried me back to the mountains and that time of my grandfather's final surrender.

SCOUTS

AUGUST 24, 1886

While at Fort Apache, July 1, to inspect the condition of the Chiricahua and Warm Springs bands who had refused to leave with Geronimo and Mangus, Miles learned from the Chiricahua Ki-e-ta, who had deserted on the hostile raid in May, that some of the followers of Geronimo and Nachite were, like himself, tired of warfare, and that the entire band might be persuaded to listen to reason and agree to surrender if two or three men they knew were sent to talk with them. Ki-e-ta consented to be one of the emissaries, and an influential Chiricahua known as Martine was selected as the second member of the ambassadorial party.

BRITTON DAVIS

THE TRUTH ABOUT GERONIMO, 1971

GERONIMO'S HANDS WERE SHAKING as Kayitah and Martine spoke to him about surrender. It was not because he was nervous. For the last three days he had been drinking the mescal liquor that Lozen and Tahdaste brought from the town of Fronteras.

Those two brave women had ridden into that Mexican town to scout about and get supplies. Messengers from the town had sent word they would not attack us if we came in to trade. Unless a Mexican town was the home of people who had injured us in the past, we always preferred to trade. Those who think that Apaches always want to fight and kill are wrong. We love peace as much as any person. If the Mexicans had not killed my grandfather's family when he was young, he might never have gone to war with them.

Along with the supplies she and her companion purchased, the Mexican traders gave Lozen a gift: three big jugs of mescal liquor. They probably hoped that we Apaches would drink the liquor and let down our guard. Big rewards were still being paid for Apache scalps. In the state of Chihuahua, they offered 200 pesos for the scalp of an Apache man and 150 pesos for the scalp of a woman.

"We are your amigos," the merchants of Fronteras told Lozen and Tahdaste. "Tell your men to come next time. We will give them a party they will never forget."

Lozen smiled as she repeated those words to Naiche and Geronimo when she got back to our camp. "It is an honest invitation," Lozen said. "If we go to Fronteras, I am sure we will never forget it. After all, dead people are not able to forget anything."

Needless to say, we did not go into Fronteras.

Lozen was that way. She often saw things that were beyond the sight of normal eyes. It was fortunate we did not accept their invitation but went around their town. We learned later that more than 200 Mexican soldiers were hidden in Fronteras, waiting for us.

"Are those Mexicans so greedy that they would just kill any Apache for his scalp?" I asked Lozen after she finished speaking with our leaders. I knew the answer, but wanted to hear what she would say.

"Not just any Apache," she said. "Listen. I will tell you a story."

There was another time years ago, she said, when she was in Mexico with her brother Victorio. Victorio had sent her and another woman into a small Mexican town to do some trading. Lozen had a bag of pesos they'd captured from a party of Mexican soldiers who attacked them. When the failed attack was over, those soldiers had no more use for pesos or anything else. With those pesos, Lozen and the other woman planned to buy food and new clothing. The people of that town were known to be friendly to the Apaches. They were as close to trustworthy as any Mexican who had not become an Apache could be. Also, Lozen and the other Apache woman were dressed in Mexican clothing. At first glance, they did not appear to be Apaches.

But as they came closer to the town, they noticed how silent it was. More than a hundred people lived there, but they heard no voices. When they entered the little square, they saw why it was silent. It was now a town owned by death. All of the people were still there, from the smallest children to the oldest grandmothers. But all of them had been killed, perhaps only a few hours before Lozen found them. All of them had been scalped.

Lozen shook her head and spat on the ground. "The Mexicans now say we were the ones who wiped out that town. It was not us. You know that we do not take scalps."

I nodded when she spoke those words. That is one of the biggest lies told about Apaches, that we took the scalps of the people we killed. Taking a scalp is a twisted thing. It may bring ghost sickness to the one who does it.

"No," Lozen said, "those innocent people were rounded up at gunpoint by Mexican scalp hunters who saw how much their hair looked like that of Apaches. The scalp hunters marched them into the town square and killed them in front of their church. With all of those scalps, they thought they were now wealthy men."

Lozen smiled then. It was not a smile that went beyond her mouth. The look in her eyes was not happy, but grim.

"We were sickened by what we saw. We went quickly back to our camp and told my brother what we had seen. 'Find where they went,' Victorio said.

"So I used my power and it told me where those scalp hunters had gone. We rode ahead of them and set up an ambush. When those evil men began to pass through a narrow canyon, we shot arrows at them and rolled down big rocks. They did not live to enjoy their wealth. We burned those bags filled with Mexican scalps in a big fire."

No one knows how many other Indians, such as Tarahumaras and Pueblos, died at the hands of scalp hunters. No one knows how many dark-haired Mexican scalps were taken during those years when fortunes were being made from Apache hair. Because no one could tell whose scalp it was after it was taken, the Mexicans also offered bounties in another way. When it came to famous men such as Fun or Nana, they wanted not just that man's hair, but his whole head. The biggest reward of all was being offered to whoever could bring in the head of Geronimo.

We'd seen Martine and Kayitah coming from far off. Two of us boys were watching from the top of the mountain. Kanseah had the field glasses because he was a little older than me, so he spotted them first.

"Are those deer?" he said.

I squinted, but could see nothing. Even with the field glasses, they seemed no larger than specks of dust. Kanseah's eyes had always been better than mine, so I handed him back the glasses.

Kanseah looked again. "*Dah*," he said. "They are men. It is . . . Martine and Kayitah. I recognize them by their walk."

No one but another Apache could have found us there, deep in Old Mexico. Captain Lawton, who we called Nantan Longnose, was the man General Miles sent into Mexico to find us. At first, he searched for us 200 miles south of where we really were. Geronimo's war medicine was so strong that Lawton and his big party of White Eyes soldiers had become confused. They thought they were following our trail when they were just becoming more and more lost. They walked until their shoes wore out and never even saw the smoke from our camps.

It was not until Nantan Longnose left the soldiers behind and just went out with a small party of Apache scouts that our real trail was found. Martine and Kayitah knew just how to locate us. Martine had fought beside Geronimo in the past as one of Juh's men. Kayitah was the cousin of Yahnozhe. They had both been in the mountains with Geronimo many times before. Even though they were now working as scouts for the Americans, they hoped that we would not kill them. They hoped we would remember that they were good men, friends, and relatives.

I went down and told my grandfather what we had seen. He and several other men came up to the lookout point. Geronimo took the field glasses from Kanseah and spent some time studying the two figures that were coming right toward us.

"Kayitah," he said at last, "and Martine." He turned his head and spat on the ground.

Yahnozhe broke the silence. "They are our brothers," he said.

"It doesn't matter who they are," Geronimo said, rubbing his forehead. He was not in a good mood. He had finished the last of that mescal liquor the night before. All that was left of it was that bad hangover. "If they come any closer they are to be shot."

"They are holding a stick with a white cloth," Fun said. "They are coming to talk."

"Let us find out why they have come," Yahnozhe said. The thought of shooting Kayitah, his own cousin, was too much to bear. "They are very brave to do this."

"*Dah*," Geronimo said. "They are only here for money. The long-knives will pay them a reward if they bring us in." He turned and looked at Yahnozhe. "When they get close enough, shoot."

"If there is any shooting done," Yahnozhe said in a slow voice, "it will be at you, not them. The first man who lifts a rifle I will kill."

"I will help you," Fun said.

"Hunh," my grandfather said. "Let them come in."

Then he looked at me and shrugged.

I understood. It was that way among our people when we went to war. You could only lead our people as far as they wanted to be led. If you gave a man a command he did not like, he could simply refuse to do it, especially if it was something that would bring injury to his own relatives. No one would hold it against him. There was no anger or hard feelings between my grandfather and Yahnozhe.

That is one reason why it was often hard for Apache men when they became scouts for the White Eyes. The army expected soldiers to do everything and anything their officers told them to do, even when it was bad or crazy. That is why so many White Mountain Apache scouts turned against the army and fought at Fort Apache when the White Eyes soldiers murdered Noche-del-Klinne, the prophet.

I looked out the window of the train. All I could see out there was darkness. But in my memory I saw again the things that happened at Cibeque Creek, the events that led to so many useless deaths.

THE PROPHET

IT WOULD BE WELL TO ARREST [NOCHE-DEL-
KLINNE] OR SEND HIM OFF OR HAVE HIM
KILLED WITHOUT ARRESTING

TELEGRAM FROM

SAN CARLOS INDIAN AGENT TO COLONEL CARR,

FORT APACHE AUGUST 1881

NOW, YEARS LATER, when I think of how the prophet died, I see how foolishly Captain Carr, who was then in charge at Fort Apache, behaved. As had happened before and would happen again, the bad decisions of white men in power caused many deaths for no good reason. As had happened before and would happen again, it began at a time when my grandfather, Geronimo, was trying to live in peace with the White Eyes.

It was 1881, the year after Victorio and his band were wiped out in Mexico at Tres Castillos. That was when Noche-del-Klinne had his vision. He was not Chiricahua, but one of the Brainless People, as we call those western Apaches in our language. (That name does not bother them. They have their own names for us, too.)

Noche-del-Klinne was a small, slender man who was no more than thirty-six years old. He was well liked by everyone who knew him. Not just his own people and the other Apache bands at Fort Apache respected him, but also the White Eyes soldiers, the white men, and the black white men, the buffalo soldiers, alike.

Fort Apache was the first place where I saw one of those black white men. My parents and I had just come into the fort the night before. We were lined up on the big parade ground with all the other Apaches there to be counted. A big broad-shouldered man came walking along our line, tallying our numbers. When he got close enough for me to really see him, I was shocked. I was very young, and the sight of a blue-coated soldier whose skin was dark as fire-blackened wood was new to me. I thought he was either a bear wearing clothing or a badly burned white man wearing a cap of buffalo hair. I had only seen light-colored white men before, whose faces ranged from the pale color of a smoke-tanned hide to the fiery red of a sunset. But as that buffalo soldier came closer I realized his skin was too smooth and healthy to have been burned. Was every other part of his body some different color? Maybe red or green or yellow? If he was naked, would he look like a rainbow? As I said, I was very young.

As he came even closer and looked right at me, the thought struck me that he was some sort of monster like those one of my uncles had told me would appear to take away disobedient children.

Have I done something really wrong? I thought.

I ducked behind my mother's skirts for safety. The black white man roared with laughter and walked away.

My mother did not laugh at me. "Do not be afraid of him, Little Son," she said. "He is not a monster. He is just a black white man, one of those whose hair is like that of a buffalo. You will see plenty of them around here."

I soon realized how right my mother's words were. In the days and weeks that followed, there were black white soldiers everywhere. From their actions and the way our men treated them, I could see that those black white men were honorable. They seemed more likely to treat an Indian with respect than the white soldiers did. But even though the color of their skins was different from that of their leaders, when they were ordered to shoot at Indians, they never hesitated.

That was also true when it came to the Apache scouts. There was only one time when they hesitated to follow orders to shoot their own people. That time with Noche-del-Klinne.

Noche-del-Klinne had been a scout himself. But he did not like war and fighting. He did not reenlist after his three months' service was over. He loved his people and wanted to bring good to them. His spirit was inclined to do that in a peaceful way.

"That is probably why the vision came to him," Geronimo said. Then he smiled. "Such a vision would not have chosen me."

The prophet's vision was a simple one. The Apaches could send the White Eyes away from this land. They could do so not by fighting, but by dancing. Noche-del-Klinne had the people gather around, like the eight spokes of a wheel, with him standing at the center. Then, as they sang and danced in a great circle, he would sprinkle them with *hoddentin*, the sacred yellow pollen that we gather from the tule rushes.

"Soon," Noche-del-Klinne told them, "those great chiefs who died, Victorio and Cochise and Mangas Coloradas, will reappear. If you just dance and sing and keep dancing and singing this will happen. Ussen will make it so that the white men will go away."

So the people danced and sang.

More and more came in increasing numbers to his camp at Cibeque Creek. My parents did not go. His message did not appeal so much to Chiricahuas. My grandfather Geronimo went once. He did not dance. He was not one of those who brought the gifts of blankets and horses that the prophet requested. He liked Noche-del-Klinne but doubted that his dancing would bring back the dead. He thought it would likely cause the opposite to happen. He was right about that.

"One problem with these white men," my grandfather said to me later, "is that they are like nervous horses. Even something as harmless as shaking a blanket can make them rear up and strike out. Everything about Apaches scares them."

The dancing at Cibeque Creek scared Colonel Carr, the commander at Fort Apache. He and the agent at San Carlos became convinced that the prophet was inciting the Indians to violence. In August, Carr could stand it no longer. He decided to end what Noche-del-Klinne was doing. He did the one thing that made it certain violence would occur. He issued orders against the prophet.

"I want him arrested or killed or both," he said.

One hundred and seventeen armed men were sent to Cibeque Creek. Among them were twenty-three White Mountain Apache scouts. The scouts looked around and saw no war preparations being made by Noche-del-Klinne and the people gathered there. Instead, they had been planting their corn.

When the soldiers arrived, Noche-del-Klinne was standing in front of his wickiup surrounded by seventeen or eighteen armed Apache men. But the little prophet came up to the soldiers and held up his hands.

"I do not wish to escape. I am perfectly willing to go," he said to the soldiers.

His followers were angry, but Noche-del-Klinne asked them to offer no resistance.

"All I ask," he said to the soliders, "is that you allow me to eat my meal before we leave."

He ate, while the nervous Apache scouts urged him to hurry up because more people were gathering. Finally, his last meal finished, the party of soldiers and scouts started off along the creek, taking Noche-del-Klinne back toward Fort Apache.

There are different stories about what happened next. Colonel Carr reported that bad Apaches attacked him and he was forced to fight back.

I heard a different story told by those who were there, including some of those Apache scouts. For no good reason, a soldier leveled his gun at Noche-del-Klinne, took aim, and shot him. The prophet was only wounded and tried to crawl away.

"Kill the medicine man," Carr shouted.

Noche-del-Klinne was shot again by a soldier who put his pistol into the prophet's mouth and fired. Still it did not kill him. Finally a white civilian guide with the party finished off the one who had danced for peace by hitting him in the forehead with an ax.

That is when the real fighting started.

I think it is likely this story is true, for the Apache scouts were so horrified by what happened that they began to defend those who had followed Noche-del-Klinne. All but one of those Apache scouts refused to fight for the army that day.

While this was happening, Lozen was watching from a hill. The year before, she had been separated from her brother Victorio before the battle of Tres Castillos, where he was killed. So she had survived and made her way back to Fort Apache, where she had been living quietly.

Lozen was always cautious around white men. She had seen the soldiers heading toward Cibeque Creek and followed them to see what would happen. What Lozen did shows how clearheaded she always was in battle. As soon as the fighting started, she rode right into Colonel Carr's camp and drove off most of the horse herd of the soldiers, leaving them on foot. She also captured those mules I told you about before, the ones that we ate, the ones that carried not just canned provisions, but also three thousand rounds of ammunition.

When the battle was over, Colonel Carr escaped, but seven white men in his command had been killed. Eighteen Apaches had died, including the prophet and six Apache scouts. Two days later, a large number of White Mountain Apaches made an attack on Fort Apache itself but were driven back with few casualties on either side. Eventually, an unquiet peace descended upon the reservation.

The way the prophet was murdered made Geronimo certain that he would be the next to be arrested and killed out of hand. He may have been right. Although only three of the White Mountain Apache scouts ended up being tried and hanged for desertion, with two others sent to prison at Alcatraz, it was rumored at first that every Indian who had resisted the capture of the prophet would be killed. Even though he had not been among them, Geronimo believed that he would be the first to die.

Soon after that rumor went around, Geronimo and Juh and seventy-two others rode out of Fort Apache. To survive, to provide themselves with food and more ammunition and other necessities, of course they began raiding again in Mexico. It was called a breakout, like someone escaping from a prison, because we Apaches had been told we were not alllowed the leave the area of Fort Apache without permission of the army. Once all of the land had been ours, but now we were supposed to stay within a few square miles.

That was the second time Geronimo broke out from a reservation. His last breakout was in May 1885. It was the result of the lies told by Chatto and Mickey Free. That third and final flight from a reservation was the one that led us to be on that mountaintop, watching Martine and Kayitah approach with their truce flag.

I HAVE BEEN IN NEED OF FRIENDS

AUGUST 24, 1886

It took but a minute to say "Surrender and you will be sent with your families to Florida, there to await the decision of the President as to your final end. Accept these terms or fight it out until the bitter end."

A silence of weeks seemed to fall on the party. They sat there with never a movement, regarding me intently. Finally Geronimo passed a hand over his eyes, made his hands tremble, and asked me for a drink.

LIEUTENANT CHARLES B. GATEWOOD

AN ACCOUNT OF THE SURRENDER OF GERONIMO

I DO NOT THINK there are any men who ever showed more courage than Martine and Kayitah did when they walked up that narrow trail. All by themselves, they came right up into Geronimo's last camp in the mountains of Mexico. All they carried was a white flag on a stick, and they knew that they might be killed. Still, they strode up there with their heads held high.

"It is over now," Martine said to Geronimo. "Every living thing, the Mexicans, the White Eyes, even the animals, are your enemies."

"This mountain," Kayitah added, "it is your shield but it is also a menace. If the trail is destroyed, you will be prisoners up here forever. How can you defend and feed the women and children with you then?"

As much as anything, their honest words convinced my grandfather to make his final surrender.

So, as I have told you before, we all rode north into Arizona with Nantan Longnose and his small band of White Eyes soldiers and scouts, leaving Old Mexico behind. It was a dangerous ride, for an army of Mexican soldiers followed us. They wanted to wipe us all out — both Apaches and American soldiers — before we left Sonora. Because of that, Nantan Longnose did not ask us to give up our weapons. The Mexican soldiers rode close enough to see that we were still armed. They far outnumbered us but were afraid to attack.

Days passed, and still General Miles did not appear. We did not know it at the time, but he was uncertain about accepting our surrender. He feared us and did not want to risk his life by coming into the field. He even sent secret orders for Lawton to wait until we laid down our weapons and then shoot us all. Finally, Nantan Longnose sent a special message to try to make General Miles meet us. Perico, always one of our best men, went, taking along Mr. Wratten to translate. Their words finally convinced the reluctant general. He agreed to meet us at Skeleton Canyon.

The name of that place came from the killing of a group of

Mexican smugglers by American volunteers a few years before. Their bones were still scattered in the canyon near the place where we camped and waited for the general to arrive.

I remember that day in Skeleton Canyon as well as I remember my own name. There were small red and blue and gray stones, and white sand in the riverbed. I could hear the sound of the small stream that flowed down through the canyon while a wren sang in the bushes. Our camp was in the rocks a little way up the canyon, where we waited for the general to arrive. A brown hawk flew up from the trees, calling loudly, just before Miles and his men finally arrived. I remember the sound of the hooves of my grandfather's horse on the sand and the small stones as he rode down. I remember the big sycamore trees where General Miles waited at the place where the stream forked.

My grandfather's hands were shaking and he was unarmed, but his back was straight as he rode down to Nantan Miles, climbed from his horse, and shook the general's hand. Standing straight, he waited to see what the tall general would do.

Nantan Miles nodded to Geronimo and began to speak words in a pleasant voice.

Wratten, who had stayed back at the fort with Perico, was not there that day to be our interpreter. That is sad, for the terms of surrender were never written down. That made it easy for the white men to lie about what happened that day. If Wratten had been there, he would have spoken the truth about what he saw and heard.

"The general," the interpreter began, "says that he is your friend."

My grandfather looked up into the face of General Miles.

"I never saw him," Geronimo said, "but I have been in need of friends. Why has he not been with me?"

When those words were turned into English all of the White Eyes officers, even General Miles, burst out into laughter.

Those white men were surprised by my grandfather's self-possession and sense of humor in such a tough situation. General Miles was as impressed as any of them. Many years later, I read the words that he put down on paper about Geronimo on that day when they first met.

"He was one of the brightest, most resolute, determined looking men that I have ever encountered," Miles wrote. "He had the clearest, sharpest dark eye I think I have ever seen, unless it was that of General Sherman when he was at the prime of life. Every movement indicated power, energy, and determination. In everything he did, he had a purpose."

My grandfather liked General Miles that day. It seemed he had a man in front of him who would speak straight words. Miles told him that his Apaches would have to accept the punishment of being sent far away to Florida, but they would be with their families, and their exile would only be for two years. Then they would be able to come home again.

I saw what happened next.

Miles knelt down and drew a line on the ground. He placed a stone by that line and spoke some words. Then he picked up another stone, gestured with it toward my grandfather, and put it on the ground about the distance of two sticks from the first one. Finally he picked up a big rock, larger than the first two together, and hefted it in his hand.

"The general says that line represents the big water," the translator told Geronimo. "That first stone is where Chihuahua is with his band. That second stone represents you. The big stone is for the Indians at Camp Apache."

My grandfather nodded. This kind of talk was simple and direct. It made him and the rest of us Chiricahuas who watched feel as if we could see what was in the heart of General Miles.

Then Miles picked up my grandfather's stone again, placing it in the hand that held the stone for Camp Apache. He reached over to put down those two stones with care beside the stone of Chihuahua, there by the line of ocean, stood up, wiped his hands, and spoke again.

"General Miles says that this is what the president wants to do, get all of you together," the translator explained.

"*Enjuh,*" my grandfather said. "Good."

So it was that my grandfather decided to advise Chief Naiche that they should make their surrender. Geronimo was so impressed by General Miles that he stayed as close to him on their ride into Fort

Bowie as a burr stuck to a horse's tail. He climbed without hesitation into the ambulance wagon with the general, Naiche right behind him. Fun and Ahnandia also got on board. Some have written that Perico and Mr. Wratten were among those who rode the sixty-five miles to Fort Bowie in that wagon, but you now know that was not so. My grandfather had sent them ahead to the fort five days before. Their job had been to carry the message to General Miles that Geronimo was considering surrender. I am as certain of this as I am that the promises made by General Miles were broken.

I have said that one of the gifts given me was that of strong memory, but there is also another. It is not one that I mention often, but I will tell it to you now, for it will help you understand how I saw so many things. The power Ussen gave to me is the power to be unnoticed, especially by white men. It is almost like being invisible, but not quite. When I use that power, white people may still notice me, and nod or scowl, depending on how pleased or displeased they are to see an Apache. But then they will look away and forget I was ever there. That is one reason why you will never see my own name mentioned in any of the books written about my grandfather, even though he kept me close by his side. Considering what foolish things have been written in most of those books, I think that gift of mine has been a great blessing.

That day, when Geronimo climbed into the ambulance of General Miles, I used my power. I climbed in with them, sat on the floor under my grandfather's feet, and listened. My grandfather had much to say. He always had much to say. That is one reason why Naiche, even though he was the chief of our band, always stood back and let my grandfather do the talking. Not only was my grandfather a great orator, but trying to stop him from talking would have been like trying to hold back the wind.

"You may wonder," my grandfather said to General Miles, "why I ran away after surrendering. It is because I was still afraid. There are two coyotes at Fort Apache who told me stories that I now know are lies. They said that I would be taken prisoner and hanged. They ran their hands across their throats and said my head would be cut off. It made me think that maybe they would even kill me themselves. It was wrong of them to joke at me that way. Those men are Chatto and Mickey Free, and they are the liars who caused all of this trouble."

I looked up at the face of General Miles as my grandfather said these words and they were translated. I saw him nodding agreement and knew that he did not doubt what Geronimo told him.

My grandfather was feeling happy. He saw his words had been taken as truth, and he took the words of the general as the same. He trusted General Miles and was no longer worried about what would happen to us.

In fact, my grandfather was already looking forward to arriving at Fort Bowie. During our last raid into Mexico, we had taken both hard goods and soft goods. Although the general had made it clear we could not keep the mules and horses, he had allowed Geronimo and the other men to keep all the pesos we had taken. Some have said that Apaches did not understand money, that when we obtained it we would just throw it away. Clearly, those who said that did not know my grandfather. He took out some of that money, a big bundle of bills he had stuffed under his shirt. As we rolled along, he began to count them.

"Does the canteen at the fort have good boots?" he asked General Miles.

"Indeed it does," the general answered with a smile.

"*Enjuh*," my grandfather said, holding up his handful of money. "That is one of the first things I will do when I get there. I will buy a fine new pair of boots."

Other things were said on that long ride, but there is one talk that I remember better than any other. As the Chiricahua Mountains came into sight, my grandfather gazed fondly at them. Of those of us in the wagon, I think only General Miles knew that my grandfather would never look at our beloved mountains again.

"This is the fourth time I have surrendered," Geronimo said.

"And I think it shall be the last," General Miles replied.

GERONIMO'S POWER

OCTOBER 22, 1886

*I was fortunate in being a fast runner, always a good accom-
plishment when you tangle with your true, everlasting friends,
the Mexicans.*

JASON BETZINEZ

I FOUGHT WITH GERONIMO

*CLACK-CLACK, CLACK-A-CLACK, CLACK-CLACK,
CLACK-A-CLACK.* The iron wheels of our train kept
up that steady song as we traveled. Even now, years later,
I sometimes wake in the night with that endless sound rattling in
my head.

Clack-clack, clack-a-clack, clack-clack. Once again we were on the
move in the direction of the sunrise, leaving Fort Sam Houston
behind. A special train with only four coaches had been prepared for
us. Two coaches contained forty White Eyes soldiers to guard us.
One coach held my grandfather and the fourteen other grown men
in our party. The women and children of our party, all eighteen of
us, were in the train car I had been loaded into. Martine and Kayitah

were also in our coach. It was now dark outside. Most of us, having eaten our dinners, were asleep. But sleep would not come for me. I could not stop thinking. I pressed my face to the window.

Our train was now approaching another depot. Of course, we stopped. Because ours was a special train with no set schedule, it meant that those running the train could decide to stay as long as they wished at any station. The stay would be longer whenever there was a group of people gathered to see Geronimo and his evil Apaches. I now think it was because those who ran our train were able to make money. Newspaper reporters and people interested in seeing my grandfather would give cash to the engineer of the train to keep him longer at the station. At this stop the biggest crowd of people I had ever seen was waiting. By now, though, after so many stops, my grandfather was feeling tired.

As soon as we stopped, the waiting crowd began chanting. I thought I heard my grandfather's name in their chant and turned to Mr. Wratten.

"What are they saying?"

Mr. Wratten shook his head at the behavior of those people. "Bring out Geronimo. That's what they're saying."

Suddenly the crowd began to cheer and point to the space between the train cars. I turned to look. My grandfather had gotten out of his seat and walked out to stand on the platform. His face was calm, neither smiling or scowling. As he moved his eyes around the crowd, people began to fall silent before his gaze. They waited, wondering if he was going to say something. Many of the faces in that crowd were as brown as our own, but from their clothing they appeared to be Mexicans, not Indians.

By now I had moved to the door of the train car, and I was standing behind my grandfather, but out of sight of the people. So I was probably the only one who heard what he said in Spanish in a soft voice under his breath.

"*Mi amigos.*"

Then he sighed, turned, and vanished back into the train car, where he pulled the blinds over his window. No matter how much the people called for him to show himself once more, he did not leave his seat or raise those blinds again until the train had finally left the station.

I have neglected something. All this time I have been telling my story thinking that you know the reason why my grandfather fought so long and hard. But you may not know why he came to hate the Mexicans. You may not know why, after hoping they would be his friends, he also came to distrust the Americans.

There are good reasons why Geronimo fought as he did. At a time when not just the other Indians, but all the Apache bands had given up fighting, he was still out in the mountains. Even though he was old, of the age when many men seek to do nothing more than warm themselves and sleep by the fire, he still chose to defy his enemies.

Many lies have been told about him. They describe him as a monster. They picture him as a being with no heart, one who loved killing defenseless children. They are as untrue as that evil tale of him wearing a robe made of the scalps of white women.

How powerful lies can be. Even those with good hearts may believe a lie. Even those with clear eyes may have their vision clouded by deceitful words spoken so convincingly that they seem true. A good liar can say that it is dark when the sun is shining, and many believe him. A good liar can say that a people who wanted to live in peace were the ones who started every war in which they fought.

It would be better for you to hear Geronimo himself tell his own story, not on paper but with his living breath. It would be best of all if you could understand our language and sit listening to him beside the fire, there in one of our favorite places in the mountains. You, too, would hear the sorrow in his voice as he spoke of how all those he loved were killed, told of all the times he and other Apaches tried to live in peace, listed all the promises that were made to them only to be broken.

But his spoken voice will never again be heard.

My grandfather tried to tell his story to a white man who turned it into a book. I was there when the man listened. I watched as he took down the words that Daklugie translated into English. But there was much that my grandfather held back from that man. If he told the whole truth, my grandfather feared, the army men would come and kill him, as old as he was. I also know that white man changed many things when he wrote.

The reasons why he fought take many days in the telling, but I will be brief. I know that most White Eyes readers are less patient than Indians and prefer short stories that are easy to understand.

Geronimo never wanted to fight the Americans. All of his life, his real fight was with the Mexicans. For generations, the Mexicans attacked the Apaches and the other Indians. They took us as captives, made us their slaves. But when Geronimo was a young man, the people of some of the Mexican towns said they wanted to be friends.

Geronimo was glad of this. He was happy in those days. His parents had raised him to be a peaceful person. His grandfather, Mahko, who was a chief of the band, did not believe in making war. What band of Apaches was theirs? I have read in that book about his life that Geronimo said his people were "Bedonkohe" Apaches. That is what the white man who was writing down that story thought he was told by Daklugie and my grandfather. But you will never find any mention of Bedonkohe Apaches before that book. It is yet another of those many mistakes about my grandfather that have been put down on paper, mistakes that make me smile or shake my head in disgust. What my grandfather, Geronimo, said to that man was that his people were Bronco Ndee, meaning they were among those Apaches who lived in the old way. *Bronco* is a Mexican word that just means "wild," and *ndee* is just Apache for "people." Their band was simply one of the southern bands of the Nednais.

Geronimo's grandfather Mahko was a generous man who always thought ahead. He would store dried meat and corn in caves so that in the winter when there was no other food he could share it with everyone in his band. When Mahko died, Geronimo's father became chief and continued to follow his own father's peaceful ways. It was during this time that Geronimo's cousin Juh came to visit. Juh's people were Nednai Apaches who lived further south in Mexico. Even though Juh always stammered when he talked, he was as intelligent as my grandfather and a fine hunter. He had already been in fights with the Mexicans and told Geronimo about his experiences. But Geronimo was not interested in fighting. He liked their peaceful life. He was already learning the secrets of being a medicine person, one who could heal the sick. Different as they were, the two boys still became close friends. When Juh left to rejoin his people, my grandfather was sad.

Then something even sadder happened. Geronimo's father became sick and died. Geronimo and his mother could not bear to remain in that place where they had spent so many happy years as a family. Everything they saw around them reminded them of their loss. So they packed a few belongings and made the long walk south to spend time with Juh's people.

It was there that my grandfather met the first girl he ever loved.

It was not unusual that he was from one band and she was from another. We Apaches frequently marry out of our own bands. We are not supposed to marry our relatives — even cousins. We cannot wed members of our own clan or clans close to ours. So it is easier to find an eligible partner far away from your own campfire. By this time, Geronimo was old enough to marry. To his delight, that young woman agreed to take him as a husband.

In that white man's story of my grandfather's life, Geronimo's wife is called Alope. That is not an Apache name. It was not her true name. I know that because after she was gone, my grandfather never spoke his first wife's true name to any man. Maybe that name was made up by that white writer. But I will refer to her as Alope, too. I wish to respect the dead as did my grandfather.

Back then, my grandfather was not yet known as Geronimo. His adult name was Goyathlay, which some have said means "One Who Yawns," but that is just because they do not understand our language. The real meaning of that name is more like "the Clever One," which my grandfather always was.

It is normal for an Apache man to join the family and the band of his wife. So Goyathlay and Alope put up a small buffalo-skin tipi in the Nednai camp. Their tipi was lined with wolf skins and cougar skins, and Alope painted its walls with beautiful designs. Since she no longer had a husband to live with and no other close relatives, Goyathlay's mother put up her own tipi near theirs. The seasons turned into years. Soon my grandfather and his young wife had three small children. It filled their hearts with contentment to just sit and watch them play. My grandfather also continued to learn songs and chants and how certain plants could be used for healing.

"Goyathlay," the old people would say in approval, "is a fine young man. He studies hard. He is well on his way to becoming a medicine man."

The nearby Mexican towns in the province of Chihuahua had said they would no longer make war on Apaches. So those Nednais felt it was safe to come out of their mountains and go to those towns to trade. It is sad that they did so. Perhaps they did not know a bounty of 200 pesos was still being offered for the scalp of any Apache.

That band of Nednais to which Geronimo now belonged traveled into Chihuahua, heading for Casa Grande. Along the way, they set up camp in the hills outside of the town we called Kas-ki-ye. That town is known as Janos to the Mexicans. Goyathlay and most of the other men went into town to trade. Because they were at peace, they left the old people and the women and children, their horses and supplies and ammunition protected by only a few guards.

While the men were trading, Mexican soldiers from Sonora led by General Carrasco attacked the Nednai camp. They killed and scalped almost every Apache. Those innocent people who were not murdered were taken to be sold as slaves. Goyathlay came home to find the bodies of his family. His wife and children and mother were all dead. In those days, our people did not keep track of dates as white men do. But I think the year was 1850.

Surrounded by enemies, with no horses or ammunition, all that Goyathlay and the other men could do was slip away to the north. But the Apaches could not forget what had happened. Especially Goyathlay. Before leaving, he burned the buffalo-skin tipi where he and Alope and their three children had lived. Into the fire went their toys, their clothing, all that they had owned as a family. He burned his mother's tipi and all of her possessions. All that he had left was a broken heart aching for revenge against the Mexican soldiers.

Mangas Coloradas, who was then the greatest of the Apache chiefs, called together other bands of Apaches to help the Nednais take revenge. This would not be a raid to take goods. This would be a war to take lives. They did not hurry. There were preparations to be made.

Great bundles of reeds were gathered to make arrows. Then those reeds were cut to the right lengths and heated over the fire to straighten them. Special white stones with grooves cut into them were used to smooth the shafts. Three feathers, from the hawk or the turkey or the quail, were fastened to the shafts. Only one-half of a feather could be used on an arrow, but those three halves were all from different feathers to be sure the arrow would fly straight. Then each arrow was painted close to the feathers to show whose arrows they were. Some of those arrows were tipped with flint. However, now that iron was easier to get, more often than not the arrowheads would be metal. These metal or flint-tipped arrows were not for hunting. They were for war, for anger, for trouble and death. Each man wanted to have thirty or forty, or even more, perfectly made arrows in his quiver, so this all took much time and care.

Other men went out and cut the long straight dry stalks of the sotol. Those stalks grow one year and are green. Then they die. Only in the second year, after they had dried out well, would they be ready. Just as was done with the arrow shafts, those long stalks, an arm's length more than the height of a tall man, would be heated over the fire and straightened. This made a lance that was strong, light, and deadly. The end of the shaft would be tipped with metal. The best tips were bayonets that we took from the guns of Mexican soldiers. Just as with the arrows, we painted our lances. Often they would be painted blue from the middle of the lance to its point, with the other half all red. We did not throw our lances like spears. We held on to them and used them to stab at the enemy either with one hand or held in both hands, from beneath or from above.

New bows were carved from white mulberry wood. Pieces of deer sinew were cut into strips, spliced together, doubled over, and then twisted to make sturdy bow strings. Shields made of cowhide were protected with war medicine so that no arrow or bullet could pierce them.

"Let no bullets go through this," each man who carried such a shield would say, and if his medicine was strong, that shield would always protect him.

War charms were also prepared over the next months, by the best medicine men. Like a powerful shield, a war charm could keep bullets from striking you. Those charms were made in the shapes of circles or crosses and only carried when you were going into battle. They were only good for that one kind of luck, not for other important things such as gambling or hunting. Goyathlay, though, carried no such charms. His power had promised to be there with him. He trusted that would be enough.

In addition to all those things that were being made by the hands of Apache men, another sort of preparation was even more important. Physical training. A strong weapon carried by a weak man is of little use. Each day the men practiced with their bows and arrows, shooting at balls of cedar bark. They fenced with their lances and wrestled with each other. They ran, up and down the hills, through the desert, into the mountains. Ah, how they ran! In those days, no one could run as well or as long as an Apache. A man on a horse was no match for one of our men in a long race. Running, then walking, then running again, a party of Apaches on foot, even with women and children along, could easily travel fifty miles a day.

Finally, after many moons had passed, they were ready to return to Mexico. As the party of men went along, they were careful to use the special language that we only speak when we go into battle.

When they spoke of the enemies they did not call them *nukai*, but *nancin*. Each man also brought along a drinking tube and a scratcher stick. When you are going to war, you must only drink water through such a hollow tube and you must not scratch yourself with your fingers, but use that stick. You may ask why things were done that way. My only answer is a man who went to war entered a world where he was set apart from all others, a place where the ways of everyday life no longer applied.

They tracked down those soldiers of General Carrasco who had attacked that defenseless camp to the town of Arispe. In the desert outside Arispe, the men made ready. They carefully checked their weapons and their war charms. They combed their hair, tied it back or put on headbands. They took off their shirts, for Apache men usually go bare-chested into battle. That way they could quickly recognize another Apache, for the Mexicans always wore shirts. Some of the men painted their faces. Goyathlay painted his face in the special way that would later distinguish him and those who fought beside him in the decades to come. He drew a wide, white band across his face, passing from cheek to cheek beneath his eyes.

Then, their preparations complete, the Apaches attacked. There at the town of Arispe they fought a great battle. Even though in those days our people had no guns but used only bows and arrows and lances, they defeated the Mexican soldiers and killed most of them.

In that battle, Goyathlay was the fiercest of all the fighters. It seemed to the frightened Mexicans as if that one Apache was everywhere and that no bullets could stop him. They did not know who he was, but as the Mexicans and Americans have always done with Apaches, they called him by a name of their choosing.

"Look out for that one," they shouted back and forth to each other as the battle went on.

"Watch out for Geronimo!"

"*Si*. There he is. Shoot him!"

"*Dónde está* Geronimo?"

"*Aquí! Aquí! El indio es muy astuto!*"

"Look out for Geronimo!"

They cried out that name so often that the Apaches soon understood who they were talking about. They realized the Mexicans were calling out that name because the young Apache was such a great fighter. Goyathlay liked that. From then on, he no longer called himself by his old name. He had become Geronimo.

Now there is one more story I must tell. It is the tale of how Geronimo got his power. All Apaches know this story, but I suspect that you have not heard it. So I will share it with you. It also explains much about my grandfather.

I have learned, from other Indians of different tribes, that among their nations it is common for a young man to go looking for power.

He finds a hilltop and sits there waiting, not eating or drinking, begging for power to come to him.

That is not the Apache way. We do not beg for power. It simply comes to us when the time is right. So it was for Geronimo. One day, in those clouded times of grief and anger after the murder of his family, during that year of preparation for revenge, Geronimo was sitting alone and weeping.

Then he heard a voice calling his Apache name. It was a breathless voice. It came from everywhere and nowhere. It called his name four times.

GOYATHLAY

GOYATHLAY

GOYATHLAY

GOYATHLAY

My grandfather raised his head to listen to what would be said next, for he realized that his power was coming to him.

"No gun can ever kill you," the voice said. "I will take the bullets from the guns of the Mexicans so they will have nothing but powder. I will guide your arrows."

It was with his knowledge of that power that the young man who became Geronimo went into that first great battle against the Mexican soldiers. No one could stand against his strength. I truly believe that no one would ever have defeated him had it not been for those two great weaknesses that we Apaches have suffered from.

If not for those two great weaknesses, I think we Apaches would have always beaten the Mexicans. We were always better men. We were tougher and stronger. We were fighting on land that knew us and helped us in our struggle. But those two weaknesses hurt us again and again.

The first weakness was our love of strong drink. Knowing this, Mexicans — and later some Americans — who wished to kill Apaches and collect the bounty paid for our scalps would give our men as much free liquor as they could drink. Then, when our men were drunk and helpless, the Mexicans would come to our camps with swords and axes and slaughter us like sheep. Only those still sober enough to run would escape.

I know this to be so, for I saw it happen as a small child. It was 1881, not long after my parents and I fled from Fort Apache following the murder of the Prophet. We were deep in Mexico. Several men and women from our camp had gone to a nearby town to trade for food. They came back pulling a cart that held many jugs of *aquardimiente*, the strong Mexican alcohol brewed from the same mescal plant that was one of our staple foods.

"Look what our good Mexican friends gave us," one of the men pulling the cart said, stumbling as he walked. They were already drunk.

My mother had been afraid this would happen. She had wanted to go into that town herself, but she had hurt her leg the day before, twisting it when she caught it between two rocks as we came down a steep path in the mountains.

"It is not safe here," she said. "We must leave now."

No one listened to her, not even my father.

"You need to rest your leg," he told her. "We can leave at first light tomorrow."

By the evening, all of the men in our camp, except for my father, were lying about drunk. Then I heard the sound of thunder. It did not come from the sky, but from the hooves of many horses striking the ground as they charged into our camp. My father grabbed his gun and ran to meet them. They were too many for him to stop, but he could slow them down.

"*Nanlyeeg!*" my mother hissed at me. "Run!"

That was the last word I ever heard her speak.

I did as she said. I ran into the dark and hid in the thick brush. I watched as my own parents were killed by the Mexicans. I kept as quiet as a small bird in an ocotillo bush when a hawk flies over. I had learned, even though I was only about six years old, that silence can save your life. I still did not speak when the Mexicans were done with their work, though I came out from my hiding place to tug at the bodies of my parents. But even though their eyes were open, they would not wake up.

When Lozen and my grandfather Geronimo found me, a day later, I was still not crying or speaking, but I was covered with my mother's and father's blood and hiding in some mesquite bushes.

I do not know for sure how they found me, but it may have been that Lozen saw what happened, even though she and Chief Naiche and Geronimo were many miles away when the massacre occurred.

"Grandson," Geronimo called to me, "Little Foot, come with me."

I came out without hesitation and walked over to him. Then he picked me up in his arms.

I have almost forgotten that I need to tell you what our second weakness was. Perhaps you have already guessed. Our second weakness was trust. Even though we were lied to again and again, we kept trusting the words of men who were more deceitful than Coyote.

When the Americans came to the southwest, one of the first things those White Eyes did was to make war against Mexico. That pleased the Apaches. Perhaps this would bring an end to the Mexican raids on our camps, to our people being taken as slaves deep into Mexico. Our leaders and our best fighters, including Geronimo, offered to help the Americans fight the Mexicans. But the Americans said they did not want our help or our friendship. I believe that if only they had accepted us then as friends and allies, none of the warfare and pain that we all suffered from would have happened. None of us, including Geronimo, ever wanted to fight the Americans.

But that is what happened — to everyone's sorrow.

BROKEN PROMISES

OCTOBER 23, 1886

The unfortunate policy adopted by the government toward the "Warm Springs" Apaches of New Mexico, who were closely related to the Chiricahuas, had an unhealthy effect upon the latter and upon all the other bands. The "Warm Springs" Apaches were peremptorily deprived of their little fields and driven away from their crops, half-ripened, and ordered to tramp to San Carlos . . .

JOHN BOURKE

ON THE BORDER WITH CROOK

A S OUR TRAIN CONTINUED to rattle its way along the tracks toward the sunrise, my grandfather sat peacefully in his seat. One leg crossed over the other, he used a kerchief to polish the black leather boots he'd purchased from the canteen at Fort Bowie before our long journey began. How he was dressed that day is as clear in my memory as a photograph. On his head was a new white straw hat with a black band. Over his white shirt, which was buttoned up to the neck, he wore a fine dark jacket. It might be said that from the waist up, his clothes were far different from those we wore before the coming of the White Eyes.

That was true of most of the other Apache men on the train. For example, Naiche's clothing was like that of my grandfather's, although his hat was taller and had no hatband. Fun wore a brown vest over a shirt with blue stripes on it. Perico's dress was almost the same, with the addition of a new brown necktie, tied in a perfect Windsor knot. Chapo, Geronimo's son, who sat in the seat across from Naiche, was just as well attired, but had chosen to put on a broad headband instead of a hat.

It was from the waist down that our clothing showed how Indian we still were, even if we preferred white man's cloth to deerskin. The men in trousers had cut out the seats of their pants and wore breechclothes. My grandfather, in fact, was not wearing any trousers at all, only his breechcloth. Old as he was, the muscles rippled in his iron calves and thighs as he put his right foot down and crossed his left to begin cleaning nonexistent dust from the other shiny black boot.

Perhaps Geronimo was as calm as he looked, nonchalantly polishing his new footwear, but I think not. He was doing as many of us did, resting when we could, but not trusting that the times were past when we might still have to flee for our lives. Perhaps, like me, he was wondering what promises made to Apaches would be broken next.

That history of making and breaking promises began well before

I was born. But I heard that sad history recited so many times by my grandfather that I knew it well. Every one of our different Apache tribes has its own part of that history of deceit.

It is especially so for the band I was born to, Victorio's people, the Warm Springs Apaches. Our people wanted to live at peace with the White Eyes. At first, the Americans recognized this. We were allowed to settle on their own land, among our sacred springs in New Mexico, not far from the present-day town of Monticello. We were given the promise, not just spoken, but in words placed on paper, that we could live there forever. Forever. My grandfather, Geronimo, was living among our Warm Springs people at that time. He still saw the deaths of his mother and his wife, Alope, and their children in his dreams. He would always be haunted by their memories, memories that would expand with the deaths of more of his loved ones in the years to come. But he had married again and had more children. He was trying once more to live a quiet life.

For our Warm Springs people, forever only lasted eighteen years, from 1858 to 1876. White gold seekers wanted our land. We Apaches never mined gold. The gold we cared for was the gold of corn that we could grow from our own land. But because of gold that land was taken. We were forced to leave. None of us had done anything wrong.

Victorio and Geronimo, Loco and old Nana, and all the leaders at Warm Springs were called to a meeting. They sat down to talk. Suddenly, they were surrounded by armed soldiers and taken to the agency blacksmith shop. Heavy iron chains were pounded onto their ankles and wrists. Then they were loaded into wagons and taken 150 miles west to Fort Thomas on the San Carlos Reservation.

The next day, escorted by soldiers and Indian scouts, all the rest of our people were formed into columns and marched over the mountains to Fort Thomas. Those low desert lands along the Gila River were terrible. Soon after we were placed there, we began to die of smallpox and other diseases. There was little or no food. The Indian agents stole from us.

Finally Victorio and Loco could stand it no longer. They gathered together what was left of us, not to raid or make war, but to go home. Geronimo, though, did not come along. He did not want to fight. He and his new family stayed at Fort Thomas, trying to remain at peace.

Victorio and Loco led us through the mountains toward Warm Springs. It was not easy. The army and the Apache scouts working for the White Eyes attacked us along the way, but rather than fighting back my Warm Springs people would just slip away each time. Finally, those Apache scouts stopped attacking, taking pity on people who wanted peace so much. So we Warm Springs Apaches reached our old homes. We begged to be left there and promised to be peaceful.

"We will fight until we die if you take us from here again," Victorio said.

So the army let us stay. The soldiers knew that Apaches at peace were far better than Apaches at war. Our people stayed there for another two years. But the demands of white men who wanted that land were too great. Again, we were told to leave our home-lands. And this time we did not do as the army asked. Victorio led us into Mexico. Seven months later, Geronimo, too, left the San Carlos Agency, following Chief Juh. But Juh and Geronimo did not find our Warm Springs people soon enough. On the plains of Chihuahua, they were attacked by a great force of Mexican soldiers and Tarahumara Indians. That is where the trail of broken promises ended for our great chief. That is when Victorio was killed. That is when so many of us, including my own parents, died. That is when, after that massacre, Lozen and Geronimo found me.

My grandfather, Geronimo, looked up at me from across the aisle of the train and nodded his head.

Yes, he, too, was remembering that time.

Then he returned to polishing his boots.

So many broken promises. Thus far, the only promise ever made by the White Eyes to Geronimo that had been kept was the promise to spare his life.

REMEMBERING TURKEY CREEK

OCTOBER 23, 1886

I wish to say a word to stem the tide of invective and abuse which has almost universally been indulged in against the whole Apache race. This is not strange on the frontier from a certain class of vampires who prey on the misfortune of their fellow-men, and who live best and easiest in time of Indian troubles. Greed and avarice on the part of the whites — in short, the almighty dollar — is at the bottom of nine-tenths of all our Indian trouble.

JOHN BOURKE

ON THE BORDER WITH CROOK

FORT SAM HOUSTON was now far, far behind us, and we were still traveling toward the sunrise. I stared out at the strange land we were now passing through. It was empty of hills. It was not the color of our deserts, but green, a green that was sometimes so bright it made my head swim to look at it.

There was water, too. Many wide expanses of it would stretch beside the train, and there would be birds in that water unlike any I had seen before. They were often as large as cranes and some of them were as red or pink as the colors seen in the sky near sunset. Also, some of them had beaks that were strangely bent. I found those birds very interesting to look at.

We had traveled so far. Would we never stop? Would we just be on this train forever, always sitting in those seats, always watching the land whip by the windows, always feeling as if our spirits were gradually being stripped from us the farther we went? Even though I was still just a child, I already knew that it was not a new experience for an Apache to have things taken away from him. Each time we had started to live in peace, that peace had not lasted. I remembered Turkey Creek.

The longest peace that I could remember was at Turkey Creek during the two years after Geronimo and Lozen found me. It began in February 1884, when Geronimo surrendered for the third time.

"You will not be killed."

That was what Nantan Lupan said to him. He even told my grandfather he did not have to stay at San Carlos, he could choose a place to live higher in the mountains on the Fort Apache Reservation. The place Geronimo chose was Turkey Creek on the Black River.

It was only forty miles northeast of San Carlos, but it was like another world. There were mountains and trees, grass, and flowing streams. We were happier there and might have stayed there in peace had it not been for the lies Mickey Free and Chatto told to Geronimo.

"I am happy to be here," Geronimo said to Nantan Lupan when we arrived at Turkey Creek. "I have been hunting for a new world. I think the world is mother of us all, and that Ussen, the Life Giver, wants us all to be brothers."

If only it could have stayed that way. Turkey Creek was such a good place for us. Although it was still a part of the Fort Apache Reservation, which had been set up for the White Mountain Apaches, it was away from those western Apaches who were so different from Chiricahuas and did not like us all that well.

To the small child I was then, it seemed a perfect place. It was a shallow valley on a tall plateau. There a cool stream wound its way through the tall grasses, and pine trees rose around the clearings. The air was sweet to breathe in every season. Protected as it was by the hills on either side, it was cool there in the Moons of Many Leaves, when the women and children would go out to gather mescal, our favorite food. There were many agaves, soapweed, century plants, and desert spoon. With digging sticks we would uproot them, cut off their leaves, bury them in a pit filled with hot coals, and then bake their hearts for a day and a night. The mescal heart had such a good taste. You could cut it up when it was cooked, the way you cut a potato. But no potato ever tasted as sweet.

At times I felt sad, having no mother or father. But I was not the only Apache child who was an orphan, and there were many adults who would bring me into their wickiups as readily as their own children. And best of all, my grandfather was there. I followed him around as if I was his second shadow, and he taught me things.

I remember Geronimo holding the long stalk from an agave plant in his hands and smiling down at me.

"This plant," he said, "has always helped us survive. It gives us food from its roots. And it gave us a great weapon to defend our people." He hefted the stalk that was twice as long as a man is tall in his hands. "From this we made our lances."

Geronimo squinted, looking back into memory. "I remember a certain person, a tall man, who was good with the lance."

I nodded, knowing my grandfather was speaking of Cochise, Chief Naiche's fearless and honorable father. Of course, now that Cochise was dead, my grandfather would not say his name.

"This tall man," Geronimo continued, "was so good with his lance that when an army man insulted him, he challenged that man to a duel. 'You use your gun,' he said to the soldier. 'I will use this.' But that duel did not happen. The army man just looked at the great man's lance and was so afraid that he ran away."

There were acorn and mesquite beans to be gathered in the

summer, juniper berries and pine nuts in the autumn. And there were antelope and deer to hunt so that we had plenty of skins to make clothing and moccasins, and did not just have to rely on the cloth and stiff shoes from the White Eyes.

There were bears and turkeys there, too. Of course we did not hunt the bears. Nor did we hunt the turkeys. That was not because there was anything special about them. We just did not care to eat them. But when we learned that Lieutenant Davis, Nantan Fat Boy, liked to eat turkey, we started to bring them to him. I had my own way of hunting turkey without using any weapon. It was fun to chase a turkey down by running after it as it flew. When it grew tired and could fly no more, I would keep chasing it until I caught up with it and could wrap my arms around it. The first turkey I brought to Nantan Fat Boy pleased him so much that he gave me ten shiny dimes for it.

There were also other creatures at Turkey Creek that no Chiricahua would ever eat. Among them were the frogs in the streams. In those days we never ate anything that came out of the water, especially fish, which were so much like snakes with their scaly skin. But it turned out that Nantan Fat Boy also liked to eat the legs of frogs. His tent was set up near the creek. Their loud croaking at night kept him awake. One night I heard the sound of a man cursing. I crept close to see what it was. Nantan Fat Boy was out there by the creek, holding a lantern in one hand and throwing stones at the frogs.

He was not a good stone thrower, nowhere near as good as we boys. If he had been in one of our mock battles, when we divided into sides and then threw stones at each other, dodging them the way grown Chiricahua men dodge back and forth in a real fight with guns or bows and arrows, he would have soon been the bloodiest and most bruised of us all. I had a bruise that night myself on my left shoulder. It had come from a rock that had been hurled all too accurately by a friend on the opposite side of that day's stone-throwing match.

"Blast you all, shut up!" Nantan Fat Boy shouted at the frogs. Trying not to chuckle too loudly, I slipped away.

The next evening, Nantan Fat Boy called a bunch of us boys to his tent. He had a pile of sacks by his feet.

"I like to eat frogs," he said. "I am hungry for their meat. I will give you a nickel for every frog you can bring to me in these bags."

So we all went frog hunting. We used our bows and arrows to shoot them, and we did well. Before long we came back to him with our bags so full of frogs that they were heavy to lift. Nantan Fat Boy was surprised. He had thought we would only get a dozen or so frogs, but we had brought far more than even he could eat. He had to borrow nickels from some of the other army men to pay us all.

Some of us thought that the most dangerous ones at Turkey Creek were the rattlesnakes. Their skins blended in, making them hard to see until it was too late. There were two kinds of rattlesnakes. There were those that crawled upon their bellies, and there were those, like Mickey Free and Chatto, who walked on two legs. It was the lying words of those rattlesnakes disguised as men that stole Turkey Creek from us and put us on the exile trains.

Before coming to Turkey Creek, we had spent many days with no food at all. That was not just when we were out on the trail or fleeing from soldiers. It was also that way when we were living at the San Carlos Agency.

San Carlos. Even thinking those words brings the taste of dust to my mouth. It is a place of hot dry plains, where the water is salty and nothing can grow but cactus. Much of the food that was supposed to be given us when we were at San Carlos was stolen by dishonest white men. Everyone knew this, including the Indian agent. Cattlemen would drive a herd of cattle into the agency, collect their money, give part of the cash to the Indian agent, and then drive that herd on out to sell it again somewhere else. It did not bother them that we were hungry and desperate. The storekeepers would take at least half of the provisions issued them for the Indians and then cart them off to sell them and keep the profit. That is the way it is with so many white men. They always seek a way to make money, even when it means starving helpless people to do it. At times at San

Carlos, the only meat we had was so old that it had maggots in it and tasted rotten. But it was all we had, and we ate it. It is no wonder that men such as Geronimo would break out to go raiding.

Of all the places in our homelands, San Carlos was the worst. The water was bad. The heat was awful. There were never any cool breezes like those that blew in the nearby mountains. There were scorpions and giants spiders, poisonous lizards and rattlesnakes everywhere. The army had originally built a fort there, but even the White Eyes soldiers had refused to live there, and the fort was abandoned. Of course, that is where they decided all the Apaches should be forced to live. The agent there at San Carlos was named John Clum, but the Chiricahuas had their own name for him. Because he was so self-important and strutted about so much, they called him Turkey Gobbler. It was Clum who was so determined to have us all come to his agency. Even though we were contented where we were, he was the one who insisted on moving us to live among other Apaches who were strangers to us.

Turkey Gobbler was like a lot of white men who have that strange habit of thinking about themselves all the time and not caring about others. They want to become great men. They want to own lots of possessions and have much money and control the lives of others. That kind of thinking is hard for us Apaches to understand. To us, a great man is one who protects his family and provides for his people. He only makes war to defend himself and his people, not to take someone else's land or to get lots of the white and yellow soft metals from the ground. People like that are ridiculed by Apaches.

"Look out," we would say whenever Clum puffed up his chest and tried to give us orders, "the Turkey Gobbler is dragging his wings."

I remember one time at San Carlos when we ate well. It was that time in February of 1884 when my grandfather surrendered to Lieutenant Davis, the one we all called Fat Boy. Geronimo had only surrendered under the condition that he could bring all his possessions back with him. After Fat Boy agreed to Geronimo's terms, Geronimo told his men to go and gather his possessions.

Soon a huge dust cloud began to appear on the horizon.

"What is that?" Fat Boy asked.

"Ganado," Geronimo answered. Before long, Geronimo's men came in sight, driving a herd of more than 300 cattle that Geronimo had taken from the Mexicans.

Fat Boy had no choice but to allow Geronimo to drive those cattle ahead of him back into San Carlos. Nantan Tan Wolf eventually paid the Mexican ranchers for the cattle that Geronimo brought to us. Geronimo's wish had been that we be allowed to keep those cattle, to graze them on our land, and use them that way for many years. He thought we could be content as cattle ranchers. If we had our own herd, we could depend on ourselves and not have to rely on untrustworthy white men to feed us. Even Fat Boy thought this was a good idea. However, the big White Eyes in Washington would not let us do that. Even though the land at San Carlos was no good at all for farming, the white men in Washington wanted Apaches to be farmers. So, despite Geronimo's objections, all the cattle he brought to us were slaughtered. However, they did allow us to have some meat from that herd. So at least there was beef that fed many Apaches at San Carlos very well for a while.

Fat Boy did not find Geronimo that time when Geronimo came in with all those cattle. Geronimo found *him*. My grandfather was seldom found unless he wished it so. Only the Apache scouts who had once fought by his side and knew all of our strongholds were ever able to find him. If it had not been for those scouts, I do not think the White Eyes would ever have caught even a single Chiricahua man. You know, Chatto became one of those scouts and was praised for his work. But if it had not been for the twisted words that he and Mickey Free whispered into my grandfather's ears, there would have been no need for Apache scouts to hunt Geronimo.

Mickey Free had been taken captive as a small boy and raised among the White Mountain Apaches. He was half-Mexican and half-Irish and the Chiricahuas had been wrongly accused of being his captors. It had led to the Army trying to take Cochise as a hostage and then to much fighting. Trouble for our people followed wherever Mickey Free went. That was especially so in his adult years when he went back to live among the White Eyes and became an interpreter between us and the army at Turkey Creek.

He would come to my grandfather holding a newspaper.

"This newspaper speaks about you," Mickey Free would say. "In Tucson they are making plans to hang you. Citizens have signed a petition asking the army to turn you over to them."

Then Chatto would agree and say that he had heard things which troubled him. He wanted my grandfather to run away. With Geronimo gone, Chatto could be the most important person among the Chiricahuas.

"Things are being planned about you," Chatto would tell Geronimo. He would not say exactly what those things were. He would just say enough to make my grandfather start looking over his shoulder, certain that he would soon see soldiers coming after him with leg irons in their hands.

Geronimo became more and more nervous. He was not afraid of battle, but the thought of being murdered or locked up troubled him deeply. He became certain that either the White Eyes planned to kill him soon and take his head, just as they had done with Mangas Coloradas, or they would send him off to the prison island called Alcatraz as they had done with Kayahtenny. He saw the way Fat Boy looked at him with suspicious eyes.

Chatto and Mickey Free did not just lie to us. They also lied to

Fat Boy and the other White Eyes leaders, telling them about all the plots Geronimo planned, how he was going to kill the White Eyes soldiers in the night and then flee the reservation. So, just as Geronimo became more and more afraid of what the soldiers would do, those same soldiers became more and more wary of Geronimo.

Geronimo and Nana, Lozen and Naiche and Chihuahua would never have fled to Old Mexico that final time if it had not been for the fact that they were certain they were going to be killed. So, on May 17, 1885, they left the reservation. With them went 38 other men, 92 women and little children, and 8 boys old enough to bear arms. I was the smallest of those boys.

Chatto and Mickey Free had made things bad. Those bad-minded men who frightened my grandfather into running away from Turkey Creek hurt us all. What they did ended up sending us all on this endless train journey toward the dawn, a journey that would have no destination for many of us other than disease, despair, and death.

NOT A FEW GATHERED

OCTOBER 23, 1886

Geronimo and fifteen of his men have been ordered into winter quarters at Fort Pickens. I trust he will draw as largely as Jumbo, for he has proved a bigger elephant to Uncle Sam. With Geronimo, and the Shipping League Convention, drawing a crowd in Pensacola at about the same time, your tradesmen should be in cheerful glee. Waiting your answer to my last, I remain, Chas. G. Hill.

LETTER FROM

CHARLES HILL, SECRETARY OF THE NATIONAL SHIPPING

AND INDUSTRIAL LEAGUE, SEPTEMBER 1886

THE APACHE ROCK CRUMBLES

A S I STARED OUT THE WINDOW, Mr. Wratten leaned over my shoulder.

"We're in Louisiana now," Mr. Wratten said. "After that it'll be Alabama. Then Florida."

Florida. Although we now knew for certain that we were going to Florida, it is also certain that none of us really knew anything about the place where they were taking us. Florida was nothing more than a name. *Florida*. I knew what that meant in Spanish. The place of flowers.

Would Florida be as beautiful as its Spanish name, or would it be another terrible place? Would our lives be as hard as they had been at San Carlos? Would this Florida just be another place where Apaches would suffer and die? All that any of us truly knew was that the place we were being taken to was a long, long, long way from our home.

It was not just the land around us that was strange. I had felt the air change, no longer dry but warm and moist as the breath of a giant. I smelled unfamiliar things on that hot, moist wind that blew into the cars when the doors were open. I was used to the high clear air of the Southwest. This new air was hard to breathe. It was not the clean air of our mountains. It smelled and even tasted of things rotting. It tasted of sickness.

Yet I must be honest and admit that at times my excitement overcame my fear. There were so many new things to see. People and places appeared before my eyes that were stranger than anything I could ever have dreamed. Despite all that I'd lost, I wasn't always filled with sorrow. There were times when I found myself almost laughing out loud at the foolishness of the White Eyes and the cleverness of my grandfather.

Our new train crept along its way like a caterpillar crawling on a branch. Each station we came to we stayed at for a long time. Those crowds of people coming to stare at us had gotten even larger. Every place we stopped, newspaper reporters shoved their way onto the train to ask questions of my grandfather and Chief Naiche, while Mr. Wratten interpreted. Chief Naiche had grown tired of always being asked the same questions, but he still stood straight and tall and responded to each question with patience. Geronimo, though, liked all the attention. He enjoyed being interviewed. It gave him a chance to tell again how we had been deceived, to explain why we had resisted for so long. To their credit, some of those newsmen actually tried to tell our story and do an honest job of reporting the words spoken by my grandfather and our chief.

To my grandfather's great delight, word had spread among those reporters about how much he and our other men valued tobacco. So those newsmen would arrive on board with one or two cigars in their pockets to offer Chief Naiche and Geronimo before asking their questions. Also — and this pleased my grandfather even more — those reporters usually were looking for souvenirs.

"Does Chief Geronimo here have anything he might sell to me?" That was what each of those newsmen would ask Mr. Wratten at the end of the interview.

Wratten would pass on that question to my grandfather, who would stand there for a time, his head lowered as if in thought.

Then, with great reluctance, he would look at his right hand and slowly remove the brass ring he wore on his index finger.

"Tell this White Eyes," my grandfather would say to Mr. Wratten, holding the ring out to him, "that I cannot number the battles I have gone into while wearing this ring."

When Mr. Wratten interpreted my grandfather's words, that newspaperman would always get an excited, eager look on his face and start reaching for his purse. Depending on how eager and excited that man looked, my grandfather would set his price at anything from $2.50 to $4.00 and grudgingly accept the money in exchange for that precious ring.

It was only after the train had left the station that my grandfather would take out another of those rings, which he had bought for ten cents each at Fort Sam, and put it on his finger.

"*Enjuh*," my grandfather would say, smiling at me. "Good opportunity."

The greatest crowd of all was waiting for us at New Orleans. Before we actually reached the city, though, we had to stop on the southern bank of the big river that Mr. Wratten told me was named the Mississippi. A crowd of people was there. A good many of them were clearly White Eyes men and women, but there was an even larger number of the black white men and women, and there were others whose brown faces and features made it seem that they might be a mixture of white and black. Some even looked as if they were Indians themselves. I noticed how all the different-looking people did not keep themselves apart from each other, as had been true at the station stops before us. Instead, faces of many colors flowed together here.

Those many-colored people had gathered there to stare at us, but they did not have much time to do so. There was no bridge here for the train to pass over. Our four train cars were pushed onto a big flat boat and taken to the other side, leaving the disapppointed crowd behind.

It was not a long trip across the wide river, but it was too long for me. The thick brown water that flowed all around that boat worried me. It was the color of soup, and you could not see into it at all. Deep water is bad enough, but this water was much worse. The thought of the creatures that might be hidden under its surface was frightening. Our boat was very wide and sturdy, but the way it rocked back and forth in the water made me feel as if my mouth and stomach were about to change places with each other. I was greatly relieved when we finally reached the other shore.

On the northern side of the river was the city New Orleans. An even bigger crowd of White Eyes waited for us there. People were waving and shouting. I could even hear music being played. It seemed to me as if everyone in the world must be there. I had never imagined there were so many people. Our train cars were hooked onto another engine. But it pulled us very slowly, and we did not leave the crowd behind. The train soon stopped, and we were told to get out. Escorted through that huge crowd by soldiers, we were taken to another train and told to board it. Our new train was much newer and cleaner. The cars did not have as many seats, and each of those seats was cushioned to make it more comfortable. But I was too nervous to take much comfort from a padded seat. The crowd was so loud that I was afraid that something very bad was going to happen soon. Perhaps all those shouting people were angry at us or eager to see us all hung.

I looked out the window of the new train. We were not going anywhere. We were just sitting. The people gathered out there seemed pleased about that. They kept shouting at us and waving. Many of them were smiling. You might have thought we were heroes and not prisoners, the way they acted. I began to relax. We were not in danger after all. Flags were waving. Food of all kinds was being sold. It smelled good, but none of us was allowed to go out and buy any of that food. Instead of food, we got newspapermen.

At New Orleans, not just one newspaper, but several sent reporters. One of them was an ugly, red-faced man who kept chewing on a small stick as he asked his questions. His clothes looked as if he had slept in them, and there were ink stains on his fingers. Unpleasant as he appeared, he seemed interested in hearing what my grandfather had to say. Mr. Wratten later read to me the story that ugly man wrote for his paper, the *New Orleans Picayune*. It showed great sympathy for us and told our story with some honesty.

Perhaps my grandfather saw what was in that ugly man's heart. At the end of their interview, he asked to borrow the ugly man's pocketknife, which the man had been using to sharpen his pencil. It was a beautiful little knife with a bone handle and silver engraving, and it was quite sharp. My grandfather used that knife to cut off one of the buttons from his own vest and then placed it in the man's hand. When the man tried to pay him for the button, Geronimo would not take his money. (However, I did not see my grandfather hand the man back his knife.)

The best part of the time we spent waiting in the New Orleans depot was the music that was being played there. It was not army music. It was music played on an instrument that I later learned was called the banjo. I had seen other stringed instruments before, not just our Apache violin, but also the fiddles and guitars that were played in Mexican towns. However, the sound of that banjo was different from anything I had heard before. It was even more pleasant than the sound of the military band had been at Fort Sam. Like the sound of the marches I had heard, it, too, made me want to move my feet.

Clearly, it also affected the black white men in that way. A number of black white men, along with several girls and boys no older than me, were dancing to that music, striking their feet in a pleasant way on the wooden boards of the platform. Others were clapping their hands or slapping their thighs and chests with their palms in time with the music. It was difficult to keep myself from staring at the musicians and the dancers, but I did not allow myself to act like a rude White Eyes. I only watched out of the corners of my eyes. When we left, I was sad to leave that music behind. I would have liked to hear more of it.

Because of the crowds and the newspaper reporters, we did not leave New Orleans until it was growing dark. Our train was now far off its schedule. I knew what a schedule was by now. I had seen how the trains that headed east used the same tracks used by those that headed west. It made me worried. So I had asked Mr. Wratten as we sat at one of the stations, waiting to depart.

"Why is it," I asked him, "that our *besh tsinagai*, our Iron Wheel, has never run into another one coming from the opposite direction?"

In reply he had pointed with his lips at the tracks beside us, where another train stood, and then looked ahead. I followed his eyes, seeing the place where the tracks joined. I understood. One Iron Wheel could be switched to the side so that another coming from the opposite direction could pass.

"But how do they know when another Iron Wheel is coming? Can they hear them?"

"No," he said, "they know when each Iron Wheel leaves one station and how long it takes to reach the next one. That is called a schedule.

They agree ahead of time which Iron Wheel will go onto a side track to let the other pass."

"*Ha-ah*," I said. I liked that answer, for I had been worrying about our train crashing into another. Now it seemed that I had nothing to worry about. "*Enjuh.* That is good. So by using that . . . sheyshool . . . the White Eyes make it so that Iron Wheel never, ever crash into each other while going very fast, causing many people to be badly injured with broken limbs and great bleeding wounds or even killed? Is that not so?"

"Well," Mr. Wratten said, shaking his head a little, "not exactly. Sometimes when one Iron Wheel gets delayed, they do get off schedule. And then they do crash into each other."

So it was that I did not lose that worry about crashing. I simply added on a new worry about staying on schedule. Later that day, my worry turned out to be justified. Halfway between New Orleans and our next stop, something happened. I heard a loud whistle from ahead of us. Then we were all thrown forward as our train was suddenly halted with a great screeching of iron wheels against iron rail. There was a long moment of silence. Then there was much shouting.

After we had all climbed back up off the floor or gotten ourselves out from under the seats where that stop had hurled us, the doors of the train were opened. We were all allowed to climb out. As soon as we did so, I saw what a narrow escape it had been. In front of our train was a bridge. There, on the other side of the bridge, was another train. The two trains had almost crashed and would have done so had not the other engineer seen us coming and blown his whistle.

We remained there for some time. It seemed that neither engineer wished to be the one to back his train up until a side track was reached. Meanwhile, the passengers on the other train, who were members of a theatrical troupe, discovered that ours was none other than the train carrying the famous Apache prisoners. They asked permission to talk with Geronimo and to purchase some souvenirs.

Soon, the men and women on board that other train were making their way across the bridge. Most of the Apache men and women, including Chief Naiche, were growing weary of talking to so many White Eyes. They went around to the other side of the train. They were happy to leave things to my grandfather, who was always ready for business. With Mr. Wratten by his side, Geronimo answered the questions asked by those theater people and took their money. Before long, he had sold his six remaining cartridge belts and all of his brass rings.

"Tell them I am going to get more personal items," he said to Mr. Wratten. "I will return with special things that are worth much to me." Then he went back behind the train.

"Quick," he said, "give me whatever you wish to sell. These people are so foolish they would buy coyote turds."

The other men gladly loaded him down with their own cartridge belts, rings, cheap necklaces, bracelets, and whatever else they had been able to pick up at our various stops. It did not take my grandfather long to sell everything.

Because of the delay, it was dark by the time we reached our next station.

"What is this place?" I said to Mr. Wratten.

"Mobile, Alabama," he said. Neither of us knew then how much the name *Alabama* would mean to us in the future. That night it was just another brief stop on our journey.

Mr. Wratten looked calmly out the window. Like our own men, Mr. Wratten did not show his emotions outwardly to strangers. I realize now how new all of those places were to him. I did not think of it then, for I was a small boy, and Mr. Wratten seemed very old and grown up to me. However, at the time of our trip he was only twenty-one years old. He, too, had never been that far away from home before. He, too, had left everything he knew behind him — even his family. When he chose to spend his life among our people, his own White Eyes mother and father disowned him. They swore that they would never see him again, and they kept their word.

"*Doo alch'ige la'adzaa da,*" he said to my grandfather, indicating the big crowd who had come to the station to see Geronimo. "Not a few gathered."

I peeked out through the blinds, which had been pulled down so that no one outside could look in. Even though it was dark, there were many people. The newspaper reports said later that there were more than a thousand people at the Mobile station. Where did all these people come from? It seemed as if there were more White Eyes than stars in the skies and they all wanted to see just one person. Geronimo.

My grandfather, though, did not stir from his seat, where he was leaning back with his hat over his eyes.

"They are waiting to see you," Mr. Wratten said. His voice sounded amused.

"They can wait," Geronimo said.

By now, even he was growing tired of dealing with eager White Eyes. He did not move from his seat until someone managed to convince one of our guards to bring in a handful of money to my grandfather. By this point in our journey, our guards were glad to do such things. My grandfather always gave them a cut of whatever they brought to him. Some of those White Eyes soldiers were very sad when their job of guarding Geronimo was done. They had never earned so much money so easily.

After counting the money and putting it into his pouch, my grandfather finally went to the door of the train and raised the blind so that the crowd could see him. He stood there, not saying a word, just staring at the awed multitude, until our train pulled out of the station.

TAKING THE MEN

OCTOBER 24, 1886

A move has been set on foot to have some of these red devils sent down to this place and incarcerated at Fort Pickens. Congressman Davidson has been consulted and he has sent a strong recommendation in favor of the scheme to the proper authorities in Washington. If Bob succeeds in this he can point with pride as having been instrumental in giving Pensacola an attraction which will bring here a great many visitors.

THE PENSACOLIAN

SEPTEMBER 18, 1886

FOUR COACHES on this new train had been reserved for us. The women and children were in the two front coaches, the men in the back two. Once again, I had managed to sneak in among the men. If something happened, I wanted to be close to my grandfather.

On the train rolled into the night. Because it was a newer train, it did not make as much noise as the others we had been on. My grandfather had slumped back in his seat again with his hat over his eyes. Chief Naiche and all the other men had grown so tired of the reporters with all their rude questions that they had finally begun to refuse interviews. At New Orleans, only Geronimo had kept answering questions from one reporter after another. Now, as I said earlier, even he was tired and trying to sleep until the next morning.

He was not allowed to do so. In the middle of the night, our train halted yet again. It was only meant to be a brief stop, while we were switched to the Pensacola track, but it was time enough for yet another reporter to board our train. The newspaperman came walking down the aisle. He held a handful of cigars. It was clear that he hoped giving those out to the Indian men might convince them to talk to him. He stopped next to my grandfather, carefully selected one cigar, and held it out toward him. Without lifting his hat off his face or turning to look, Geronimo reached out one big hand. As quick as an eagle snatching a fish from the water, he took not that one cigar but the entire bunch the man had been holding. The man stood there looking at his empty hand with his mouth open.

"Whaat-whaat?" the man said. He sounded like an injured duck.

Then he turned and spoke to Mr. Wratten. I couldn't understand his words, but I could see that he was looking for sympathy. Instead, Mr. Wratten gave a short laugh and jerked his thumb toward the door.

"Interview over," Wratten said.

Clutching his one remaining cigar, the newsman scuttled out, and the train started up again.

It was still long before first light when our train rolled again to a stop. Was this our final destination? Had we reached the place of flowers? I tried to look out the window to see where we were, but it was too dark. I rubbed my eyes.

"*Bil nzih*," my grandfather's soft voice said. "You are sleepy." He reached out one hand to pat me on the shoulder. I leaned back into the cushioned seat. I closed my eyes, believing that there was no way I could sleep, but I did.

I slept deeply. And I dreamed. I opened my eyes to the place of my birth. The tree that had been planted there was tall and covered with fruit. I could hear the voices of my parents speaking just behind me. They were arguing with each other in that joking way they had always done. It made me feel so happy to hear them talking that way again that there were tears in my eyes. I did not turn around to look at them. I was a very young child, and I had just learned to walk, and I knew if I tried to turn around too quickly I might fall. But I also knew that soon one of them would come and pick me up. So I held my arms out and closed my eyes again. Sure enough, I felt my father's strong arms lift me up, and I leaned my head against his shoulder as he carried me.

Then I heard my mother shouting. "They are taking them," she cried. "They are taking our men!"

I opened my eyes.

"They are taking our men!" came that cry again. But it was not my mother's voice. It was She-gah, one of Geronimo's wives. She was in the seat just ahead of me, looking out the window and striking the palm of her hand against the glass. All around me other women were shouting and wailing and children were crying.

I looked around. Where was my grandfather? Where was Mr. Wratten? When had they left the train car? I was too confused at that moment to realize what had really happened. While I slept, either Mr. Wratten or one of our guards had gently picked me up and carried me back into one of the cars with the women and children.

"They are going to kill our men here!" another, younger woman's voice called out from behind me, so loudly that it cut through me like a knife. At first I could not tell who it was, for her voice was distorted by fear. "Kill us with them," she cried. It was Tahdaste, the wife of Ahnandia. She leaped out of her seat and began to try to push her way past the guards to reach the door of the train.

I scrambled into the empty seat Tahdaste had left behind and stared out the window, still wiping the sleep from my eyes. It was morning now. I had slept through the rest of the night and kept sleeping even after our train stopped at the station that I later learned was Pensacola. The morning light shone on the two coaches that held the Chiricahua men of our party. But those coaches were standing still, and we were moving. They had been separated from us and shunted onto another track next to ours. We were still connected to the engine that was now pulling us out of that station. We were about to leave my grandfather and the other men behind.

If they are going to kill the men, I thought, *I should die with them.*

I bent over to slip under the arms of the two guards who were holding back Tahdaste and pushed down the aisle toward the door. Someone took hold of my wrist. I struggled to pull free.

"Grandfather," I cried. "Grandfather."

The one who had grabbed at me, the white soldier we called Red Face, threw me back into the nearest seat and shook one long, bony finger in front of my face. Then he held his hand up to show he would strike me if I tried to stand again.

Despite that threat, I began to move my hand down toward the boot where my knife was hidden. But then words, words that I heard as clearly as if my grandfather had spoken them, came into my mind.

Grandson, do not just think of yourself.

I stopped my struggling. I understood. I had to act like a man for the sake of those who were weak and needed protection. I had to be brave and stay with our women. I looked out the window as the two cars holding my Geronimo and Mr. Wratten and the other Chiricahua men grew smaller and smaller. I could see my grandfather through the window of that train car. He was sitting calmly, his eyes holding mine until our train's tracks bent us around a big stone building and he was lost from sight.

ST. AUGUSTINE

OCTOBER 24, 1886

CAN TAKE SEVENTY-FIVE PRISONERS, BUT
RECOMMEND AGAINST SENDING ANY.

COLONEL LOOMIS L. LANGDON, COMMANDING OFFICER

FORT MARION SUBPOST OF ST. FRANCIS BARRACKS, SAINT

AUGUSTINE, FLORIDA, TELEGRAM DATED AUGUST 21, 1886

S OME OF THE WOMEN continued to wail and cry as we went on. The sun was so bright that everything around the train seemed to glow with light, yet there was no light in their hearts. However, as our train left that last station further behind, they no longer fought to get off the train. Instead, some of them did as Tahdaste did, covering their faces with their blankets as our half-a-train continued on. On we went, further toward the direction of the sunrise. Worn out by their sobbing, some of the women grew quiet and slept.

Not all of the women were crying. Ha-o-zinne, the young wife of Chief Naiche, and U-go-hun, her mother, sat together quietly, looking ahead. Ha-o-zinne's father, Beshe, was one of the men who had just been left behind. The two women's hands were laced together like the branches of trees that grow side by side. I could feel the strength being shared between them.

I did not sleep. I kept my eyes open. If anyone tried to harm the women, I would fight them. However, I soon discovered that I was wrong in thinking that all of the grown men among us had been left at Pensacola. Martine and Kayitah, because they were army scouts, had been allowed to remain on the train. They came into our car after we had been traveling long enough for the sun to rise the width of three hands above the horizon. They moved about, speaking words of comfort.

"My sisters, all will be well," Martine said.

"Do not worry," Kayitah reassured us, "your men left behind will not be harmed. I am sure you will be reunited with them."

"Yes," Martine said. "Maybe they will just question them and then send them to join us on another train."

I tried to follow their example. I moved to the empty seat next to my grandfather's wife, She-gah, and rested my hand on her wrist. She did not turn toward me, but placed her arm around my shoulder and drew me close to her.

The other women and children were still crying, but their crying was softer now, and as we went along they gradually stopped. Even though you may have a good reason to do so, you cannot cry forever.

Compared to the great distance we had already traveled, the rest of our journey was not long. It only took the rest of that day to come to a stop. It was early evening when the Iron Wheel halted near a big stone building. It was, I later learned, the place called Jacksonville. The one whose name that town carried, Andrew Jackson, was the president who sent the Cherokees and many of the tribes of the South into exile. I was not surprised to find out that a big town had been named for a White Eyes chief who robbed other Indians of their land.

As we were being unloaded from the train and counted yet again, I stumbled. It was growing dark outside, and I had been sitting for so long that I missed the first step. One of the new white men waiting outside the door of the train caught my arm to keep me from falling. His grasp on my arm was firm, but it was not rough. He righted me at the bottom of the steps, then looked down at me and said something. He did not have hair on his face like many of the White Eyes. That made him look less threatening to me. It took a long time for me to get used to seeing men whose faces were like that of a bear or some other animal, all covered with thick hair. He repeated his words and waited. I suppose he was asking me if I could speak English.

"Uh-one, uh-two," I said to him.

That made him roar with laughter. He was still laughing and waving at me as we were led with the others to a ferryboat. The water it crossed was not as wide as the Mississippi had been. On the other side, yet another train was waiting for us. It took us the remaining forty miles to St. Augustine, the shortest train journey we had yet experienced. It was so short that we were surprised when that train stopped and we were told to get off. But an even bigger surprise awaited us.

The shapes that stepped out of the darkness into the light shone on the platform by hissing gas lanterns had familiar faces. They were Apaches. To my great surprise, there at the St. Augustine station, we were met by Chief Chihuahua and several men and women of his band.

"*Hondah*, my relatives. You are welcome," Chief Chihuahua said. "*Nanohkah*. Come. Come with us to the wagons."

"*Shina?* Are you hungry?" said a woman who placed something in my hands. "Here is some bread."

"Are you cold? Here is a blanket," said a man who gently took my arm.

"Who is here with you?" said a woman to Tahdaste.

"Where is Chief Naiche?" a man asked Ha-o-zinne.

"Where is Geronimo?" someone asked.

I tried to answer. But, although tears began to flow from my eyes, words would not come from my mouth.

How did those other Apaches get there? Chief Chihuahua and the others of his band, over 300 people, had been sent to Florida several months ago. They now knew their way around enough to be our guides. The *nantan* of Fort Marion, General Ayres, was not a bad man. He thought, rightly, that we would be less upset if we were greeted by people of our own kind. So I heard not only words in English, but those good Apache words, greetings and questions about our well-being and our health, spoken in our beloved language.

This place, St. Augustine, Florida, was where Geronimo and the others of our band had been told that all the Apaches would be held. They had been promised that they would be united here with their beloved families. But that was just another lie. It was like all the other promises made by General Miles that turned out to be no more than dust blowing in the wind.

It is hard to explain just how much it meant to us, seeing other Apaches waiting for us, wearing clean clothes, speaking our language to us. Many of us had still expected to be taken off the train at any time, lined up, and shot by a firing squad. But that night when I arrived at St. Augustine, the sight of Chief Chihuahua gave me hope. Perhaps the White Eyes were going to keep their word. We might be prisoners in exile in a strange, foreign place for a while, but we would be with our relatives. That would give us some happiness.

Chief Chihuahua and the others continued to speak kind words as we went along in the growing darkness of those wagons. It was good that they did so. Even the adults among us were as confused as small children by the strangeness of this place, by the moist heat, by our exhaustion from one train passage after another, steps on a journey that had seemed to have no end.

Clop, clop, clop, the sound of the hooves of the mules that pulled us were loud on the stone road, yet those sounds were soothing. The sound of hooves was welcome, and so much more natural to hear that I fell asleep on that jolting wagon. When I opened my eyes again, it was to see the huge stone fort looming above us. Its gate was open.

"Castillo de San Marcos," Chief Chihuahua said. "*Nohwigowa*," he added. "Our home." The tone of his voice was ironic.

Lanterns burned to light our way through that gate, guarded by soldiers who held guns. Big moths were circling around those lights, which made hissing sounds as they burned. One of those moths came flying at me, and its wings brushed my face like the touch of a lonely ghost. Going through that gate was like walking into the mouth of a hungry giant. When the last of us had passed through, that big gate closed behind us. Below us there were dungeons, cells where prisoners had been kept. But at least they did not put us down into those cells. They took us up some stone stairs to a big place that was open to the sky. On each corner there were little square places with windows, places where they kept soldiers as lookouts. There was a wall all around that flat place that was as high as my chin. Many tents were pitched up there on that hard stone floor. That was where we had to stay.

The small parade ground inside the fort is surrounded by walls in which were casements once occupied by the garrison, but the terreplain above became so dilapidated that water leaked down into them rendering them uninhabitable. Therefore I have pitched tents — eighteen of them — on the terreplain to shelter eighty additional persons, but the sanitary conditions will be bad. . . . Besides the danger of being drowned, the prisoners would have to face the diseases peculiar to the low grounds of such localities.

COLONEL LOOMIS L. LANGDON, COMMANDING OFFICER,

FORT MARION SUBPOST OF ST. FRANCIS BARRACKS, SAINT

AUGUSTINE, FLORIDA, LETTER DATED AUGUST 23, 1886

THE NEXT MORNING, as the first light that comes before dawn woke me, I got up and went over to the stone walls. It was not easy to do so, for the people were packed tightly together here, and I had to be careful not to step over anyone who was sitting or lying down. It is a very impolite thing to step over another person. Even though I wove my way in and out with great care, I still felt uneasy by the closeness here. It was hardly possible in this little space to separate one family from another. Yet all were doing their best to be polite and respectful and maintain their dignity. When I finally reached the parapet and looked out over the stone walls of the old fort in the direction of the dawn, I saw what seemed to be a wide plain.

But as the sun rose above it, that bright surface wavered and changed. Its color was not like that of any land I had ever seen before. Then I realized that it was not land but water. It was water that stretched on as far as I could see. I had caught glimpses of that water before as we traveled, but I had never realized how big it was. For the first time, there in Florida at St. Augustine, I truly saw the ocean.

We have come, I thought, *to the very end of the earth.*

I began to walk around our *kotah*, our little village of tents on top of the old stone fort. It was better in the daylight. Many, but not all, of the familiar sights and scents of an Apache were camp here. Freshly cut firewood was piled in stacks by the conical army tents. If I squinted at them just right, they almost looked a little like Chiricahua brush wickiups. The smoke that brushed across my face from the cooking fires was reassuring. The good smell of tortillas being made and stew being cooked made my stomach grumble. But not for long. We are a people who always feed our hungry children. Women's hands began reaching out to me, placing tortillas in one hand, a small bowl in another. Soon I had my first taste of Fort Marion stew. I'd grow to know it far too well in the days to come, that thin soup which used the few pieces of stringy beef that were rationed out to us each day. But at the time it tasted wonderful.

I was greeted warmly by many people, some of whom hugged me even before they spoke those polite words of greeting in Chiricahua that remind us how much we always show respect to each other. Ih-tedda, the youngest of Geronimo's three wives, grabbed me in a hug that almost squeezed the breath out of me and danced me around in a dizzy circle.

I saw other familiar faces that I had thought I would never see again. Among them was my favorite of all the adult women, Lozen. I had not seen her since my grandfather's surrender to Nantan Longnose. She had been among those left behind when our small band took flight. Although I had never worried about her when we were out in the mountains, hunted by armies of Mexicans and White Eyes looking to kill us, I was greatly concerned about her being in captivity. I remembered her words about going so far away that she would never see home again.

Suddenly, there Lozen was. I came around a tent and found her sitting on the stones. She was not cooking, as were many of the other women. She was sharpening a knife. I was so glad to see her, almost as glad as I would have felt at seeing Geronimo. I felt as if my heart had wings. But as Lozen looked up at me, I saw how worn her face looked. She no longer looked strong, and her shoulders were slumped. She did recognize me right away. Her eyes grew brighter for a moment, but she did not stand or say a word. All Lozen did was nod and then return to the sharpening of her blade. I felt a heaviness in my heart as I walked away from her.

I began to find friends, children of about my own age whom I had played games with. I began to feel more hopeful seeing them, a part of the life I had lived before. There were boys I had hunted birds and rabbits with, girls who had teased me. We greeted each other, made jokes, shared stories of the strange things that had happened on each of our journeys to this place. As best we could in this strange place, we found things to do. We chased each other, threw sticks, explored the fort and the grounds around it. Our hearts were not completely in it, but being able to behave again with all the freedom that even the White Eyes guards allowed to children was a good thing. There were even times when we forgot we were prisoners as we walked by the ocean, awed by its size and a bit frightened at the thought of what monsters might be hidden beneath its waters.

On that awful train trip, I had often wished for an icy stream like the one my grandfather used to send us boys into each morning in the mountains. Now, although there were no cold streams here, there was at last a chance to bathe. But bathing was not easy.

There were just two places for bathing, one for the women and one for the men. Each had just one tub of water. There were now almost 400 Apaches in the Castillo de San Marcos. So we had to stand in two long lines, waiting and waiting. Many stood there through most of the day.

Some of us boys, though, went down to that wide water, which we had thought at first was a wide rippling plain. We were timid at first, just wading in. Before long, though, we were running around and playing in the water. We soon learned that it was unlike the fresh, clean water of the streams in our homelands. That ocean had a taste even stronger than its smell. Its waters made our eyes burn and left a white film of salt on our skins when it dried. At least, though, it cleaned us. At least we were able once again to smell more like real human beings and less like skunks.

You may wonder what it was like for us Chiricahuas, people who came from the dry deserts and the mountains, to be imprisoned at that fort by the ocean. It was hard. Very hard. We were all crowded together into a small area, hundreds of us. Back home, we always set up our homes so that we did not crowd each other. We Apaches respect each other's privacy, and so we always put a respectful distance between our houses. Also, whether we stayed in a round wickiup or a conical tipi covered with skin or leafy branches, we would always make sure that our doors faced toward the rising sun.

I remember how, when I was a small child, my father always got up every day before sunrise. He would go outside and stand there with his arms upraised, waiting to greet the sun. Then he would pray as I do to this day. He would pray to Ussen, the Giver of Life. He would first give thanks for our lives and all the gifts of life. Then he would ask for the strength to survive the hardships that are a part of every life. When I was a child, I thought that was a good way to pray. I still think so.

Here, though, at Fort Marion, we were pushed like sheep into a pen, always walled in. Those few tents they gave us were almost on top of each other. It was not possible to make sure that all of our doors faced the sunrise. We tried to be courteous to each other, but there was no privacy at all. You had to share a tent, as I did with six other boys. You could not open your eyes without seeing more than you wished. You could never escape from the smell of too many people pushed into too small a space. It made me feel at times as if I was being held in a giant fist and squeezed.

It was also always hot and moist there by the ocean. The sunlight was not healthy and dry as it had been back home. Here it made us feel tired and dizzy. Then there were the mosquitoes. Unfortunately, we already knew what it was like to be eaten by hungry insects. One of the reasons that our people hated the San Carlos Reservation was because of the mosquitoes there. We had noticed how people became sick at San Carlos with a shaking disease that none of our old medicines could cure. I know now that disease was malaria, and it was brought by the bites of mosquitoes. Just as at San Carlos, the mosquitoes of Florida were carriers of death.

As bad as San Carlos was, at least when we were there we were not far from the mountains we loved so well. There, if we went only ten or twenty miles, we could find good running water and trees. In those nearby mountains we could find familiar plants that gave us food: prickly pear, mesquite beans, piñon nuts, juniper berries, yucca, and acorns. There was even some game there to hunt, rabbits and deer. There were bears also, but we never hunted them. When someone lives a bad life, his spirit does not go to the Happy Place when he dies. Instead, that person comes back as a bear. So if you were to kill a bear you might kill a relative. No one would even touch a dead bear, much less skin one and use its hide. However, that does not mean we saw bears as bad creatures. Sometimes, in fact, bears try to help people. They protect those who are helpless and come to the aid of those in need. There are stories of children who were lost in the mountains and cared for by bears until their families found them. When a bear raises up on its hind legs and raises its paws toward you it is greeting you as a friend.

Lozen was standing by the wall of the fort, looking inland. I came and stood beside her.

"No mountains here," she said.

We were not allowed to leave that high stone courtyard without permission and an escort of soldiers. Even when we went out into the town or down by the water, everything was strange. It was so flat that it made me feel empty in my stomach. All of Florida, it seemed, was hot and flat and monotonous. A land without mountains to an Apache is like a body without a heart. Being there filled us with sorrow. It drained our spirits and weakened our hearts. All we could do was wait.

I still had my knife. They had not searched me for weapons as they had the grown men. I kept it with me wherever I went. If one of those White Eyes soldiers tried to kill me, I would make sure he did not do it without a fight. We all knew the terrible things that the White Eyes often did to Indians. We knew how they liked to cut off our heads and keep them as souvenirs. White men and Mexicans had paid bounties for Indian scalps for many years now.

Scalping is not something that we Apaches did. Before the white men introduced it to us, we had never even heard of it. That is what all my elders have told me. Even after many of our own people were killed and scalped, we seldom scalped anyone. I know that there are still stories told about how many people Geronimo scalped. They say that when he arrived at Fort Sill he brought with him a robe he had made of the scalps of white women he killed. Those stories are all lies. It made me feel sick to think of someone doing that. But I knew that some white men liked to keep Apache scalps hanging in their rooms. Some white men even liked to skin Apaches and use their skins as shades for their lights. So I kept my little knife close at hand. If they tried to take my skin they would pay for it with their blood.

There at Fort Marion with us were Apaches who could speak English. Most of them were men who had served as government scouts. I looked at some of them as coyotes who had hunted their own people.

I often saw Chatto, but I would not talk to him, nor would many other Chiricahuas. We disliked him because of his treachery, because of the lies he and Mickey Free told about Geronimo that led to so much trouble. However, we were glad to see him there with us.

Chatto had a look of confusion on his face that was pleasing for other Chiricahuas to see. That look said, "How is it that I am here with these renegades after having hunted them for my White Eyes?"

Chatto had been in Washington, D.C., trying to gain influence so that he could be a very big man when he went back home. He thought he was important to the White Eyes. But when word came that the last of the hostile Apaches led by Geronimo had been captured, the train Chatto and the other Apache scouts were on was diverted to the federal prison in Leavenworth, Kansas, where Chatto and his men were locked up. Now that Geronimo was in captivity, they no longer needed other Apaches to hunt him. Chatto and his men were shipped to Florida, like those same Apaches they had spent so much time trying to capture.

I learned later that some of the White Eyes leaders did not want to see this happen. "If you put our good Apache scouts in detention along with the bad Indians they were hunting, those bad Indians will kill them." That is what they said.

But they were wrong. To their surprise, no one ever tried to physically attack even one of those former scouts. In part it was because many of those who had agreed to work for the army were honorable men. They wanted peace and thought it was the right thing to do. They had courage, too. Men such as Martine and Kayitah had nothing to fear. But what about Chatto, who was disliked by so many? Ah, it was more pleasant to watch his discomfort than it was to harm him. So we watched him with amusement — and he knew he was being watched — all through his years with us there in Florida, in Alabama, and in Oklahoma.

One day passed into the next, and still Geronimo and the men who had been taken from the train did not arrive as Kayitah and Martine had suggested. We waited for them, but we did not have much hope. Perhaps the army had just lined them up and shot them after all.

Gradually, bit by bit, we began to hear news. It trickled down to us the way water seeps through a beaver dam. A drop here, a drop there, but never enough to quench your thirst. I was learning more English and could now understand the soldiers when they talked with each other. Because they assumed I didn't know their language, they would sometimes talk of things related to our captivity. Of course, they spoke often about Geronimo. They were both excited and fearful about his being brought to Fort Marion.

"I hear Geronimo is a-comin' next week," one would say.

"Ain't no way," another would answer. "Haven't you heard they're earning two bits a pop just to let folks take a look at him? No way they're going to give that cash cow up to us."

Those Whites Eyes spoke just as much about Geronimo as we Apaches did. It was always that way with Geronimo. Even those who hated or feared him could not stop talking about him.

Some Apaches were angry at Geronimo, blaming him for their exile. If he had not broken out from the reservation, they thought, we would not have all been punished this way. If he had not run away from General Crook when everyone else surrendered, we would still be in Arizona.

But there were just as many others who felt that the White Eyes would have done this to us anyway. They felt they could not trust the promises of any white soldier, any white government. At least Geronimo and those who followed him had enjoyed a little freedom, taken some revenge on those who killed our families, before he was finally forced to surrender that final time. Those who felt that way longed to see my grandfather. They felt as I did. He was still the one who carried our hope in his strong old hands.

"Tomorrow," I told myself each night. "Tomorrow my grandfather Geronimo will arrive here at Fort Marion and things will begin to go better for us."

I did not know how wrong I was.

STONE

OCTOBER 28, 1886

Won't see Mexico no more.

UNIDENTIFIED APACHE (PROBABLY AHNANDIA) BEING

LOADED ONTO THE FERRY TO FORT PICKENS

THE APACHE ROCK CRUMBLES

ALTHOUGH HE WAS OFTEN in my thoughts, I did not think of Geronimo all of the time. There was so much that was new and hard about this place by the endless water. The hardest of all was the place where they had us put up our small tents. It was in front of the big stone soldier house. The ground was all stone, a strange, smooth stone that was all flat. That stone surface felt strange to our feet. During the day it became so hot that you could not touch it without burning yourself. But at night it lost its heat and became cold. It felt and looked nothing at all like the living stones of our homeland. In our homeland, the stones flow like the wind and are soothing to our eyes. Some of the stones on the mountains and ridgetops look like people. During those days when we were in the stronghold with Geronimo I would sometimes look up at such stones and feel comforted. I felt they were watching over us and keeping guard. The courtyard stone here at Fort Marion, though, was not alive. It was as dead as our hopes of freedom.

"The White Eyes make this stone," Kayitah said to me one day. "They are good at making things like this stone and those iron posts."

He gestured with his chin toward the barred windows of the fort. "I think it is because their own hearts are just as hard as this stone and that iron."

I thought Kayitah might be teasing me. I found it hard to believe that the white men actually made stone. Then I saw them repairing a place where the stone had cracked. They mixed water with a white powder to make a kind of paste. When that paste was poured onto the ground, it dried and became that stone. The White Eyes love that kind of stone surface more than they love the soft earth where grass or flowers or moss or the roots of trees can find nourishment. That is why they put it everywhere in their cities, which seem to be all made of that material. They call it concrete. Perhaps one day they will cover the whole earth with that concrete stone. I do not want to live to see that time.

One day passed, and then another. I was learning more English. I have always found stories easy to remember. New words, for me, were like the start of stories about to be told. So I put more and more words together and found that those sounds were, indeed, turning into stories. But none of those stories answered my biggest questions. There was no sign of Geronimo, no certain word about the men who had been taken off the train. In the past, we had always relied on Mr. Wratten to tell us what the White Eyes said or planned. But Mr. Wratten was not with us. He had been in the train that took away my grandfather and the other men.

So there were only rumors and wild tales of the sort that come to you in bad dreams. Perhaps they were being tortured. We knew how much the Mexicans loved to torture Apaches, and some of the Americans had proven just as bad. Perhaps our loved ones had been shot or hung, their bodies mutilated so that their spirits would not be whole when they reached the Happy Place.

Perhaps, on the other hand, the White Eyes were going to keep their word.

Although I kept hoping each day as the sun rose that the train would arrive carrying the rest of our men, that wait turned out to be longer than any of us expected. Day after day, sunrise and sunset, sunrise and sunset, and still there was no word, no sign.

Finally, we learned what had happened. Martine and Kayitah came to us from the office of the commanding officer.

"Geronimo and the others," Martine said, "are safe."

"But they are not coming here to Fort Marion," Kayitah added.

"They are being held at another place in Florida called Fort Pickens."

It was a comfort to us, but it was also another loss. The promises that we would all be together here had been broken. A train bringing our loved ones back to us would never arrive at Fort Marion. The only trains that came were not to give back our lost ones but to take more away. It would be eight months before I would see my grandfather again, and it would not be in Florida.

But it was just as some of us expected. Lies from the mouths of the White Eyes seemed as certain as the sunrise each morning in the east. Even when they wrote their promises down on paper, they still did not keep them. Paper lies are even easier to burn.

FISH

OCTOBER 29, 1886

Fish was not eaten. It was not an Indian food in the old days.
We classed fish with the snake and thought it could bite. We
thought it could bring evil influence.

UNNAMED CHIRICAHUA MAN

AN APACHE LIFE-WAY

THEY FED US AT FORT MARION. We did not starve. They gave us boxes of flour and coffee and sugar. But those rations were slim. No one's stomach was ever full. And even if they had given us more of those supplies, we still would not have felt satisfied. We were hungry for real food. There was no mescal here, no deer to hunt, not even any rabbits.

I tagged along behind some of the men when they went to speak to the nantan at the fort. That is what boys were supposed to do. We would try to make ourselves useful in whatever way we could to the men. Even the smallest child would wait at the edge of the camp whenever the men came home from raiding or hunting, hoping to be chosen to take the reins of a man's horse and lead it into camp. A

192

boy had to go on four successful raids with the men before he could be admitted into their company. He would cook the food, gather firewood, and do all the things that needed to be done to help out.

Here, even though there were no raids, no horses, no men's jobs to carry out, I still followed the men whenever I could. I think it made them feel good, too, to have us boys following them. It made them feel as if they still had things to teach us, even if our lives had been made so small that we could carry them between our fingertips.

"We need more meat," Martine said to the White Eyes colonel. "We need to hunt."

"There is no hunting allowed here," Colonel Ayers said. "You can go into the town and try to get some meat. But there is plenty of meat, and you do not need guns or money to get it. It is right out there."

Then he pointed to the ocean. He meant that we Chiricahuas should go and catch fish!

Martine was so shocked that he just turned around and walked away in silence. I followed behind him, shaking my own head.

Fish. No Apache would ever eat fish in those days, no matter how hungry he or she was. As I have told you, scaled things were regarded in the same way as snakes. Things that came out of the water were dangerous. I had heard the stories about the monsters that hide under the surface of the water in the rivers and in springs, waiting to grab someone foolish enough to approach too closely.

Fish. It made me feel sick to think about that, the way a White Eyes might feel if you told him he had to eat spiders or worms.

Fish. They smelled bad, even when they were still alive and flopping around. Their skins were slippery and left slime on your hands when you touched them. Their eyes never closed like the eyes of the animals we hunted for food. They had no legs, as wholesome creatures do. Their eyes were always wide and staring, even in death — just like the eyes of snakes.

Finally, some people did eat fish. But no one liked it. We only did so because we had no other choice. It was not until years later when I met other Indians whose homelands were by the ocean, and who talked about salmon the way we talked about deer meat, that I realized there were any Indians at all who liked to eat fish.

I was an orphan with no mother or father and no close relatives to care for me. But people always shared their food with me. I had friends among the children and sometimes would end up sleeping in the tent of their families. We all knew each other, and everyone tried to care for the children. Every child was precious to the Apaches, and it was even more so because there were now so few of us. The only good thing about Fort Marion was that we were there together, trying our best to take care of each other.

That is why it was so terrible when the White Eyes soldiers came and began taking away the children.

TAKING THE CHILDREN

NOVEMBER 9, 1886

I recommend that the whole party of prisoners be sent as soon as possible to Carlisle, Pa. I have been told often when these Indians surrendered they were promised by the Government officers that they should not be separated from their children. A breach of faith in this respect — a separation — is what they constantly dread. Even a present of clothing to their more than half-naked children excites their mistrust and makes them very restless, because it looks to them like preparing them for a journey, a separation from their parents.

COLONEL LOOMIS L. LANGDON, COMMANDING
OFFICER, FORT MARION SUBPOST OF ST. FRANCIS
BARRACKS, SAINT AUGUSTINE, FLORIDA

"ASA, BENJAMIN, CHARLES, Daniel, Eli, Frank." That is what the man at the Carlisle Indian School in Pennsylvania said as he walked down the line of Apache boys and young men who had been lined up according to height. Because he was the tallest, Daklugie was at the head of the line. So his name

195

became Asa. It was a name that he hated then and still hates to this day. No one who really knows him ever calls him Asa Daklugie. He is just Daklugie. The son of Mangus was the last one in that short line of Apache boys. So he became Frank Mangus.

That story about being renamed at Carlisle was told to me later by Daklugie. On the day when I watched them take Chiricahua children away, I saw Daklugie and he saw me. But there was no chance for us to talk.

That day began like so many others at Fort Marion. There was the bright, hot sun rising over the endless ocean and the little breeze at the start of the day, a cooling breeze that never lasted long enough. There were the sounds of the army around us — the bugle calls, the loud voices of white officers giving orders, the shuffling of marching feet from below. There was the rattle of wagons and the clop of horses' feet on the cobbled streets outside the fort as white- and black-skinned people, free to move and act as they wished, began their daily jobs. There were the sounds of our own camp, where we were crowded together too close for comfort or privacy.

But that day felt different to everyone. What made it different was that we knew a train was coming again to take some of the children away. That December day it would include four of the children of Chihuahua. Chihuahua and his wife were being allowed to go to the train station to see them off. So when they walked out of the gate of the prison, I went with them. No one stopped me.

Perhaps it was because I was so small that they did not find me threatening.

In fact, some of the white people had been very kind to me. That was especially true of the white women in long dresses whom we were told to call sisters. Whenever we were sick, they came in and helped care for us. Their hands were always gentle, and they never shouted at us. They often gave us little things to eat — which was very welcome because our rations kept being cut. They also handed out small presents. I myself was wearing around my neck one of those presents. It was a chain with a little cross on it. Back then, before I started attending the little school the sisters ran at their house, which was called a convent, I thought the cross stood for the four sacred directions that we Apaches know. I didn't know it was a symbol of an awful thing white people used long ago to torture their god and kill him.

Many of the things those sisters did helped me understand that white people are very much like real human beings. Ussen made human beings in such a way that their hearts would naturally be good and kind to children — just as those sisters often were. However, those sisters also suffered from some of the other weaknesses that seemed to be shared by so many White Eyes. It was hard for them to respect us. In their school they tried to teach us that everything we knew as Apaches was bad.

No one tried to stop me as I walked along with Chihuahua's family. I had learned that if you do something while acting as if you know what you are doing, white people will assume that you have been given permission to do that. So I kept my head up and behaved in a confident way as I tagged along behind Chihuahua and his family. They had not told me I could come with them. But they also had not forbidden me to do so. In fact, a little smile came on Chihuahua's face when he first noticed me. But that smile did not last long. It was gone as quickly as a ripple on the water and replaced by a look that might have seemed calm to some. But I knew what that look meant. I saw the sorrow. Chihuahua was trying not to show how worried and upset he was about his four children going so far away.

When the train pulled up to the station, I spotted two familiar faces looking out at us through the windows. It was Daklugie and the son of Mangus, who later became known as Frank Mangus. Frank was the grandson of Mangas Coloradas. His father, whose name was Mangus, was the leader of the last band of free Chiricahuas. Daklugie, who was already old and strong enough to be a capable fighter, had been with that band. Like me, Daklugie was an orphan and we thought of each other as relatives. His mother, Ishton, had been Geronimo's favorite sister. His father, the great chief Juh, had died in Mexico several years before. I was glad that they were alive, but it made me sad to see them on that train. I knew what it meant. Mangus's band, too, had now surrendered. The last of the free Chiricahuas were captives.

Indeed, on November 10, Mangus's band had arrived in Florida.

Just as with our exile train, the men and older boys had been separated from the women and children, who continued on to join us at Fort Marion. The adults and older boys of the Mangus band had been sent to join Geronimo and the others held in Pensacola at the other prison fort. Now Daklugie and Frank Mangus were being separated yet again from their people to be shipped off to the United States Indian Industrial School at Carlisle.

Daklugie and Frank Mangus gave no outward sign that they noticed us on the platform, but I knew they were just as aware of us as we were of them. One of the four children of Chihuahua boarding that train was his oldest daughter, Ramona. Of course, she did not have the name of Ramona yet. It was well known that words had been spoken more than a year ago about Daklugie and her marrying. Her parents had agreed it should happen. It was a marriage that Ramona and Daklugie had looked forward to. The two of them were well matched. Both of them were tall and handsome. They both carried themselves with great poise and seriousness. Of course, even though there must have been joy in their hearts at being reunited, they did not look at each other. They would not sacrifice any of their dignity in front of the White Eyes soldiers by showing emotion.

A white woman in a blue dress came down from the train to speak through Concepcion, one of our two interpreters, to Chihuahua before getting back on board with the four children. It seemed that one of the guards had brought his wife with him. That made me feel a little less worried. When there were White Eyes women along, there was less chance that the white men would behave badly with the children or hurt them.

But I knew that Daklugie had to be uncertain about this train trip, as I was of mine. I am often able to see some small distance into people's hearts, to take note of things that help me know what others are thinking and feeling. It has been that way with me ever since I went with Geronimo that last time into the Sierra Madre. So it was that I noticed a small gesture Daklugie made as Ramona was brought on board that train. He reached up one hand as if to arrange the thick braid of his hair that hung over his left shoulder. I felt a tingling in the back of my neck as he did that. It was as if I could feel with my own fingers what his hands were touching inside that thick braid. Daklugie had concealed a small, sharp knife in his hair, wrapped it into that thick braid. I knew his thought. He would use that knife to protect Ramona if any of those white men tried in any way to harm her. If they had to die, he would make sure that they died fighting.

Chihuahua had not been given any choice about sending his children to school. But he had been granted one favor.

"The officers say they are going to take all of your children to school," Concepcion had said to Chihuahua as they stood in the office of Colonel Ayers at the fort. Concepcion was an Apache who spoke English well enough to be a good translator. Even though he was one of the scouts who had been with Chatto in his party sent to Washington, he was not envious or deceitful as Chatto was. Chihuahua would not let Chatto or Mickey Free interpret for him. It was only Concepcion or Sam Bowman, the army scout who was Choctaw Indian by blood but had learned to speak Chiricahua, that he would trust.

"Tell the *nantan*," Chihuahua said, "he must leave me at least one child or I will die."

Nantan Ayers looked hard at Chihuahua after Concepcion translated those words. Nantan Ayers had been told about Chihuahua by Colonel Langdon, the commander who had been at the fort when the first Apaches arrived there in April of 1886, five months before us.

"Of all the men at Fort Marion," Langdon had said to Ayers, "there is no one whose word is more true than Chihuahua's."

Langdon knew well that Chihuahua always spoke the truth. He had learned this soon after the Apaches' arrival, when he called Chihuahua in to speak with him. Chihuahua had not gone alone to that conversation. One of his sons, Eugene Chihuahua, the same one who was allowed to stay, accompanied him and told me later about what happened that day.

His father had been worried about being called in. Perhaps this officer was going to punish him for the things he had done while making war. Perhaps, because he had been a scout for Fat Boy before resigning in disgust, he would be accused of desertion and hung as Dandy Jim and Dead Shot and Skippy were in 1881 after Cibeque. They were three of the White Mountain Apache scouts who turned to fight against the army when Noche-del-Klinne, the prophet, was murdered.

Colonel Langdon stood turned away from Chihuahua and his son, with his hands behind his back. "Ask him if it is true that he ambushed and killed many soldiers at Guadalupe Canyon," he said to Concepcion.

As soon as those words were translated, Chihuahua drew himself up straighter. "*Enjuh*," he said. "It is true. I did it. My men and me, we did it. I am proud of it. I just wish we had killed every one of them."

"Ask him why he did it," Nantan Langdon said in a level voice.

"*Han'te bigha?*" Concepcion said. "Why was this done by you?"

"*Hagosha?*" Chihuahua said. "Why? Why did they kill my mother? Why did they kill the women of our families? If they wanted to fight, why didn't they fight men? Why women and children? Your soldiers were fighting women and children."

Then Chihuahua turned his own back and sat down on the floor. His son and Concepcion looked at each other. They were certain that the next thing they would hear would be Chihuahua's death sentence.

But when Nantan Langdon turned around, his words surprised them.

"Chihuahua," he said, "you are a brave man. You speak the truth. I like that. I cannot blame you for what you did. Had I been in your place I hope I might have had the courage to do the same. I would like to let you go back into your own country, but I cannot do this. But I will make certain that no one can order you to dig in the earth or cut wood or carry water."

Chihuahua stood and turned to face Colonel Langdon. He was surprised not just at his words, but that the *nantan* knew how much it had troubled Chihuahua to be ordered around like a slave by some of the soldiers at the fort. As a chief who had led his people with honor, such treatment hurt his pride.

"You will not be with me all of the time," Chihuahua said. "How will others know that I cannot be ordered to do such things?"

"I will give you the uniform of a captain. You have been a scout and worn the uniform of the United States before."

"Not the pants," Chihuahua said.

For the first time, Nantan Langdon smiled broadly. "The whole uniform," he said. "That includes the trousers."

So, rather than being hung, Chihuahua had left the office of Nantan Langdon with the uniform of a captain, the two double bars of his new rank on his shoulders. And he did wear the trousers, but only after cutting the seat out of them, with his breechcloth worn over the top.

Now, just as Langdon had done, Ayers himself saw the truth in

Chihuahua's eyes. Chihuahua meant what he said. He would die if all his children were taken. So, Colonel Ayers agreed that his son, Eugene, could stay with him.

Just like Chihuahua, no Apache parents wanted their children taken away. They wanted to keep their children with them. What Apaches wanted, though, was thinner than our fingernails. It meant little or nothing to the white men who ruled our lives. It was decided that the children would go to school, whether they liked it or not. While I was at Fort Marion, they eventually gathered up most of our young people between the ages of twelve and twenty-two, as well as some who were older. They even forced some married couples to go off to school, where they were separated and not allowed to live as husband and wife. Even though I was old enough in years to have been among those taken to be students, I was so small that I looked younger than my age. The little children were allowed to remain at Fort Marion. At least for a while.

The first time they took away Apache children was in October of 1886. None other than Captain Pratt, the superintendent of Carlisle, came to Fort Marion to take away some of our young people. Captain Pratt was a tall, broad-shouldered man who did much smiling. None of us smiled as he looked us over. No one wanted to catch his eye and be taken away. Pratt brought with him an Apache boy who was already at Carlisle. Even though that boy had relatives among us, it was hard for any of us to recognize him as an Apache. His hair had been cut off, and he wore a full military uniform that did not have the bottom of the pants cut out. He even had a new name and acted just like a white man.

Captain Pratt had all of the children called onto the fort parade ground.

"Line up," he said. "Form a line."

He did this so that he could look at us and judge who was old enough. I kept my knees bent to appear smaller. Others tried digging their feet down into the soft sand to make themselves shorter. Since Captain Pratt could not be sure of our actual ages, he was choosing people by their height, taking the tallest children. There was only one thought in my mind. I must not let them take me. If I were taken to Pennsylvania, I would never see my grandfather, Geronimo, again. It was a fearful time for all of us. Some of the smallest children hid behind their mothers or even crept beneath their skirts to avoid being noticed.

Captain Pratt stepped forward, a big smile on his face. Then, in a voice even bigger than his smile, he began to speak as he strode up and down in front of us.

"I am again looking for candidates for my school. Here in front of you, you see one of your own relatives. He has done well at Carlisle and so can you. Come along now, who will volunteer?"

No one raised a hand. No one even looked up. But that did not stop Captain Pratt.

"Ah," he said, stepping forward. "Here is one." Then he reached out, grabbed hold of the wrist of the tall boy next to me, and hoisted his hand up into the air.

The soldiers pulled that boy out of the line as Captain Pratt moved on to choose his next unwilling volunteer. I held my breath, my eyes focused on the toes of his shiny black military boots as he loomed in front of me. He paused for only a heartbeat.

"Not yet," he said. Then he moved on to choose a girl on the other side of me. I had escaped.

Even though I was relieved, I was not happy. All of us shared the despair being felt by the families whose children were pulled from that line, one after another — like rabbits being snatched by a coyote. Mothers and fathers were wondering if they would ever see their children again. They feared their beloved sons and daughters were being taken away to die. Years later, as I remember that day, I grow sad when I think about how right those parents were. Although Captain Pratt may have had the best intentions, may have thought that his school would give us a chance for a better life, just the opposite happened. At Carlisle young Chiricahuas quickly learned to read and write and do math. They excelled at learning the skills of industry. But there was also sickness there.

GERONIMO'S WIVES

NOVEMBER 15, 1886

I come to White Painted Woman,

By means of long life I come to her.

I come to her by means of her blessing.

I come to her by means of her good fortune,

I come to her by means of her different fruits;

By means of the long life she bestows, I come to her;

By means of this holy truth she goes about.

CHIRICAHUA APACHE DANCE SONG

FROM THE GIRLS' PUBERTY CEREMONY

O NE OF THE JOBS I took upon myself at Fort Marion was to do all that I could to help the three wives of Geronimo. I had promised Geronimo I would do so, and I kept my word. Whenever She-gah or Zi-yeh or Ih-tedda went into town, I would go with them to help them carry things. Even though I was a small boy, I also had it in my mind that I could protect them. You might think this was foolish of me. But even though

I was small, I was a Chiricahua. I had seen hard things and learned things that many grown white men had never known.

That first morning I was at Fort Marion, after I finished staring at the wide ocean that went on forever, I went to look for Geronimo's family to see how they were. None of us who were with Geronimo had seen Ih-tedda since Geronimo came in for that first surrender in January of this year and then fled after he feared treachery. She and one of Geronimo's daughters had been kept by the army. He was most concerned about her, and so I went to seek Ih-tedda first. I was surprised to see that she had a little baby.

When she had arrived at Fort Marion, Ih-tedda had been pregnant. She gave birth to a girl in September. Geronimo had a daughter that he did not even know about!

Lieutenant Colonel Langdon, who was *nantan* at Fort Marion when Ih-tedda arrived there, had been especially concerned about the welfare of the little children. In that way he was much like an Apache, and people liked him for that. So, I am told, he was close by when Ih-tedda gave birth.

"This little girl's name will be Marion," I am told he said. Then he wrote that name down in his record book:

Marion, infant daughter of Ih-tedda, born September 13th, 1886.

However, that was not the name everyone called the baby. To all of us, she was Lenna, and that was the name she was known by all of her life.

However, Ih-tedda told me some sad news. The four-year-old daughter of Geronimo's, who had not yet been given her final name — and was just known by the childhood nickname of Little Girl — had died. Little Girl was not Ih-tedda's daughter, but the daughter of yet another of Geronimo's wives who was taken by the Mexicans and never seen again. Little Girl had not been well, even when we were out in the mountains. That was why Geronimo had sent her back with Ih-tedda when the army took those members of our band as hostages. The long train trip had been hard. When Little Girl arrived at Fort Marion, there was little life left in her.

"Nantan Langdon tried to save her," Ih-tedda said, shaking her head. "He told his doctor to do his best. They gave Little Girl medicines and special foods. But her body was too weak to hold on to her spirit."

Little Girl's body was buried on Anastasia Island. So, without knowing about it, Geronimo had lost one child at Fort Marion and gained another.

Next I went to Zi-yeh. Her little boy, Fenton, was playing in front of her tent, with a toy he made from some sticks and round seed pods. It looked like a train, and he made a growling sound to imitate its engine as he played.

"Second Grandmother," I said, greeting her that way because she was the next to the youngest of Geronimo's three surviving wives. "My grandfather asked me to tell you that he is well."

Zi-yeh had no bad news and seemed as happy as a woman can be when her husband is locked away from her. But that was always the way with Zi-yeh. Even though she was a tiny woman, not much larger than me, she had a big happy spirit. Her father had been like that, too. He was a well-liked person, a fine singer who enjoyed a great reputation as a man, even though there was no man in the band smaller than he. Even some boys of my own age had greater height. He was not even as tall as an old-fashioned musket gun. He had been born outside as a white man, but grew up as a White Mountain Apache and then joined the band of Juh and Geronimo. He died as one of us, fighting in Mexico.

The last of Geronimo's wives I went to see was She-gah. I was shocked when I saw her. Her face looked tired and gray. She-gah truly was in need of help. The bad air and the insects in Florida had made her weak and sick. This troubled me greatly. She had always been the strongest of Geronimo's wives, the one on whom everyone could rely. Now, even carrying a small bundle was too much for her.

"How can I help you, Grandmother?" I asked.

"I would like to take a walk," she said, "but I find it hard to do now, even with a stick."

I almost wept when she said this, remembering how she used to stride with such strength up the steepest mountains, never tiring.

"Lean on my shoulder, Grandmother," I said. And that was how she walked, with me by her side, helping her keep her balance.

I know that it is unusual for a white man to have more than one wife at a time. I can understand why this is so when one lives as do the White Eyes. Their lives are not surrounded by enemies like the lives of the Apaches were when I was a child. There is little chance that a white man might come home and find his house burned and his family dead. Or that Mexican raiders might sweep down in the night and carry off his wife and children as slaves. Or that army soldiers might take away his wife and children as captives. All of those things happened to Geronimo. Had it not been so, had his first family not been wiped out, I think he might have lived out his life happily with only one wife. But it did not happen that way. And each time he lost a wife, because he loved and respected family so much, he married again.

That was why, when both Zi-yeh and She-gah and his three children were taken captive by the U.S. Army in 1885, he married Ih-tedda.

The Bureau of Catholic Indian Missions was given a contract to run a school for the small Apache children. So every morning, we were paraded through the town from the fort to the mission where the sisters at St. Joseph's Convent taught us. That walk was sometimes hard to take. Sometimes white children made fun of our ragged clothing, and even the grown-ups, who had obviously not learned how to behave politely, would point and stare at us. Once we reached the grounds of the convent, we were free of people staring or teasing, but I often felt as if those sisters saw us as pitiful and strange beings. We were not allowed to speak our own language. We had to either speak English or be silent. The sisters were kind, but when they were not teaching, they would sometimes talk to each other as if we Apache children were not there. I think they believed we could not understand what they said unless they spoke to us directly. We talked about them, too, but we were polite enough to only do it when they were not around.

One day, while we children were eating the small midday meal they served to us, their conversation turned to the married Apache women.

"Those poor women. They are such pathetic things," the tallest of the sisters said. We called her Sister Flat Nose because her nostrils seemed to be as wide as those of a horse. We children joked with each other about not getting close to her face for fear she would take a breath in through her nose and suck us into it.

"You would not believe, not believe at all, what I learned today," the smallest of the sisters twittered to her. She was the one who never seemed to be able to sit still and was always fluttering her hands about. The nickname we had given her was Sister Constantly Moving Bird.

"Wha-a-a-at? Te-ellll," said the round and heavy sister, who always measured out her words the way an Indian agent would weigh out flour to an Apache — one small, slow scoop at a time. It took her as much time to say one word as it took Constantly Moving Bird to say two sentences. So we children named her Sister Words from a Stone.

"Well, well," Sister Constantly Moving Bird said, moving her hands so fast it seemed as if she were about to fly up to the ceiling, "I found out that three of those women are Geronimo's wives. Three of them all at once. Three! Can you believe that?"

"No-o-o-o-o," Sister Words from a Stone said, nodding her head in a way that showed she not only believed but expected such awful behavior from Indians.

"Those poor dears," Sister Flat Nose said. "What an awful fate to be married to that evil old man."

"Well," said Sister Constantly Moving Bird, patting her thin chest with both her hands, "the poor dear heathens just don't know what marriage is, do they?"

"No-o-o-o-o-o," Sister Words from a Stone agreed, the tone of her voice making it clear that she certainly understood what marriage was, even though the poor dear heathens did not.

"We have so far to go in our mission to civilize the savage," Sister Flat Nose said, smiling broadly as she did so. Then she clapped her hands, and we children became visible again to them. "Back to your lessons."

It was strange for me to hear such things said by women who had no husbands at all. It made me want to ask them what they knew of marriage. But I did not speak up. When we spoke out of turn we had to stand in front of the class with a tall hat on our heads. Sometimes we were told to close our eyes and hold out our hands so that Flat Nose could strike our palms with a flat stick.

I know that it is common for white men to marry again if their wives die. What if a white man's wife should be thought dead, but then turn up alive after he remarried? What would he do then? (I learned that according to the White Eyes' laws, that man would have to send the new wife away. No Apache man would show so little respect for a woman.)

I did not speak up to those sisters, but I wanted to tell them that most Apache men have only one wife. Only a man who is a great provider could have more than one. And when an Apache man has more than one wife it does not mean that he has less respect for marriage than does a white man. I think it is the other way around. We Apache men knew, in those days, that we could not survive without our wives. They were the ones who knew how to make clothing, who gathered and prepared most of the food that a family ate. Not only that, they were the ones who brought new life into the world and kept our people alive. It is the sacred blessing given to all women that they are able to bring children into the world.

Even though I know they might not have understood it, I also wanted to tell those three sisters another reason why Apache men sometimes had more than one wife. For generations now, the Spanish and the Mexicans and now the Americans had been trying to kill every Apache man they could catch. So there were always more women than men. Sometimes being a second wife was the only way a woman could enjoy those blessings of having a family, bringing children into the world, and extending the life of our people into another generation.

TALKING BY PAPER

NOVEMBER 25, 1886

It would be well to keep [the intention of removing the Apaches]
as secret as possible because all the railroad interests of Eastern
Florida and the influential men of that region will make the
most strenuous endeavors to prevent it by beseiging the War
Dept. with petitions and remonstrances against the change
which will divert a great deal of travel from that country and
cause a loss to the railroads and hotels in that side of the state.

COLONEL LANGDON, COMMANDER AT FORT PICKENS

REPORT TO THE INSPECTOR GENERAL

MARCH 24, 1887

WHERE WAS GERONIMO? All of those eight hungry months that we were at Fort Marion he and the sixteen other Apache men the army regarded as the most dangerous of the hostiles were still being held 400 miles away at Fort Pickens on the gulf coast of westernmost Florida.

Yet while people died at Fort Marion, no one ever got badly sick at Fort Pickens. While we struggled by on half the food we needed, the seventeen Chiricahuas at Fort Pickens ate well every day.

Perhaps it was because they had to do so much physical labor that the Apache men at Fort Pickens were fed better than we were at Fort Marion. Perhaps, too, it was just that it was easier to care for seventeen able-bodied men than it was to provide for almost 500 men, women, and children. But I think there were two other reasons for their better treatment. Both of those reasons were white men.

The first of them was Colonel Langdon. With the return of Colonel Ayres from leave, Colonel Langdon had been transfered from Fort Marion in October, just in time for the arrival of Geronimo and the others. Langdon was assigned to command Fort Barrancas on the mainland and restore Fort Pickens on the barrier island of Santa Rosa to the point where it could be a secure facility to hold the hostiles. Rather than bloodthirsty demons or surly prisoners, he found the Apaches to be cheerful, intelligent, and hardworking. The first thing he did was to set up a schedule of six hours a day, six days a week to clear up the place. There was less complaining than he would have heard from a squad of white soldiers, more hard work, and much more good humor. But I think it did not surprise him. He already had gotten to know our people through his five months with Chihuahua and the seventy-two members of his band, and his briefer experience with the remaining 452 Indians who arrived in September. Langdon gave our people the best treatment he could.

The other reason, of course, was Mr. Wratten.

"We are here," Chapo said to me when we were finally reunited, unfolding one finger from his fist. "And here," he said, unfolding the finger next to it and bringing the two together, "here is Wratten."

As the translator for Geronimo and the others at Fort Pickens, Mr. Wratten not only spoke their words truly but also wrote letters. Those letters went not just to Washington and to the army, but to influential people all around the country. He told of the unjust treatment given to men who had been taken as prisoners of war. He told of the broken promises and how our families were separated from each other. With such a man as Mr. Wratten speaking for us, our voices were heard.

And he helped us hear each other, for some of the letters he wrote — as my grandfather slowly dictated them — were not to white people, but to those Geronimo loved.

I remember well the words in one of those letters that Geronimo dictated and Wratten mailed to Fort Marion.

One morning, when I went, as I usually did, to see how I could help She-gah and Zi-yeh and Ih-tedda, I was surprised to see all of Geronimo's family gathered together. Zi-yeh was holding an envelope in her right hand while she grasped the hand of her small son, Fenton, in the other. Ih-tedda was holding Lenna in her arms.

Dohn-say, who was a grown daughter of Geronimo's, and her husband were also there.

Zi-yeh shook the letter up and down and tapped her feet on the stone as I came close. Ih-tedda was standing close to her, one arm around Zi-yeh's shoulder and looking just as excited as she rocked little Lenna in her other arm. She-gah sat at their feet. Her face was still gray with fever, but her back was straighter, and she seemed to have more strength. There was even a small smile on She-gah's lips as Zi-yeh handed me the letter.

"Grandson," Zi-yeh said, "I know you have been learning from the sisters. Can you read to us this paper that talks? We have heard it read once, but want to hear it again. Read it first as it is written. Then we will hear our friend Wratten's voice. Then speak it to us in our own tongue and we will hear your grandfather."

I unfolded the letter. Slowly, but with not much difficulty because the words were as clear as the sentiment they held, I read it aloud in English.

My dear wives, Faith-si-se-la and Tede and My Son and Daughter,

How are you at Fort Marion? If so how do you like it there? Have you plenty to eat, and you sleep and drink well? Send me a letter and tell me all the news. I am very satisfied here, but if I only had you with me again I would be more so. I work every day, excepting Sundays. It is very healthy to work. My work is not hard. It consists of hoeing and raking in and around the fort. It seems to me that the great Father and God are very closely united. I do hope he will let us see one another soon. As sure as the trees bud and bloom in the spring, so sure is my hope of seeing you again. Talking by paper is good, but when you see one's lips move and hear their voice, it is much better. I saw General Miles, heard him speak, and looked into his eyes, and believed what he told me, and I still think he will keep his word. He told that I would see you soon, also see a fine country and lots of people. The people and the country I have seen, but not you. The sun rises and sets here just the same as in our country, but the water here is salty. The government is good and does not like to see the Indian imposed upon. It has given us pants, and coats with pockets on, and shoes, and enough to eat. I think of God, the President, and you in the same light. I like you so well. When I get your letter I will think well over it. I hope you think the same of me as I do of you. I think you have influence with the sun, moon and stars. If the government would only give us a reservation, so we could support ourselves — Oh wouldn't it be fine? We are at peace now, and by God's help will remain so. There are seventeen of us here, and not one of us thinks or acts bad. Everybody is well and contented. Chatto is a bad man, and has caused us lots of trouble.

His tongue is like a rattlesnake's — forked. Do not let him read a word of this letter. Do what is right, no matter how you may suffer. Write me soon a lovely letter.

Your husband

Geronimo

It was easy to read, but it was hard for me to speak it. My eyes became clouded with tears. It was difficult to keep my lips from trembling. But I did not pause, and my voice stayed clear and straight, despite the pain in my heart. When I spoke it again in Apache, though, those tears vanished. It did seem as if I were hearing the voice of Geronimo. I felt his power touching my lips, and a great calm came over me.

"We will all live to see him," I said as I handed the letter back to Zi-yeh. "It will be soon. I know this."

FORWARD MARCH

MARCH 1887

Of the eighty-two adult male Indians confined in Fort Marion, sixty-five served the Government as scouts during the whole or a portion of the time that Geronimo was out, viz. from the spring of 1885, until the fall of 1886.

COLONEL ROMEYN B. AYRES,

COMMANDER AT FORT MARION MARCH 25, 1887

OUR REUNION was not as soon as I hoped. The months stretched on. I could easily say them now in English. There was November. That was when the letter to his wives came from my grandfather. November is also when the White Eyes celebrate the only time when all give thanks. That seemed strange to me. We Chiricahuas are all used to giving thanks to Ussen every day. Then came December, when a fat white man dressed in red tied a cloud-white scalp to his chin and tried without much success to coax us Apache children to come close to him so that he could put us on his lap. His name was Saint Nicholas, they told us. But I knew that his other name was Sergeant Smith. January started when the white men fired off guns and shouted out and did much drinking because their new year was beginning. February arrived when they celebrated the births of their two greatest leaders — Washington and Lincoln, both of whom killed many Indians. Then came March, which did not seem important enough to the White Eyes for them to have any special celebration.

I learned all this as I learned more English from the sisters.

However, as my knowledge of English improved, my understanding of why all of the Chiricahuas were being treated this way did not. I could understand why the White Eyes might hate and fear Geronimo and those of us who held out so long to fight. But few who fought the army were being held here at Fort Marion. Almost all of the Apaches here were scouts who had remained loyal to the army and the families of those confused men. One minute they had been given medals, the next they had been sent into bitter exile. Among us were even two of the old chiefs who had stayed at Fort Apache throughout every outbreak and convinced many of their followers to do the same. There were some who were not even Chiricahuas, but had just been living among us and were swept up by the army. Why were harmless people who spoke for peace or those who fought on the side of the Americans being kept here as prisoners? What wrong had their elderly relatives, their wives, and children done? It made no sense to me.

I was no longer angry at the scouts. I had forgiven them for fighting against their own people. I realized now that nearly all of them had done so because they thought it was the only thing to do to help their people. They trusted the White Eyes to honor their promises. They thought of themselves as soldiers serving the United States just as loyally as any white man or black white man in a uniform.

So how could they have ended up like this? Some of them came to the same conclusion I did. It was the only explanation that made any sense. Martine explained to me one day when I asked him and Kayitah why he and the other scouts and their innocent families remained captives.

"I think it is easy to answer," Martine said. "The leaders of the White Eyes are all stupid or crazy."

"Or both," Kayitah added. Then they both laughed.

Yes, they laughed and I did, too. That is one thing about us Apaches. When we realize we have no other option than to suffer, we try not to make our suffering worse by feeling sorry for ourselves. Even though there was little for us to do at Fort Marion and the idleness was hard, even though we were so crowded together and the heat was so great that we sometimes found it hard to breathe, we were still breathing. And because there was still breath within us we made jokes.

"Brothers, I have been thinking about why we are here," Martine said one hot April morning to the group of men and boys standing around in the courtyard. "And it has given me an idea about how we can leave this place."

"How is that, brother?" Kayitah asked.

"We are here because we are Apaches," Martine said. "But look, we are now wearing parts of the uniforms of the White Eyes soldiers. And we are learning to speak their language."

"We are even eating fish," Kayitah said.

"We have learned how to salute," Martine added.

"We have learned how to obey orders that make no sense," Kayitah said, nodding his head.

"We are learning how to walk as the White Eyes walk."

"As if our feet hurt all the time."

"As if our necks and our backs were made of wood."

By now, Martine and Kayitah were not just talking, but moving about and demonstrating how much like the white men they had become. They had even changed the tone of their voices so that, even though they were still speaking Apache, they sounded like white men.

"Tenshun," Martine said, his voice exactly like that of an officer.

Not only he and Kayitah, but several other of our men who had been scouts immediately snapped to attention, although they were careful to do so in such a sloppy way that it was obvious they were imitating raw recruits.

"Bout Face," Martine barked, and all of the men turned on their heels, some to the right, some to the left, some spinning round and round without stopping, and not one of them ending up facing the same direction.

"Forward march," Martine shouted. At that, some men walked backward, some stumbled to one side or the other, while others just stared at their feet in mock confusion.

Chihuahua, who had been leaning against a wall and watching all of this, could contain himself no longer. He stepped forward, cupped his hand, and put it over his mouth in mock astonishment.

"Ah," he cried, his voice a perfect imitation of Commander Ayres, "you men are all real white men. You are not Apaches. You must not fraternize. All of you must quick march now to the gate and leave this fort. You are all discharged."

Heeding his words, a group of about twenty former scouts, led by Martine and Kayitah, began to form up and march toward the gate.

"Hup, do, tree, fo-wah," they chanted, more or less together.

I am not sure how the guards at the gate would have responded to them, but they only managed a few steps together before Martine and Kayitah and all the other "real white men" fell onto the ground because they were laughing so hard.

LEAVING AGAIN

APRIL 1887

Notwithstanding the many reports that have been sent abroad about the bad health and ill treatment of those confined at Fort Marion, it is a fact that they are generally healthy and contented, so much so that when the news of their intended transfer was conveyed to them, they received the news with wild manifestations of dissent, and since have made the ramparts of the fort nightly re-echo with the wild yells and incantations of the medicine dance.

PENSACOLA COMMERCIAL

APRIL 30, 1887

DESPITE OUR JOKING, there was much to make our hearts heavy. Soon after the arrival of Chief Chihuahua's group, Chiricahuas began to pass on at Fort Marion. All the while we were there, our people continued to pass on. I will not mention their names, but there were men and women and children of all ages. They left behind families who loved and mourned them.

Death is always a terrible thing to us. It is so awful that we try not to speak about it at all. I remember my mother telling me never to say in our language that someone died. Instead, I was either to remain silent or just say that person had passed on. When someone passes, their clothing and all their possessions are burned. In fact, when someone is very ill, they are sometimes taken outside before they die, because if they die inside their dwelling place, their house, too, must be burned.

It was not the death of that first Chiricahua who passed on at Fort Marion itself that was most terrible. It was what happened after he passed. The soldiers took the man's body. His relatives were powerless to stop them. The women had only begun to wail their grief. The soldiers sewed the man's body into canvas with heavy weights and then rowed out into the bay and dumped him into the deep water.

The thought of what they did still makes my flesh crawl. We Apaches fear deep water. It is where the worst monsters dwell. A proper burial is done in the earth, in a secret place where those things can be properly done to return a body to the soil and ensure that the spirit's journey to the Happy Place will be successful.

That bad burial caused much anguish to all the Chiricahuas held at Fort Marion. Colonel Langdon soon realized that he had made a big mistake. It was too late to get that man's body back, but from then on whenever an Apache died, Chiricahuas took care of everything. There is a place secret to us along Anastasia Bay. That is where the bodies of the twenty-four who passed on during the year our people were held at Fort Marion were taken. I will not say more about it.

Before long, it was April, When It Gets Warm. It was so hot and cramped on the stone grounds of the fort that Colonel Ayres realized we needed a better place. Some of us were allowed to move out of the fort itself and set up our tents on the east side of the North River. That was better for more reasons than just space. It allowed in-laws to avoid each other in the proper, courteous way.

That first evening out under the moon and stars, I stood and stretched my arms up to the sky and took a deep breath. There was still the taste of salt in the air, and there were still mosquitoes coming to buzz about us, but I felt closer to freedom. A pale bird flew inland from the ocean, the sunset reflecting off its wings. I imagined my arms becoming wings. For a moment I felt my spirit lift and fly free with that bird. I was ready to fly without stopping until I saw the snowcapped sacred mountains. But then I felt the sand beneath my feet and remembered my grandfather and all those other beings held captive here. I lowered my arms. I could not fly alone.

White curiosity seekers from the town came there to look at us. Captain Ayres had now forbidden access to the actual fort to anyone but Apaches and army men, but tourists could come to see us by the river. Some of those White Eyes visitors were rude and nosey. They stared at us as if we were strange animals. Others were friendly, gave us presents or bought some of the crafts that we made. Just as at Fort Bowie, the men were allowed to make such things as small bows and arrows and wood carvings, while the women made jewelry and wove baskets. Like my grandfather, we were able to do good business. Many of us also found those white people amusing to watch. The ways they dressed and acted were often quite comical. We could make each other laugh hard by imitating White Eyes tourists after all of them had left for the day. It was a change from the monotony and the tight quarters of the fort.

I was one of those who went to camp by the river. It was no less hot or unhealthy there, but it was outside those stone walls. Even a few steps away from the fort seemed a little closer toward freedom to me.

Then, once again, what little freedom I was enjoying was threatened. Captain Pratt arrived again from Carlisle. We did not see him at first. Instead, several of the boys who had been chosen six months before suddenly appeared. They had been sent ahead by Captain Pratt to recruit more of us for Carlisle. And this time his plan was to not just take the older children. Captain Pratt and his daughter were staying at a hotel in town. These boys who had been real Apaches only a few months before had been given the job of convincing more of us to join their ranks. They now wore stiff uniforms and caps and tight boots; their long hair was cut short. It was hard to look at them.

"Come and join us," one or two of them said. "It is good at Carlisle."

But their words sounded hollow. And the others did not even try to speak such words. They simply embraced their relatives and could not hide the sorrow in their eyes. I also noticed that one of those Carlisle boys kept hiding his mouth to cough into his hand.

"Tomorrow," the Carlisle boys told us, "Captain Pratt will come to collect his new recruits. Who will volunteer?"

That was an easy question for us Chiricahua young people to answer. No one. Not one boy or girl wanted to leave.

So once again we were lined up for inspection before the fort. I stood there with no expression on my face, but in my mind I was frantic. What could I do? Pratt was stalking down the line like a wolf ready to pounce on its prey. I could already feel his rough hand grasping my wrist and lifting it up as he was now doing to one young person after another. Then I saw a motion in the crowd of adults gathered around and watching helplessly. I looked up. It was Lozen. Her eyes were on me, and she made that small motion again, just a slight turn of her head to point off to the side with her chin. I turned my head slowly to look.

Sam Bowman was standing there, only fifty feet away. As I've said, Sam spoke our language and was not a Chiricahua, but a Choctaw. He had been the head of the reservation scouts at San Carlos. With Mr. Wratten gone, he and Concepcion had been the main interpreters for us here. Over the many years our people had known Sam Bowman, we had grown to trust him. Although his wife was back in Arizona, he had agreed to remain for a time here in Florida to help. Sam had been one of the first to teach me a few words of English, and I knew that he liked me. At the moment, while Captain Pratt was making his choice of those who would be taken, he was not interpreting. He had casually stepped to the side.

Sam Bowman was not looking at me. In fact, he was making it a point to look in the opposite direction. But he was leaning on an empty wooden barrel that had been placed upright, with its open end downward. The scout was leaning on it in such a way that it was half tilted off the ground. I understood.

"Let me be invisible," I whispered under my breath. "Let me not be seen."

Staying low, I crept along behind the line of nervous young people, some of whom moved closer together so that their bodies would block me from the eager captain's view. Perhaps, to the White Eyes, I truly was invisible just then. In any case, if anyone other than a Chiricahua, such as one of the soldiers guarding us, saw me move, they did not betray me. I reached the barrel and slid under it. Sam

Bowman tipped it back and then sat on it. It was dark, but I could still hear the voice of Captain Pratt.

"I thought," he said, "that there was a fine young fellow just here. A little lad who would be perfect for civilizing. Now where did he go?"

I knew he was talking about me. No one answered him.

By the end of his walk down the line, Captain Pratt had rounded up sixty-two young men and women. He and his soldiers herded them away like cattle. They left that Saturday afternoon, taken by train to a seaport. There a steamboat carried them all the way up the coast to New York City, where they took another train to Carlisle.

A few days after Captain Pratt's last raid on our children, Colonel Ayres called everyone to the parade ground, stood up before us, and made a short speech.

"You must pack your belongings," Sam Bowman said, translating the Colonel's words. "They are sending us all to a new place."

On the following nights we held dances around the fire. Women's voices pierced the darkness whenever the names of Child of Water and White Painted Woman were sung. The masked dancers came, those we refer to as the *Gans*, the Mountain Spirits of each of the four sacred directions. Their dances were done before the rest of the people did social dancing. The coming of the Mountain Spirits is always meant to bring good things to our people. The *Gans* help us look ahead toward a brighter dawn. Those nights before we left Fort Marion, our dancers came to us. Through their dancing they asked the Mountain People, whose spirits they carried as they danced, and Ussen, the Good Spirit, to care for and guide us. They also asked for guidance and long life for all of those children who had been taken from us. They asked help in assuring that our children would still be able to find their way back to us now that we were being moved yet again.

I listened to the words of the songs and observed the dancers closely. I saw how they avoided bumping into each other as they danced, how they moved together in unison, the horns of their headpieces in line with each other. I was no longer afraid of the clown dancer we call Gray One. When I was a little child I had been told that he would carry away the children who did not behave. Now I just watched as he clowned about, carrying messages to and from the four main dancers. He did not wear the elaborate dress of the other four. As always, he was just naked, his whole body painted white, his big nose sticking out from the middle of his leather face. I looked over at Chief Chihuahua. He had one hand over his mouth and his big stomach was shaking. Despite all the weight of worry Chief Chihuahua was carrying, the antics of Gray One were making him laugh.

Before one becomes one of the four main dancers, he may first be Gray One. As foolish as his antics might seem to those who do not know our ways, he is just as sacred as Great Black Gahe, Great Blue Gahe, Great Yellow Gahe, and Great White Gahe. Someday, if I lived to grow into manhood, I hoped to be one of those chosen to be painted and masked and carry the message of the Mountain Spirits to our people. I prayed that I would have a long enough life to become a man.

The sun rose on our final day by the ocean. As I trudged through the gate of Fort Marion for the last time, I tried to keep my face brave. But there were tears in my eyes at the thought of those who had died and been left behind. There were now twenty-four graves of our people hidden near the shores of Anastasia Island in the bay. Like everyone else, I was worried about the fate of the young people on their way north. We did not know then how many Apache graves would be dug in other places far from our homeland.

What gave hope to some of us was the thought that we were finally being taken back in the direction of the sunset, away from the wide, strange waters of the ocean. Our journey would turn out to be no more than a few hundred miles, but it was a heartbeat close to the homeland we ached for.

Now, too, the wives and families of those who'd been separated from us would be allowed to rejoin their men.

Soon, I thought. *Soon I will see my grandfather's face.*

TO PENSACOLA

APRIL 27,1887

Wednesday night's train No. 21, second section, arrived at Union Depot having eight passenger coaches filled with Apache Indians en route from Fort Marion, Fla., via the S.F.& W.R.R. for Mount Vernon, Ala., and Fort Pickens, Fla. One coach stopped here and discharged its cargo of 20 squaws and a number of papooses and children. A lieutenant from Fort Barrancas with a squad of men came up on the government launch and conveyed the dusky dames to their liege lords now sojourning at Fort Pickens. We suppose that Geronimo's cup of happiness is overflowing now that he is surrounded by his papooses and wives. The meeting must have been a joyful one to all concerned.

THE PENSACOLIAN

APRIL 30, 1887

ALTHOUGH IT SEEMED as if we had few possessions, the bundles that many carried onto the train were sizable. People filled the big canvas bags that had been given us by the army to use as suitcases. Men packed away their personal items, their tools, half-finished bows and arrows, and whatever crafts they had not sold to White Eyes visitors. More than one man carried a saddle. Though we had yet to find horses, there was still the hope that we would do so in the west. It is hard to feel complete without a horse. Women put away their pots and pans, their baskets and jewelry, their bolts of cloth and blankets. As is our custom, everyone wore as much of their clothing as possible. A bag may be taken away, but it is harder to remove the clothes from a person's back.

Accompanied by fourteen soldiers, we crowded into a special train that took us first to Jacksonville. It seemed a quick trip, and this time, having been there before, the station looked familiar and almost friendly to me. People waved at us and smiled. A few women even handed bouquets of flowers to us. No one seemed afraid of Apaches anymore.

I, too, was without fear. I had none of that deep feeling of dread that I had experienced when I had seen a train for the first time seven months ago. Then it had been the time we Chiricahuas call When the Wind Blows Hard. That hard wind had seemed about to blow us right off of the edge of the world. Now it was When It Gets Warm, the season that promises many leaves and ripe fruit. It was a hopeful time, though I now realize that we Apaches hoped for more than we would get.

Another train was waiting for us in Jacksonville. I read what was written on the sides of the coaches. Savannah, Florida and

Western Railroad. That word *western* brought a small smile to my lips. There were eight coaches. That made it very tight for 385 Indians and fourteen soldiers. Yet the last coach, the one that I made sure to get into, was less crowded than the others. It held twenty women and twelve children. Among us were the wives and children of Geronimo and Naiche and Mangus and other men imprisoned at Fort Pickens.

This journey toward the west was different from our first train journeys. Back then, no one knew what fate awaited us. To be honest, neither did our captors. For all they knew, they might have been taking us to be imprisoned forever or hanged the next day. Now, no one feared being executed. And we knew that we were being taken either to be reunited with loved ones or to go to a place that we'd been told was much better than the old fort by the big saltwater.

I had understood much of what Colonel Ayres spoke in English as he explained things to our head men, Chief Chihuahua, Chief Loco, and Nana. The main group of Apaches was to be transported to a place called Mount Vernon in Alabama. They would have fresh water and hills and many trees. There would be room to spread out, freedom to roam around, to build homes a respectful distance from each other. They would no longer be crowded together like prairie dogs trapped in a hole. But I wondered if it would be true.

"Is it good where they are sent?" I asked Sam Bowman as we were being loaded onto the train.

He didn't answer for a long time. "Might be," he finally replied.

I didn't know it then, but those were the last words I would ever hear from Sam Bowman. He climbed into one of the forward cars, and I got into the last one. When we reached Union Depot, our car was sidetracked from the others. Sam and the rest of the Apaches continued on to Mount Vernon. It would be a year later before I saw Mount Vernon. By then, Sam Bowman had been given permission to go back home to his family in Arizona. That was more than any Chiricahua would ever be given.

REUNION

The Commercial *is allowed to say that the restrictions now placed upon visiting the Indians confined within Fort Pickens will be removed possibly next month. The recent advent of the squaws and children from Fort Marion, and their proper disposition, the latter has not yet been effected, render visiting for awhile very objectionable.*

PENSACOLA DAILY COMMERCIAL, MAY 10, 1887

A
T PENSACOLA we left the train car. We were marched down to the bay where we were told to climb onto a sort of platform. To my surprise, as soon as we were on board, a great growling noise came from beneath it, the whole thing shook and then the platform began to move out onto the water. The squad of soldiers with us did not appear frightened, so I kept my face calm and tried to show no fear. Neither did the other Chiricahuas. By now we had experienced so many strange things, it would not have surprised us if the thing we rode had risen up into the air and flown above the moon.

As that motor launch, for such it was called, roared across the water, big creatures began to come up to the boat. They were larger than the fish I had seen at Fort Marion, and they swam next to us, swift as arrows, leaping out of the water with their whole bodies at times.

"Porpoises," the White Eyes lieutenant said to me as I watched them.

Even though I had been taught that evil creatures live in the deep water, those porpoises did not look at all bad to me. I could see that they had smiles on their faces. Their presence added to the excitement I felt as our boat drew closer to Santa Rosa Island and Fort Pickens. There were other boats around us, curiosity seekers taking to the water to see our arrival.

But they did not come close to us, and they were left behind as we drew close to the dock and the stone walls of Fort Pickens. Colonel Langdon, the same officer who had been *nantan* before my arrival at Fort Marion, had given orders that there would be no visitors to see the Apaches for a while. My grandfather, I learned later, had become the biggest tourist attraction in the whole state. Thousands of people had come in excursion boats over the past six months to see him and the other "wild Apaches," bringing much money and business to the town of Pensacola. Colonel Langdon, though, had grown to respect our people. So we would be allowed as much privacy as possible for our reunion.

They were all waiting for us, those who had been kept there with Geronimo at the old stone fort on the island. You have heard most of their names before, but I will say them again here.

There was Naiche, the young chief who was the son of Cochise. At that time he had about thirty-five years. I saw how his eyes quickly found his wife, even before the boat reached the dock. I saw, too, how her eyes grew brighter as they met his, and she drew herself up taller.

There was Mangus, son of Mangas Coloradas, also in his mid-thirties and also a chief.

There was Chapo, Geronimo's son, about twenty-two years.

There was Perico, who Geronimo called brother, but who was a second cousin as white people figure such things and was perhaps thirty-seven years old.

There was Fun, Perico's half-brother. He was only some twenty years of age and, though a second cousin, also called brother by Geronimo.

There was Ahnandia, another second cousin and brother of Geronimo, and perhaps twenty-six years old.

There was Yahnozhe, who was about thirty-two. He was the brother of She-gah, Geronimo's wife, and also a first cousin of Naiche.

There was Nahba, one of the older men, who had about forty-five years.

There was Laziyah, Nahba's brother and a year or two older.

There was Beshe, who was even older than Nahba and Laziyah, maybe even older than Geronimo himself, who was over fifty then. Beshe was the father of Naiche's wife, Ha-o-zinne.

And for all of those men there were wives among us, women who had stayed strong and cared for their children, and dared to hope this day of reunion would come. Many of those women were crying, and there were tears in the eyes of more than one man, even though they all tried to maintain their dignity. There was a lump in my own throat.

There was Kithdigai, about thirty-five and one of the few men there who had not been separated from family, for he was unmarried and had no relatives among those of us who had been at Fort Marion.

There was Mohtsos, also about thirty-five.

There was Tissnolthtsos, perhaps twenty-one.

There was Zhonne, a half-brother of Naiche's wife, about twenty and not married.

There was Gozo, who had been with Mangus. He was no more than nineteen and also had no wife.

There was Hunlona, perhaps nineteen and unmarried.

And there was my grandfather. He was much shorter than tall Chief Naiche, who stood by his side. Yet I think that even those on our boat whose eyes sought their beloved husband or father noticed Geronimo before anyone else. His power drew your eyes to him, but it was more than that. I also felt the love that seemed to radiate from him the way warmth rises from a stone that has absorbed the heat of the sun. Seeing him looking so strong and well made my heart leap. I had been worrying that the sicknesses that had struck so many at Fort Marion might have come here, too. I had feared I would never see him again or that he would have become old and sick like She-gah. But he stood as he was. He stood unchanged.

He wore those same boots that he had bought when I was with him in San Antonio. His legs were bare above those boots. The long army pants that some of the men wore were not for him that day. An old-style breechcloth was his choice. A long, clean calico shirt hung down past his waist, and he had necklaces about his neck, with a big abalone shell pierced at either end. On his head was the dark hat he had also gotten at that army post. His face and the faces of the other men were not painted as they would be on other occasions when there were dances or when tourists came and photographs were to be taken. There was a way that Geronimo and his men always painted. Their faces would be painted purple, with a yellow band drawn from ear to ear, just below the eyes and crossing the bridge of the nose. Today, though, they wished their loved ones to see their faces.

I felt like leaping out of the boat and running up to him. But it would not have been right to do that. Instead, I stayed with Geronimo's wives, taking little Fenton from his mother Zi-yeh's arms and putting him on the dock, then handing little Lenna to Ih-tedda. Lastly, I helped She-gah out of the launch. The illness that had weakened her had not left her, despite the touch of the Mountain Spirits and the many songs that had been meant to help her regain her health. But she was determined to make this journey, to reunite with my grandfather. She tried to stand straight and walk strong, but if it had not been for my shoulders to lean on, I think she would have fallen.

One by one, led by She-gah, the three women and their children made their way to my grandfather. One by one, they put their arms around him and embraced him as he returned their embraces with a quiet dignity that did not conceal, for me at least, the deep emotion that he felt at that moment. He held up Fenton, then Lenna — the daughter he had never seen until now. He knew that two of his children were missing. His grown daughter, Dohn-say, had not chosen to come with us but had gone on to Mount Vernon with her husband, Dahkeya. Geronimo's other little daughter was in one of those hidden graves left behind on Anastasia Island. But Geronimo did not mention either of their names.

Then Geronimo held out his hand to me. I thought he might pick me up, as if I were a little child. But he did not do that. Instead he bent down and put his arms around me.

"Little Foot," he said in a soft voice, "thank you for caring for our family, grandson. You have grown tall."

NO HORSE

The Apaches have the soldiers' quarters in the fort and live comfortably. They are served with rations daily, including fresh meat three times per week. At first they could not eat pork, but after seeing the relish with which it was eaten by the whites, they experimented and became converts. Even now they will not touch the lean, prefering the fat. The beef they cut up in strips and hang in the sun until it dries and is stiff. The Indians claim the juices are preserved intact by the sun, and give the flesh a fine flavor. They love corn best. Geronimo says that corn is for men . . .

WILLIAM HOSEA BALLOU, *CHICAGO TRIBUNE,*

MARCH 5, 1888

THE FIRST THING that impressed me as Geronimo led us back into the fort was how clean everything was here, how uncrowded it felt, even with the arrival of the thirty-one of us. The two casements, the big stone rooms where the Apache prisoners had to live, were furnished with bed frames and mattresses stuffed with straw, and there were plenty of blankets.

While we had been dressed in rags at Fort Marion, Geronimo and the others had been provided with army fatigues to wear, as well as those new clothes they had bought at Fort Bowie.

Chief Naiche was dressed in an army officer's coat. All of the men had several changes of clothing. There was also an open hearth in the middle of each of the casements, two big open rooms made of stone and masonry. Cannons had once been placed in those casements to shoot out through the openings in the fort walls at enemy ships in the bay. Now one casement room was the camping place for Chief Naiche and those men who stayed with him, the other for Geronimo and his relatives, among them Fun, Ahnandia, Perico (two parrots now flapping their wings on his shoulder), and of course, Chapo.

That division did not mean the two groups of men were on bad terms. It was just a better and more normal way to do things. For example, Yahnozhe, who was She-gah's brother and Geronimo's brother-in-law, was among those in Chief Naiche's casement. Among our people, in-laws try to keep a respectful distance from each other.

We new arrivals divided ourselves among those two groups. Chief Naiche's family and the wives and children of his men went into his part of the fort, and Geronimo and the rest of us went into my grandfather's casement room. She-gah was settled onto a cot where she could watch Ih-tedda and Zi-yeh unpacking their pots and pans and settling in. All of the wives of the men were examining with approval the supplies that had been piled up for them in each of the kitchen areas — so much more than they had even been given at Fort Marion, including some big pieces of beef. I knew that I would soon smell tortillas and stew cooking.

My grandfather drifted away from the women. He knew enough to get out of the way of his wives now that they were taking over the cooking area.

"I have no horse here for you to hold for me," Geronimo said, putting his hand on my left shoulder.

I smiled at that remark. My grandfather's words were meant to remind me of all the times he came back from going out to scout around. We boys all lined up at the edge of the camp waiting. I was the one he usually chose from all the other boys to take the reins of his horse and follow him back into camp with it. It had always been a great honor. He was honoring me again by reminding me of those times.

But, as was often true of words spoken by Geronimo, my grandfather meant more than that. It was a way of telling me what he believed. He believed that one day we would again have horses to hold, again be free to ride them. Perhaps he saw that day. Maybe his power told him we would again have horses. Perhaps it was just his wish. But his words gave me hope.

My grandfather gave my shoulder a squeeze. I was glad that he chose that shoulder. I might have winced if he had done that to my right shoulder.

The day before we left Fort Marion, my friends and I had had one last mock battle. We lined up twenty paces from each other at the edge of our camp outside the fort and had a great fight that lasted much of the afternoon. The rocks at Fort Marion were not good. It was mostly sand there. So we had used our small bows and arrows. The tips did not have arrowheads on them, and I had dodged almost every arrow shot at me and even caught two of them with my hands. However, because I was the best arrow dodger of all, the other boys had showed their respect for me by making me the main target by the end of our game. And one arrow that had become splintered at its tip had pierced into the muscle of my shoulder. I had to pull it out and wrap my headband around the wound to slow the bleeding. But it did not stop me or our game. That only ended with the quick coming of evening. It had been one of the very best battle games we boys ever had.

Mr. Wratten came up to me and Geronimo. He nodded at me and smiled, then spoke to my grandfather.

"Nantan Langdon needs to speak with you about some requests being made to visit the fort," Wratten said. "He asks if you could please come to his quarters."

Geronimo squeezed my left shoulder one more time and then walked off with Wratten. Chapo strolled over to me. His wife, too, was busy with settling in and cooking. Even though both he and his wife would have liked to just spend time together, they knew this was not the time to do so. Chapo dropped his hand onto my right shoulder and shook it in a friendly way. I did not wince.

"Let's walk about, nephew," Chapo said.

He led me up to the top of one of the walls of the fort. The embankment sloped up and was covered with grass that had been planted by our men as part of their work in fixing up the grounds. Being in this fort was not at all like being inside Fort Marion, where the walls were high and steep. Here if you wanted to get outside you just had to walk up the embankment and step out. The army men around us seemed relaxed and even friendly.

"It was not so good when they brought us here," Chapo said. "The White Eyes did not know they could trust us to keep our word not to run away. Also, this place had not been used since the White Eyes fought the war against their own brothers. Maybe twenty harvests. Weeds everywhere, grass, trees." He pointed with his lips toward the top of the stone building.

"A pine tree was growing out of that chimney up there. So our first job was to clean everything all up," Chapo said, pointing with his chin in first one direction and then the other.

I looked at it all and took a deep breath. I was not free, but I felt that the wind here was cleaner, the sky more open.

"You did well," I said. But I did not look back down into the fort. Instead, I looked across the water, to the north and the west.

We will go that way, I said to myself. We will go back that way toward our homeland.

WHITE PAINTED WOMAN'S BLESSING

JUNE 10, 1887

GRAND INDIAN WAR DANCE!

The Willie C *will leave Palafox Wharf this evening (Thursday)*

to take to Fort Pickens all interested parties having passes

to attend THE WAR DANCE.

PENSACOLA DAILY COMMERICAL

JUNE 9, 1887

ONE OF THE YOUNG WOMEN who came with us to Fort Pickens was an orphan like myself. The name that Colonel Ayres had given her while we were at Fort Marion was Katie. So that is what I will call her.

She-gah had been especially concerned about Katie. Perhaps it was because She-gah felt that her own life was ending just as this young woman was about to begin her womanhood, to be White Painted Woman. And now, only a few days after our arrival at Fort Pickens, Katie's time of womanhood had come. It was good that it was so, that it should happen after our families had been brought back together. No one was better equipped among all of us than my grandfather to see that her ceremony was done properly.

"Willie," a familiar voice said. I turned around to look. It was Mr. Wratten. During the last few days I had seen him often about the fort, but he had been kept busy. This was the first time we had talked.

I greeted him in the proper way, in Chiricahua, and he answered. I lifted my head to look right at him. He knew what I was doing, and he smiled at the way I was imitating that rude White Eyes way of staring into another person's eyes, something we Chiricahuas do not do unless we are challenging someone.

"How you know name Fort Marion soldiers give me?" I asked, speaking English. I had not yet grasped the fundamental use of such parts of English speech as articles, but my meaning was clear enough.

Wratten smiled, stroking his mustache as if he were thinking. Then he answered me in Chiricahua. Even though he always spoke it with a white man's accent, he spoke it well.

"Is it not better I call you by a White Eye's name than speak your true name when all can hear it?" Wratten said. Then he dropped back into English. "To answer your question, the lieutenant who accompanied you here told me that he thought that Willie, the young boy who spoke such good English, was a promising lad."

"Ah," I said, trying not to show how proud Wratten's words made me feel.

"If you are not busy," Wratten continued, "I would like you to come with me in the motor launch. They are going to take me over to get supplies."

"*Enjuh,*" I said, a little quicker than I had intended. I had meant to act as if I was considering his words, as if I had other important things to do. The thought of another trip over that water, which no longer frightened me, of seeing those smiling animals, was so exciting I could barely contain myself.

That evening, when we returned to Fort Pickens, both of us were laden with many things that had been purchased for the special occasion that was coming. We had cloth and ribbons and things to be given away, things needed for Katie's ceremony.

Colonel Langdon, after consulting with Naiche and Mangus and Geronimo, had decided that vistors from the town would be allowed to come over and see the ceremony as well. That did not bother any of us. Such a ceremony is meant to bring blessing to the world. And that day would give us good opportunity to do some trading. Since our families had come back together, we had been spending time getting ready for the return of tourists to the island. Yahnozhe, who had first started making crayon drawings on paper of Chiricahuas and cowboys on horseback when we were at Fort Bowie, had become quite a good artist. He had no trouble selling his pictures for as much as fifty cents each.

Every family had their own goods to trade, especially the bows and arrows that the White Eyes tourists never could get enough of. It was amusing to watch certain White Eyes men after they bought a bow and arrows. They would actually start shooting arrows at each other. Unlike us Apache boys, White Eyes tourists are not good at dodging arrows. More than one left the island bandaged, and it sometimes did not end there. Wratten told me that fights often broke out on the excursion trains that took those tourist parties from Pensacola. So we kept a close eye on any White Eyes man, especially one who had been drinking heavily, who bought one of our weapons.

My grandfather, in fact, no longer made bows to sell. He had better ideas. His wives had been helping with the making of a new item for Geronimo to trade. They were little beaded pouches with his name on them.

"I will get at least a dollar for each of these," my grandfather said, lining up the pouches in front of him. "Good business."

Good business, indeed. And unlike some of the other men — who I will not name — my grandfather did not gamble away his money by playing hoop and pole. His plan, even then, was to use that money to buy livestock when the day came that we would have a ranch of our own.

There were many who came that day. I learned later that word went around that we were doing a war dance. Some of them were disappointed when the promised war dance failed to happen. The thought of their being disappointed made me laugh. If we had done the anger dance, which was never done just for show, it would have been to prepare us to go out against the enemy. Those fat, curious White Eyes who came to watch us would not have enjoyed seeing us as our enemies did. A Chiricahua man who had prepared himself to fight was often the last thing those enemies ever saw. But there was no danger to those people who flocked to the island in the excursion boats. We Chiricahuas longed to be free, but we had given our word never to fight the White Eyes again. There would be no such war dance, despite what their newspapers promised.

Instead, when the evening came, they saw a ceremony that I believe to be our oldest and most sacred. In that ceremony, the girl who is entering womanhood actually becomes White Painted Woman. She is painted with pollen and then with white paint. Each part of the ceremony recognizes her connection to the continuance of life, to the blessing of our people by White Painted Woman. When she gets up to run in a circle, she is following the path of life. Then the children get up and run behind her, pretending to race her, but being careful never to run past her, for that run is both a blessing and a prayer for a long and healthy life. Many were blessed with that prayer on that night. I wish that blessing could have come true for more of us, including Katie herself.

The Gans came and danced as the fire burned. Among those who carried the spirit of one of the Mountain People was Chapo. No one danced better or looked stronger than Chapo did that night. As

Geronimo sat in the circle of men who sang and kept the drum rhythm, I knew that he was aware of every sure step that Chapo made. Chapo was close to his father's ways, yet he was also learning the ways of the White Eyes. Perhaps, one day — a brighter day, when we had finally been allowed to return to our real home — Chapo would take his father's place.

I could feel how proud my grandfather was of his grown son. I shared that feeling of pride. Yet as I think back on how strong and full of life Chapo appeared that evening as he danced, that pride melts away, and I find myself left with sorrow.

A WHITE STONE

SEPTEMBER 28, 1887

Why it is I am asked how we like it here? People go around and see where I live, the fort, the waste of hot sand and water, the old guns, the guards ever armed, how we live, and what we evidently have to live for. I can't understand why we are asked such questions. . . . Here we have plenty to wear and eat, but it is charity. . . . We are tired of salt water and sand.

They want us to be like white men. If so, this is no place for us. . . . Give us good farms and we will show you we can act like white men.

NAICHE

CHICAGO TRIBUNE

MARCH 5, 1888

THE MOONS ABOVE the saltwater and the sand grew full and waned and grew full again. I sat at Wratten's desk and practiced writing English. Sometimes Ahnandia helped me, although today he was working with Katie. Since her womanhood ceremony, she had been spending more time with Ahnandia, and they sometimes smiled at each other as she tried to speak English words.

Ahnandia still had that beloved book of grammar he had carried with him on the train. He was the best of us at speaking English and could write good sentences on paper. Like all of us, though, whenever White Eyes visitors came we would not converse with them in English but simply use gestures and signs or allow Wratten to interpret if the person was a reporter writing a story about us. While we were at Fort Pickens, several such men came, and more than one of them seemed sympathetic. They became even more so when they were told of the promises made to Chief Naiche by General Crook and Nantan Short Arm, General Howard.

"Will they let us go home?" I asked Wratten.

Wratten stroked his mustache. Then he shook his head. "Not yet. Back in Arizona," he said, "they still have hard feelings about the Apaches. But I think they may let us go join the others in Alabama sometime soon."

But soon was not very soon. More moons waxed and waned, and the sunsets came a little earlier. The moons and the lengths of the days were the only real way of telling what time of year it was here. There were no real seasons. There were no aspen leaves changing color as they had in our mountains, no welcome winter winds bringing the fresh whiteness of snow. There was only sun and sand, relieved only by rain and fog. We all worked whenever we could.

My grandfather was working even now by the wall of the fort with Yahnozhe and some of the other men. They were readying an area for the planting of more Bermuda grass. Geronimo had his favorite wheelbarrow, a bright red one. He was using it to move sand from one place to another. He had told me in a very amusing way, making faces and gesturing as he did so, how hard it had been for him to tame that wheelbarrow. It was worse, he said, than a stubborn wild mustang. It had been so difficult for him to learn how to balance a wheelbarrow, especially with a heavy load in it. Now, though, he handled it so well that he allowed no one else to use that wheelbarrow but himself. Since our group of wives and children had arrived at Fort Pickens, he had made that wheelbarrow a part of our games.

"Come," he would say, "take a ride on my one-wheeled mule." Then we would climb on top of whatever he was carrying and giggle as he trundled us along. Now and then he would even make braying sounds like a donkey.

My grandfather noticed me standing there and watching him. He nodded at me and then looked at his load, offering to take me for a ride.

I shook my head, and he nodded and continued on. There was too much going on in my head. Too many things were troubling me. It was good that we could work here, I thought. Work was a way to keep ourselves busy. But I also thought about how the soil here was no good for growing much, and there were no animals to hunt.

I walked down to the water. The cottage of one of the white

soldiers, Sergeant Henry, was there near the dock. His wife was a very friendly person. She smiled a lot and sometimes gave us candy. She was sitting on a chair surrounded by several women. Ih-tedda and Zi-yeh were there, happily conversing with Mrs. Henry by way of hand signs and a few words that were mutually understood. Katie was there, too. But She-gah was not with them. Her coughing had become worse. She had no longer been able to get up from her bed. She had been taken to the hospital on the island. The doctors were trying to help her, but she was not doing well.

Mrs. Henry gestured at me, but I pretended not to notice. I was in no mood for candy. I continued walking, a fist forming inside my belly. I walked past the racks where men were hanging up strips of beef to dry. Fenton and Mike gestured to me to come over and wrestle with them in the sand. I shook my head and continued on. I wished that I could walk and keep walking, walk over the water, walk along the railroad tracks until my walk became a run. I would run and run without looking back, run until I saw the beautiful mountains wearing caps of snow rising before me. I would run and I would not be alone. Geronimo and Chapo would be with me. So, too, would Ih-tedda and Zi-yah and She-gah and Fenton and Mike and Lenna, Ahnandia and Kanseah, Lozen and Wratten. Everyone. The Apache scouts who tracked my grandfather and then were betrayed. Even Chatto. Everyone would be running with me, all running free, running home.

I thought of what it would be like at that time back home. It would be the time when the wind blows hard, the time when the leaves are blown from the trees, the time when one season passes and another begins. I walked on to the hospital, but I did not go inside. I could hear her coughing, even from outside the window.

She-gah passed on that night.

There was no way to give her a secret burial. Geronimo and Wratten went with her body in the motor launch the next day. I climbed into the boat with them, but no other Apaches came along. As I have said before, our people avoid death whenever we can. Yet I felt a duty to She-gah as if I had been her blood grandson. I know that my grandfather was glad to have me beside him. We went over to the mainland. There the soldiers had dug a grave in the Fort Barrancas cemetery. That is where she was placed, and then the sand was shoveled back in. Twenty-four of our people had passed on at Fort Marion, but She-gah's is the only marked grave of a Chiricahua in Florida. A big tree grows there, the biggest one in that whole cemetery.

A white stone stands over her grave. I still see it in the eye of my mind. A cross is carved at the top followed by her name, spelled as the White Eyes heard it.

GA-AH

GERONIMO

Apache Indian

September 29, 1887

CAGED TIGERS

APRIL 1888

What shall be done with the caged "tigers" and their kindred Chiricahuas? Their children at Carlisle evince uncommon aptitude for learning. All long for education, and some have made commendable progress. Yanosha is an artist in the rough. Geronimo has vanquished the untractable wheelbarrow which first defied his awkward attempts to trundle it. As willing and efficient laborers, his compatriots are promising; as herdsmen and farmers on inalienable lands alloted in severalty, they have demonstrated ability to subsist, and even amass wealth; as traders, they are of the keenest and most acquisitive . . . Quick to apprehend, obedient to authority, faithful to their friends, they are worthy of higher destiny than that of exhibition as caged "tigers."

"THE CAGED TIGERS OF SANTA ROSA"

BY RICHARD WHEATLEY

COSMOPOLITAN MAGAZINE,

AUGUST 1889

WHEN I THINK BACK on those eleven months I spent at Santa Rosa Island, I realize that my stay there was brief. Yet while I was there, the days moved so slowly that it seemed at times as if the sun was stuck in the sky and it was always noon, always too hot, too sandy. It seemed that the taste and sticky touch of salt would never be gone. I longed for hills and trees, for mountains and the change of seasons, for drifts of snow and clear streams rippling over the stones. And when night finally came, more than once I would wake from a restless sleep and listen, hoping that I would hear the call of a coyote. But I never did. All that I had of the sounds and smells and the beautiful sights of our homeland was what I could remember or see in the eyes of our people or experience in a story.

When the days grew shorter and the nights lengthened, my grandfather told us stories.

"Although we cannot see snow upon the mountains in this place of sand and saltwater," Geronimo said, as we gathered at night around the fire, "I know the white blanket now covers the earth of our home. So it is time for me to tell you of the old one, the foolish one, it is time to hear about the things Coyote did way back when."

If it were not for those stories, stories that still make me laugh and think to this day, I am not sure I would have been able to survive. I am sure that telling those stories helped my grandfather as much as hearing them helped those who listened.

One evening, when we children came to gather around the fire and hear stories from my grandfather, and he sat down in front of us, we were all shocked at what we saw. It was hard for us to remain polite and not stare at Geronimo. At first he kept a straight face and pretended not to be aware of the way we were all avoiding looking at his hair. Then he began to laugh.

"Young people," he said, "do you see how I have become a white man?" Then he held both hands up to his neck and his ears. He had cut his hair short, almost as short as the hair of those Apache boys who had come back to us from Carlisle wearing military uniforms.

If you do not know much about my people, then the fact that Geronimo cut his hair that way may not mean anything to you. But in those days, no man ever cut his hair. It was always allowed to grow long, held back only by a headband around the forehead. Sometimes women would cut their hair, but they only did so as a sign of mourning when beloved relatives had died.

Of all the Chiricahua men at Fort Pickens, Geronimo was the first to do this. I see now that he had good reason to do so. It was yet another way for him to show those who held us as prisoners that we Apaches would no longer be a danger. We were harmless people. Even Geronimo, their once fearsome enemy, was going to be just like a white man in every way he could. He would even cut his hair. In the days that followed, other men followed his lead, even though it was no small thing to do. Before long it was common to see Chiricahua men with hair shorn up to their ears.

Colonel Langdon wanted to send those of us who were young enough off to Carlisle. Some of us, like Chapo, believed that going off to gain that kind of education was important, and he was ready. Others were not so eager to leave friends and family behind. In fact, the first of us to be sent to Pennsylvania was far from prepared to leave.

It happened in this way. I saw it all happen. Ahnandia came up to Naiche. Naiche was the proper one to approach, for Katie had no living parents.

"I wish to marry Katie," Ahnandia said. "I ask your permission."

By now it was well known how the two of them felt about each other, and Naiche gave his blessing.

Colonel Langdon did not. The thought of Ahnandia marrying so young a girl was not a pleasing one to the colonel. He also knew that Ahnandia already had a wife and young son, both of whom had been sent to Alabama. He quickly obtained an order from the Department of the Interior to send Katie to Carlisle.

Ahnandia came to ask Langdon to change his mind. I heard his quiet request and Langdon's firm reply.

"Marriage," Langdon said, "is not a good thing for Katie now. She is a young girl and needs to go to school to fulfill her promise."

ALABAMA

MAY 13, 1888

I have the honor to transmit herewith, for the information of your Department, of telegraphic instructions to the Commanding Officer, Division of the Atlantic, directing the transfer of Indian prisoners now held to Fort Pickens, Florida, to Mount Vernon Barracks, Alabama, and also directing the transfer from Fort Pickens to the Indian school at Carlisle, Pa., of five youths.

MESSAGE FROM SECRETARY OF THE INTERIOR ENDICOTT

MAY 12, 1888

W E'RE GOING TO ALABAMA. Pack your things." That was just how sudden our departure was. We had no idea that we were to leave that day, but no one wasted any time after hearing words spoken by Colonel Langdon. Some of us were already turning away to begin getting ready before Wratten could finish his translation of the order.

The newspaper articles that had been written about us, the words spoken in favor of our being reunited with friends and families by Colonel Langdon and Major Sinclair, who was *nantan* at Mount

Vernon, had finally changed the minds of the White Eyes leaders in Washington.

Another step toward home, I thought. I would not be sorry to leave this place behind, the saltwater, the small insects that flew up from the sand to bite us by day and night. I had heard that the place we were going would be larger and there would be space for us to have our own homes and not be crowded on top of each other like prairie dogs in a burrow. There would be trees and fresh water. And I would see my friends, boys I had spent so many hours playing games with, even when we were together at Fort Marion. I wondered if they would be surpised at how much I had grown over the past year.

And then a thought crept into my mind the way a scorpion crawls into a moccasin left on the ground. How many of my friends really would be there? Even before I left Fort Marion I had seen many of them sent off to Carlisle. Perhaps more had been taken over the past year. Rumors had come to us that many of the Apache young people at Carlisle had become sick.

Yet more were to go to Carlisle, and some of them were willing to do so. Five of them were here at Fort Pickens. They were Gozo, Mike, Zhonne, Hunlonee, and Geronimo's son, Chapo.

Chapo had been speaking to me about going to Carlisle. He did not like the thought of being away from his family. He would have to watch his wife and child go on to Mount Vernon without him. If his father had objected, he would have remained. But both he and Geronimo thought it would be a good thing for him to get more education.

"My father agrees that we have to learn to think as the White Eyes think," Chapo said to me as we sat together on top of one of the big rifles that were still placed around the fort. When the White Eyes fought each other in their War of the Two Brothers, those cannons had been used by the southern White Eye soldiers to throw death at the ships of the northern White Eyes. Chapo slapped the cannon with the palm of his hand. "We do not know how to make these and many other things they use to kill us. They are many and we are few. If we want our grandchildren to survive and go to our rightful home, we will have to be able to speak to them with their words."

I looked up at Chapo. He had so much of my grandfather's spirit in him. I could easily imagine him helping our people find a brighter day.

"Are you going to come with us?" Chapo asked.

What did I want to do? There has always been a part of me that wants to see and learn new things. It is still that way, even now that I am a grown man. So it is easy to remember how I felt on that day when Chapo asked me to go with him.

"They have told me that they play many games at Carlisle," Chapo said. "You would be the fastest runner there, especially now that your legs have gotten so much longer."

I looked down at my legs and smiled. Chapo's words about sports had almost convinced me. But that little voice inside my head also spoke, and I found myself repeating what it told me to my friend Chapo.

"*Ao*," I said. "I need to stay by my grandfather."

So when we were loaded onto the launch to take us to the mainland and the waiting train, not all of us left Fort Pickens. The five young men chosen to go to Carlisle remained behind, waiting for their transportation to Pennsylvania to be arranged by the War Department. The five of them stood tall as they watched us depart. The tallest of those who watched was Chapo, standing as straight as a pine tree, his eyes as bright as an eagle's.

MORE MOSQUITOES

MAY 1889

We had thought Fort Marion a terrible place with the rains and mosquitoes, but this was worse. The only way it was better was that it was larger . . . It rained nearly all the time and the roofs leaked. On top of that the mosquitoes almost ate us alive. Babies died from their bites. It was hot and steamy. We had been accustomed to dry heat in Arizona and could take it, but that humidity. It was worse than at St. Augustine — it was terrible. Everything moulded — food, clothes, moccasins, everything . . . it was a good place for Apaches to go — and die.

EUGENE CHIHUAHUA

INDEH

I SLAPPED MY CHEEK and repeated one of the string of words I had learned from the soldiers here. It had been easy to learn those curses because the White Eyes soldiers stationed at Mount Vernon shouted them out a thousand times a day when they, too, were bitten by mosquitoes.

"I think there is now more Chiricahua blood in those mosqui-toes," Nana said, "than in all of our people combined."

I smiled at his words and slapped my other cheek. It was good to be able to listen to Nana. I had missed him while I was at Fort Pickens. Even though he was the oldest man here, he still had the vitality and determination of someone a third of his age. He never gave up. That was why, even when he reached that time of life when many men are content just to be grandfathers sitting around the fire, he was still out scouting about, taking goods from our enemies, and fighting to protect our people. When the White Eyes saw him, all they saw was a small, skinny elder. But if they saw him when they went up against him in battle, his old determined face was some-times the last thing they ever saw.

Despite his long years of fighting and all the hard times he had known, Nana never lost his spirit. Nana was not a storyteller or a medicine person like my grandfather, but he had lived through many harvests and was happy to share his knowledge. So it was that, as on this day, he was usually surrounded by a circle of boys, ready to listen to his words of wisdom. We young men also loved to be around him because he had twice the sense of humor of most other men, as his remark about those mosquitoes showed.

"Perhaps it would be better for us to sign a treaty with the mos-quitoes. If they become our allies, together we can defeat all the

White Eyes," Nana said as he cupped a hand and used it to catch a mosquito that was buzzing in toward him.

The boy next to me nudged me, knowing that whatever Nana said next was sure to be good.

Nana bent over his closed fist and whispered into it. "Go," he said, "tell your people we want to parlay. And if you cannot do that, then at least go and take blood from Chatto."

Nana opened his hand and blew the mosquito off it. To our delight, it flew off in a straight line toward Chatto's camp to the west of where we sat on the high point of the long plateau. Up here, where the winds blew above the trees, there were usually fewer mosquitoes, and it was good to be able to see more than just one tree after another. All of us longed for the wide vistas and the big skies of Arizona. In the sunrise direction we could see below us the broad Mobile River. Far to the south, in the direction of the White Eyes city of Mobile, the river emptied into the Gulf of Mexico.

When the air was clear and there were no rain clouds gathering and the wind was just right, we could sometimes hear the trains coming up from Mobile toward Mount Vernon.

It was almost a year since one of those trains had brought those of us who had been at Fort Pickens to the station at Mount Vernon. The new depot itself had not yet been built. There were only piles of lumber there beside the tracks and holes dug in the earth. Aside from a detail of White Eyes soldiers, no one was there waiting for us. Not even one Apache.

Chief Naiche looked insulted, but my grandfather had not been surprised. He knew that there were Chiricahuas who were still angry at him. They felt his deeds — especially running away from General Crook as he had — were the reason why all of them were being punished. He also was certain that Chatto had been speaking bad words about him and Naiche and our little band. Guided by the soldiers, the forty-six of us, along with Mr. Wratten — who had chosen once again to stay by our sides — walked up from the station to Apache Village.

What I saw as I looked around me was far different from the place we had left. There was green everywhere, trees and plants of all sizes. But it was also different from our homeland. It was hot, but not the healthy dry heat of the desert and the mountains. What I felt at Mount Vernon was a wet heat like the moist, drooling breath of a giant animal. And it is not exactly true that the only ones who took notice of us when we arrived were the soldiers. Clouds of mosquitoes descended upon us. Their numbers only lessened as we approached the smudge fires that were burning outside some of the tents and cabins that were scattered about. The tents were army issue. The cabins were new and made of logs. Every tent flap was closed, and blankets hung down to cover the cabin doors. Were we to be outcasts among our own people?

My grandfather, though, was undaunted. He stepped forward in front of all of us and stopped there in the middle of the village. Without a word, he stood there, his arms at his sides, waiting. There was no expression on his face, and I tried to show no emotion, either. I held my breath. I could feel the tension of hidden eyes watching, and even the air seemed to tremble.

The flap of one of the tents was pushed open, and a young woman came out. She began to walk toward us, slowly at first, and then, as she became overwhelmed by emotion, tears began to run down her cheeks and she ran toward Geronimo with her arms open to embrace him.

"My father," she cried out in a choked voice. It was Dohn-say. She was sobbing now, her whole body shaking as she embraced him. "My father," she said, "my father, you are truly here."

I was close enough to see that my grandfather's eyes were also moist, but he kept the emotion that I knew was almost overwhelming him from his face. He held his daughter to him, his eyes looking about the village of tents and half-finished cabins. And then, as if drawn out by my grandfather's strong, calm gaze, more people began to emerge and come toward us. Soon we were surrounded by a crowd of people. Whatever had been in their minds at first was now gone, as they came out to welcome us from all directions.

"Young man, you have grown tall," said a familiar voice. I turned to look at Chief Chihuahua, his broad face smiling at me. When I had seen him last a year ago my head had only come up to his waist.

Now my eyes were at the level of his barrel chest. His hug almost cracked my ribs. Then Lozen came. Her face was gray and she did not seem firm on her feet as she grasped my hand, but she still pulled me to her and gave me an embrace.

That was a good day. I will never forget it. All of us were greeted in the proper way, welcomed as friends and relatives. I saw many familiar faces, but I also looked for some in vain. One face I did not see, nor had I wanted to see, was that of my grandfather's old enemy, Chatto. Chatto had been the main force behind the attempt to shun us. When his plan did not work, he had made himself scarce.

By the end of that day, my grandfather and Chief Naiche had each been settled with their families in one of the new log cabins. Geronimo's cabin was in the center of the village.

I helped Mr. Wratten make a count of our numbers the next day. Counting our 46 souls, there were now 87 men, 179 women, and 129 children. Some of those children were new little ones. They had blessed their mothers and fathers with their births here in Alabama. But there were fewer adults and children than had been on the train that left Fort Marion. While only She-gah had passed on at Fort Pickens, far more Chiricahuas had set their feet on the final trail here in Alabama. There were now more than a dozen graves hidden in the forest around Apache Village.

The shaking sickness, malaria, was part of the reason. When one suffers from that illness the body feels hot as fire one moment and cold as ice the next. One is weaker than a newborn puppy and the mind wanders wildly. That sickness eventually touched everyone in Apache Village. There were those who did not survive it, despite all the best efforts of Doctor Walter Reed, who did much to try to help us when we were ill. Even Doctor Reed, who was a kind and caring man and who went on to be famous and honored among his people, had not discovered then what everyone knows now: the clouds of mosquitoes that attacked us night and day were the bringers of malaria.

Yet it was not just the Chiricahuas at Mount Vernon who were growing sick and dying. Many of those young men and women at faraway Carlisle were suffering from an illness even worse. We called it coughing sickness, for those who suffered from it were racked by a cough so terrible that it tore the body apart and blood came from the mouth. I learned later that the name the White Eyes give it is tuberculosis. And it did not just stay at Carlisle.

That day as we sat with Nana on the plateau, I was the first to hear the train coming. We all listened close, hoping to hear its whistle blown in a certain way. Two long blasts and one short. Every Chiricahua knew what that signal meant and waited eagerly for it. You see, the woods around us had many wild longhorn cattle in them. They were animals with as much meat on them as on a big elk. We were not allowed to hunt for them, but the train often did our hunting for us. Those longhorn cows were so stupid that they often wandered onto the tracks and were struck by the train and killed.

The railroad had a rule that their workers were not allowed to eat those cattle. Whenever one was struck, they sounded that cattle alarm, which was a call for the railroad workers to go out and find the dead animal and bury it. But if we Chiricahuas got to it first, we would bring it into our village, butcher it, and cut it into strips of good meat to hang on our drying racks by the fire. Because it saved the railroad men a lot of work, no one complained.

The cattle alarm did not sound that day. But I heard that voice in my head again. It told me to go to the station. I began to run, and my friends ran with me. They tried to keep up, but I left them far behind as I dashed along the trails through the thick woods, passed Apache Village, and continued on down to the new depot building that had only recently been completed. It was a fine structure, painted brownish gray and trimmed with bright red and dark green. It looked much like some of the buildings I had seen almost two years before, when our train had stopped in New Orleans.

I did not look at the depot, though. My eyes were on the train that pulled into the station. I knew what I might see after it stopped. I hoped that I was wrong.

But I was not wrong. Nor were the other Chiricahuas who had come down to meet this train. One of those who stood up from where he had been waiting on a bench was my grandfather. Geronimo held out one hand, and I went to stand beside him. Our eyes were on the door of the train and on the two brown-skinned young men who came slowly down the steps. We had heard them coughing before they appeared in the doorway, a coughing that they were now struggling to control, now that we could see them. Sick as they were, they still had their pride.

I looked at them feeling as if I was caught in one of those dreams where bad things happen, where more bad things will happen soon, and there is nothing that you can do. You cannot even turn your head or try to run away.

Both of those young men had short black hair and were dressed in the White Eyes clothing that Carlisle students wore. Their faces were gaunt, and they were stooped as they climbed down, holding on to the train rail like old people. Both of them held handkerchiefs in one hand. Carefully as those handkerchiefs had been folded, I could still see the red flecks on the white fabric. They were too weak to carry their own cloth carpetbags. An even darker-skinned porter, his face grave and sad, held up their valises behind them.

The first of those young men took one step, his eyes bright with fever, only half-seeing those who stepped forward toward him.

"My parents," the young Chiricahua man said, as he stumbled and fell into the arms of his mother and father, who embraced their dying son.

LESSONS

JUNE 1889

*The interpreter at Mount Vernon Barracks, George M. Wratten,
is a person not calculated to advance the interests of the Indians
nor our relations with them. He is in the habit of writing for
the Indians there, discontented letters, in which I see more of the
Interpreter than of the Indians themselves. Two or three of
the boys who have been here sufficient length of time to acquire
the English language, and proper habits of industry, with
reasonable ideas of their own and their people's relations to whites,
sent to Mount Vernon as Interpreters and helpers and the discharge of Mr. Wratten, would benefit the service in every way.*

LETTER TO THE WAR DEPARTMENT

FROM CAPTAIN PRATT, SUPERINTENDENT

CARLISLE INDIAN INDUSTRIAL SCHOOL, 1889

A SUDDEN WIND BLEW through the pine trees around us. It made their branches rustle so loudly that for a moment I could not hear the words spoken by Miss Stephens as she pointed to the blackboard. It made me aware, for just a moment, of the small children who were gathered in the class across from us, where Miss Booth was using her side of the blackboard to teach the basics of the alphabet.

Our outdoor classroom, here in the tall grove of pines to one side of Apache Village, had existed for three months now. There were now twenty men on our side of the clearing, and almost thirty little children with Miss Booth on that other side of the blackboard.

Our school still did not have a building of its own, but it had come a long way since the first class, when I had been the only student sitting on the ground and waiting for these two White Eyes ladies to begin teaching me. I had been a little worried about the whole thing, but my grandfather had urged me to go and hear their lessons.

"You have learned much from our friend Wratten," Geronimo said to me, "but I think you will learn even more from these teachers. Those skills will be as important to you as the bow and arrow once was. Also, if those teachers do well here, then maybe the army will no longer take our children to that place."

I understood what my grandfather meant by "that place." The Carlisle Indian Industrial School. More than a hundred of our young people had been sent there. And so many of them had become ill. We knew this not just from the letters that they sent home to us, letters that Wratten would translate and read to anxious relatives. Whenever an Apache boy or girl became too ill to do their work at Carlisle, they would be sent back to Mount Vernon.

Once someone became ill with the coughing sickness, that person never recovered. Among those who returned from Carlisle to die were Gozo, Mike, Hunlonee . . . and Katie. The coughing sickness was now among us here at Mount Vernon, too. The relatives of those who came home sick and those who cared for them often became ill themselves. One of those who had shown no fear of that sickness, but done all she could to help care for those dying young people, was Lozen. Nothing ever brought fear to her heart. But there was now fear in my heart for her.

I had been walking by her tent and heard the sound of a harsh cough from behind it.

When I looked around the corner, I saw Lozen there, sitting on the ground, looking weaker than I had ever seen her before, her hand over her mouth.

"My Aunt," I said to her, "are you well?" I started toward her, but she held up a hand to stop me.

"No," she said. "I am not well."

I still wanted to help her, but I respected her wishes and stepped back. As I walked away, I spoke those curse words I'd said about the mosquitoes again, but this time I directed them toward Carlisle.

By now every Apache was terrified at the thought of Captain Pratt swooping down among us yet again like a hawk to carry away more of our people to that place. Even though he had wanted to do just that, there was now real opposition to his wishes. Once, Major

Sinclair and Wratten and even Geronimo had thought that sending some of our young people to Carlisle was a good thing. Now they were against it and fought it every way they could.

Dr. Reed and Major Sinclair spoke to the War Department, telling them that Carlisle was not a healthy place for our young people. Wratten wrote letter after letter, not only to his superiors but to those White Eyes groups that tried to help Indians. He told them of the fears that Naiche and Chihuahua, Nana and Geronimo had for the young people. Geronimo was worried in particular about Chapo, who continued to do well at Carlisle but wrote letters home that worried us all, for they spoke of how many Apaches had grown sick. Like other Apache parents, Geronimo kept those letters from his son displayed in his cabin in a lovingly beaded frame.

"Let the Chiricahuas remain among their own people. Send teachers here to them," Wratten wrote. "Let the Chiricahuas at Carlisle come home before they become so sick that they cannot recover."

Captain Pratt did not want to give up any of his students. He held on to them the way a mountain lion fastens its claws into a piece of meat. He wanted more.

"Gentlemen," Miss Stephens' voice brought me back to our lessons. She had a strong voice, but she always was polite to us and did not treat us as if we were fools — the way many White Eyes tourists did when they came to visit Apache Village. Miss Stephens and Miss Booth had both taught Indians before. Miss Booth had been at Hampton Institute, and Miss Stephens was a former teacher at Carlisle. They had learned that they would only get real respect from our people if they also gave it. They were not surprised that Apache men would listen to a woman's teachings. They knew enough about Indians to know how strong our women really are. Only a very foolish man will not listen to a woman whose knowledge can help our people.

I could see one such strong Chiricahua woman sitting right across from me. Today, the first young Chiricahua woman to join the school was sitting there with the little children. Her name was Annie. She was as determined in her way as I have always been in mine. Even though she was old enough to marry, and a capable and very good-looking person, she had given no encouragement to any of the Apache men who looked at her with interest. She was so strong-minded that her father and mother agreed to let her come to the school. I had a suspicion about why she had such a strong desire to learn to speak and write English. I noticed the way she looked at Wratten and had seen him return her friendly glances more than once.

To one side of the little children sat none other than my grandfather. He held a stick in his arms, just like the stick he used to hold those mornings when he woke us boys before dawn. He had appointed himself as the disciplinarian of the school. He looked just as much at ease urging the little ones into the waters of learning

English as he had been when he was ordering us to dip into the freezing waters of a high mountain stream in the Sierra Madre to toughen ourselves. Miss Booth smiled at Geronimo and greeted him warmly each morning when he showed up to take his post. Each day, at the end of classes, my grandfather would remain to help both teachers put away their materials.

I think my grandfather was always the happiest when he was around children, watching them learn the things that might help them live long and useful lives. Perhaps, too, it helped him worry less about his own family. There were fewer people living in his cabin now. His wife Ih-tedda and his daughter Lenna were gone.

A CHANCE TO SURVIVE

FEBRUARY 1889

*I am not at all in sympathy with those benevolent but injudicious
people who are constantly insisting that these Indians be returned
to their reservation.*

PRESIDENT GROVER CLEVELAND

FROM HIS FOURTH ANNUAL MESSAGE,

DECEMBER 3, 1888

IH-TEDDA AND LENNA had not died. What happened
was something both sad and happy at the same time. You may
remember that Ih-tedda was taken by Geronimo from the
Mescalero Apaches during his breakout from Fort Apache in 1885.
Even though she had begun as his captive, she had grown to love my
grandfather and was content to be his wife. But it was still known
that she was Mescalero, not Chiricahua.

When the army sent our people into exile, they meant to send
only Chiricahuas. But because one Apache looks like another to
most White Eyes soldiers, some of those who were swept up and put

on the trains were not Chiricahuas at all. Twenty of them, including Ih-tedda, were Mescaleros.

Back in New Mexico, the relatives of those Mescalero Apaches did not forget them. They kept asking the government to set their people free. "We are peaceful people," they said. "Our relatives were not fighting you. They are being punished wrongly."

So, in February, When Leaves Start to Grow Large, the War Department gave its consent. Those Mescaleros held at Mount Vernon could go back to New Mexico.

I sat quietly on the stoop of Geronimo's cabin as he spoke with Ih-tedda. I knew it was a private moment between them, but I felt awkward about moving and drawing their attention to me. So I sat there, waiting for a chance when I could slip away.

"My wife," Geronimo said, "I want you and our daughter to have a chance to survive."

Ih-tedda turned her face toward the wall, not wanting to listen.

"Do you hear what I say?" Geronimo asked.

"No," Ih-tedda said, her voice small. "We can live here."

My grandfather stepped closer to her and spoke more softly, but I could still hear his voice. "People are dying all around us," he said. "This place is not healthy. You can save your life and the life of our daughter. You will both be free there at Mescalero. You'll see the snow on the mountaintop, and you will hear the song of the coyotes. You will find another husband and have a long life. It will be good."

Ih-tedda turned and put her arms around him. I stood and walked away, leaving them to say their good-byes to each other.

Ih-tedda and Lenna left the next day with a party of ten other Mescaleros. They traveled safely to New Mexico. Just as my grandfather had said, they survived there in that good dry air, with the sacred mountains all around them. Six months after their arrival, Ih-tedda gave birth to a boy who was named Robert. She married again and took another name and never saw my grandfather again. But she and Lenna never forgot my grandfather. When Robert grew to be a man, even though he had grown up without his real father, he changed his last name to Geronimo.

THE SINGING BOX

JUNE 1889

We have fine lady teachers. All the children go to school. I make them. I want them to be white children.

GERONIMO TO GENERAL HOWARD

APRIL 1889

THE APACHE ROCK CRUMBLES

I PUT MY HAND ON THE SINGING BOX that had been set up in the open area between the two rooms of my grandfather's cabin.

"It is an organ," Giles said. "That is what our teacher, Miss Shepard, calls it."

Our first two teachers, Miss Booth and Miss Stephens, had now left us after spending half a year as our teachers. I missed them, but I liked their replacement just as much. Like them, Miss Shepard truly seemed to enjoy being with our people and behaved as if she loved us.

I have to admit that because of this wonderful new thing she had gotten for us, I liked her even more. I was eager to hear what else the big box could sing. She had tried it out when it arrived the day before. Miss Shepard had pushed with her feet like someone trying to walk while sitting, and then pressed her fingers down. The sound that came out was so loud that it almost hurt my ears, but so pleasing that I was sorry when she stopped.

"Tomorrow," she said. "On the Sabbath itself. We shall only use this for Sunday school."

Miss Shepard was a smart person. She knew how much we all loved music, and this *organ*, that was the word, would draw us together with its songs. Miss Shepard explained to my grandfather that it had been a gift from a White Eyes Sunday school class in a faraway place to the north called Connecticut. By getting my grandfather's permission to keep it at his cabin, she had made certain that it would be both safe and in the very heart of Apache Village.

"Our singing will improve with the organ to accompany us," Miss Shepard said. "The hymns will sound better."

"*Enjuh,*" my grandfather agreed.

We were all growing used to hymns. Every class, whether for the children or for the adults, always ended with everyone getting up, one by one, to write their names on the blackboard. Then we would all sit down and sing together.

"Are you ready to go?" Miss Shepard would ask.

"*Ou,*" we would all call out. "Yes."

"When will you return?"

"*Iscargo*," we would say. "Tomorrow."

Then all would kneel and bow their heads as Miss Shepard led the prayer.

> Dear Savior, make me good,
> And help me every day;
> Forgive me all my sins
> For Jesus' sake I pray.
> Amen.

"This Jesus road is not a bad thing," Geronimo said to me as the people began to gather in front of his cabin. He looked over at Zi-yeh, his one remaining wife. She was holding their new baby daughter, Eva, in her arms. Once again, another child had come into my grandfather's life. He would never forget those he lost, but he would always be able to open his big heart to new little ones. And he would do whatever he could to care for them.

My friend, Giles Lancey as he was now named, was one of the returned Carlisle Apache students, and he had taken up the job of being Miss Shepard's interpreter. Giles had recently taken special care to explain to my grandfather how the Christians believed that their Jesus loved and protected little children and the weak. So although Geronimo himself had not yet done so, he had made certain that both Zi-yeh and Eva had been baptised.

My grandfather was wearing his finest clothes. That included not only a fine hat with a shiny band and the new cloth coat he had recently purchased in town, but also one special adornment on the front of his coat. It was a large shiny medal. It had been sent by the Boston Citizenship Committee, one of the sponsors of the fine new school building that had almost been completed. Not only Miss Shepard, but also the new post commander, Major Kellogg, was impressed by Geronimo's devotion to the children and the school.

Just two months ago, Nantan Short Arm, General Howard himself, came to visit Mount Vernon. He was now the commander of the Atlantic division of the army, and our post was under his command. As soon as my grandfather saw him, he ran up to him and threw his arms around the general. He remembered first meeting the general many years ago, when my grandfather had been with Cochise. He remembered well that Howard was the kindest of all the *nantans*. We called General Howard Nantan Short Arm because he had lost part of one arm in the war of the brothers, when the White Eyes fought each other. General Howard was the one who set up the Warm Springs Reservation and treated the Chiricahuas and other Apaches like human beings. My grandfather was sure that had Nantan Short Arm not been sent away, but allowed to stay in charge, none of the wars that followed would have happened.

My grandfather was so excited that he forgot what English he knew and talked Chiricahua so fast that even Howard's interpreter found it hard to keep up. Finally they got Mr. Wratten to help.

"Geronimo is telling you that he is pleased for you to see him, to see how he has now become a white man," Wratten said. "Mostly, though, he is telling you all about the school."

Nantan Short Arm was both impressed by his visit and saddened to hear that so many of our people had passed on. Like many of those White Eyes who at first either dealt with us with suspicion or fought us, he had learned we were honorable people. He could not forget the Chiricahuas. General Howard added his weight to the recommendation that Geronimo be honored. So that special medal was made and presented to my grandfather. Now, whenever he posed for photographs, my grandfather wore that medal.

Miss Shepard sat down at the organ, and everyone grew quiet. She pumped with her feet, and as her hands pressed down on that wonderful singing box, a great music that touched all our hearts filled the clearing in front of my grandfather's cabin.

MORE VISITORS

The last time you saw me there were lots of us; now there are very few of us left. In winter time, when the ice freezes, it stays the same size, but when the hot weather comes, it all melts away; so with us, we have, since you last saw us, been melting away like ice in the summer.

NOCHE

JULY 1889

THE APACHE ROCK CRUMBLES

"I NEED THE BEESWAX, grandson," Zi-yeh said, bending over her beadwork.

I put down the new arrow I had been straightening and picked up the yellow block of beeswax to hand it to her. When the string upon which beads are strung is waxed, the beading is much easier. More visitors were coming soon, and my grandfather's wife wanted to finish what she was working on before their arrival. It was a fine-looking beaded buckskin cap with a tall crown of erect turkey feathers and silver ornaments on it representing the sun, moon, and stars. When the visitors arrived, my grandfather would be wearing it as he sat among his display of bows and arrows, quivers and canes. Most of those items had not really been made by my grandfather but by other Chiricahuas. They had now learned that the fastest way to get their trade goods sold was to have Geronimo do it for them and take a small cut.

I could already hear Mr. Wratten explaining to some eager White Eyes that it was Geronimo's own war bonnet and that he would part with it for no less than $25. Of course, since it belonged to the most famous of all Indians, that eager visitor would come up with the money. Then my grandfather would take a dry twig, sharpen its end, dip it into the inkwell he kept handy, and carefully print his name inside the headband.

As Zi-yeh continued to bead my grandfather's "favorite war bonnet," I went back to my arrows. Because this was a Saturday, I did not have school, nor did little Fenton, who sat by his mother's side playing with a stick that he pretended was a rifle. So I was using my little knife, which I no longer kept hidden, to make more arrows, just as the men used to do when we were in the Sierra Madre and having many arrows meant the difference between life and death.

I was not making them to sell, but to use in other ways. Although there were no longer any deer in the woods around us, there was still some small game, and I always brought something in when I went out hunting. Also, I kept one or two of my best arrows aside to use for our games. One of the games we boys played was winning the others' arrows by shooting an arrow into a target and then trying to be the one to strike it or put the next arrow closest to that first one. The winner got all the arrows that had been fired. That was almost always me. But I did not keep all those arrows. At the end of the game I would select the very best ones, put them in my quiver, and then take all the rest and throw them up into the air for the other boys to grab.

Another good game we boys played, one that I have mentioned before, was to divide into two sides and shoot untipped arrows at each other, trying to dodge or catch them.

The last way I used the arrows was to get money. The White Eyes visitors never tired of watching us boys display our marksmanship by shooting at coins placed on top of sticks thrust into the ground. Of course, those visitors supplied the coins, which we were allowed to keep whenever we hit them. The pockets of those visitors were always much lighter when they left us.

"Baddy, baddy," Fenton said in a delighted voice, putting down his stick.

I looked up from fletching my arrow and nodded to Mr. Wratten. "Baddy" was the name all our little children called him. We do not have that "wrah" sound in Chiricahua.

"Willie," Wratten said. "Know who our visitors are today?"

I waited. Wratten often asked questions like that, ones that he fully intended to answer himself. That way of Wratten's sometimes made my grandfather angry at him, and even though Wratten remained his favorite interpreter, there were times when Geronimo stopped talking to him. But we never had any doubt of Wratten's loyalty to us. His own White Eyes family had disowned him because he had chosen to stay with Indians. While he was with us here in Alabama, Wratten's father had died, but his family had not even wanted him at the funeral. Wratten would soon be even more of a Chiricahua. He had asked permission from Annie's father to marry her. That permission had been gladly given.

Wratten smiled, seeing how I was waiting him out. "Well," he said, "we got some important visitors coming today from the Indian Rights Organization. A Professor Charles Painter and none other than our old friend John G. Bourke, who is a captain now."

Bourke. I was happy to hear his name. He had liked us so well when we were at Warm Springs that he had learned to speak some of our language. He had been with the Gray Fox when Chief Naiche and Geronimo surrendered that first time, before we became frightened and ran. Whenever Bourke had spoken, he had spoken straight words.

That night, Painter and Bourke sat and watched the ceremony. Just by chance, their visit came at the time when another of our girls was to enter womanhood and became White Painted Woman. So, when the meeting took place the next day, we all were feeling the way you feel after blessings have been bestowed.

Maybe, I thought, *maybe this visit will also follow that blessings path. Maybe it, too, will help bring long life to us.*

From the way those two men had watched the night before, quietly and with respect, I had hopes that they would be good listeners and speak on our behalf when they left us.

Painter began. "The Indian Rights Group," he said, "wants to buy land in a better place for the Apaches to live. They hope to get a tract for a reservation in the east in a place called North Carolina. There are other Indians there called Cherokees who are willing to part with some of their land and have your people live near them. There are mountains there, and the seasons change there. You could have livestock and farms."

It sounded good, but no one spoke when Painter paused and looked around. We had heard promises before. It was hard to be hopeful.

"The old Indian road is shut up," Painter continued. "The white man has built railroads across the Indian road, forcing the Indian road to lead only to ruin. The man who wants to follow the Indian road will find that it leads to utter annihilation."

He paused to see if anyone disagreed. Again everyone sat there in silence. There was no answer we could give to that. After all, we were prisoners in a foreign place.

"If we were still in Arizona," Painter said, "then you all could teach me how to live. But now, to walk the white man's road, you must learn other things. You need a school. I am grieved to hear that your children have become sick at Carlisle. I want the children to stay with you as they study. But if we buy this land, we want to hear from you that you will stay there. We want to hear the message from you that we can take to our friends."

Painter and Bourke both leaned forward to pay close attention to whatever was said in response.

Chatto, because he had been a sergeant under Bourke, was given the honor of speaking first. He and my grandfather were still enemies. Apache Village was divided between those who had loyalties to one man or the other. But for a meeting as important as this, differences were laid aside. Everyone knew that Chatto's words would be closely listened to by his former commander.

"I was a successful farmer before," Chatto began. "I pray to God that we could once more have a farm, that someone would come to talk about it where we could raise cattle and crops. I pray for such a home every day."

Then, as he always did whenever he met important White Eyes, Chatto took out his medal that President Arthur had given him.

"When I went to Washington," Chatto said, "I talked the same way. They gave me that medal. Everyone has seen it. I think I have said enough."

Painter looked out at the men gathered there. "I ask all of you Apache men who feel as Chatto does to say so."

At that, with one voice, everyone spoke.

"*ENJUH*," all said.

My grandfather now stood.

"I like your talk," Geronimo said to Painter. "I am glad to hear your voice. I'd like to be like a white man. I have walked in the white man's path many days. I don't think I am an Indian anymore. I think I am a white man. Look at our houses. Look at our clothes. We are all like white men. We are behaving ourselves."

I understood my grandfather's words. We would always be who we truly were in our hearts, but we could look like the White Eyes and walk the road they set before us.

Many spoke that day. It was as if we had one voice. We wish to live as white men. We have promised to live in peace and never fight you again, and we have kept our promise. Allow us to have farms in a better place than this. Allow our children to return to us. Allow us to survive.

Both Bourke and Painter bought hickory canes from my grandfather as souvenirs before they left. They had those new canes in their hands as they waved good-bye to us. When Bourke held his up as he waved, I could read the letters my grandfather had carefully carved into that cane. G.E.R.O.N.I.M.O. Like so many other White Eyes, those men were taking my grandfather's name out into the world.

WARRING GENERALS

I certainly would not form a plan to move the Apaches if there was any probability of their turning like snakes upon the government. The Apaches are broken in spirit and humbled to the dust.

GENERAL CROOK

"GERONIMO HEAP GOOD INDIAN"

THE NEW YORK TIMES, JANUARY 28, 1890

THE RAIN WAS FALLING HARD. It was a gray rain, one that made the cold go deeper into your body than snow could do. That was how it often was at this season here in Alabama. Back home, it was When Grass Starts. But here, in this month the White Eyes call January, the grass never rested under a cleansing blanket of snow. Here there was just heat one season and rain the next. A rain that made me feel tired and sick.

My mind drifted away from the calisthenics lesson we were being given. I looked out of the window of the school, wishing I could see something other than that forest of trees closed in around us like a green fist. My body moved automatically at Miss Shepard's commands.

"Bend and touch . . . and bend and touch."

Then I thought I saw movement in the trees. Was someone coming up the path? A covered vehicle had come up from the train station early that morning. Word always spread like fire here at Mount Vernon. Even that never-ending rain could not stop news of visitors from quickly reaching us here in Apache Village. That covered vehicle had stopped at the office of Major Kellogg, the post commander at Mount Vernon. The boy who observed it had seen a tall old white man with gray hair and a younger man, who kept close to his side, climb out.

The movement in the trees resolved itself into the shapes of three men. One of them was Major Kellogg. One was a young officer I did not recognize. But it was the face of the third man, a man dressed not in a uniform but in somewhat shabby civilian clothing, with a slouch hat on his head, that made me stop my calisthenics. It was Nantan Lupan, the Gray Fox, General Crook himself.

The three men came in through the door, water dripping from their clothing. Miss Shepard was surprised at their arrival and held up a hand to halt our class, even though most of us had already stopped bending and stretching long ago. We didn't stare at our visitors. We were too polite to do that, but we all turned in their direction.

"Children," Miss Shepard said, "lift up your heads and greet our guests."

"No," Major Kellogg said. "Just carry on. The general wants to see the school in operation."

We went back to our exercises. But all of us, including Miss Shepard, were so self-conscious that I know we did not do well. Nantan Lupan's only remark, as he turned and went out the door, was proof of that.

"Not that impressive," General Crook said.

Even though I wanted to be present at the meeting with our leaders that was now going to take place, I was not allowed to leave until school was over for the day. On my way to the meeting place, I passed by Geronimo's cabin. To my surprise, I found my grandfather sitting there, a rather sad look on his face. I did not ask him why he wasn't at the conference, but he answered the question that he knew was in my mind.

"Our old friend Nantan Lupan does not like this old man," Geronimo said. "When I tried to join his conference he waved me away and spoke words about me to Wratten that I am certain were not kind. It was not right for him to do that." My grandfather shook his head. "I think Nantan Lupan's heart is not good."

"I will stay here with you, Grandfather," I said.

"No," Geronimo said. "You go and listen to what is said. Then you can come back and tell me."

I did as my grandfather asked, even though I was now feeling angry at the Gray Fox. I sat at the edge of the council area and listened as our other leaders spoke and spoke well. They told Nantan Lupan how hard our lives were here. They also told him, when he asked, that none of us had been captured by General Miles, even though he was now telling everyone that lie. Instead, we had come in under terms of surrender. That was the only thing that made General Crook smile. It seemed that he and General Miles hated each other even more than either of them ever hated their Indian enemies.

The thing I liked best was said by Chief Chihuahua, after telling Nantan Lupan that he was worried about his daughter at Carlisle and his other relatives there and wanted to see them soon.

Chief Chihuahua looked up at the dark wet pines that loomed around us like a great smothering blanket. "There are trees all about," Chief Chihuahua said. "I would like to go where I can see."

Despite his rudeness to my grandfather, General Crook spoke to the War Department about our sad state. He said that we should not remain at Mount Vernon, where we were dying. He also said — and this made Captain Pratt his enemy — that our children should be brought back to us from Carlisle, a place that had proven fatal to them. But Nantan Lupan did not think we should go to

North Carolina and live with the Cherokees. His plan was that we be sent to Fort Sill in the Indian Territory.

As soon as General Miles heard that General Crook wished us to go to the Indian Territory, he did everything he could to see that we would be sent to North Carolina. General Miles said that Indian Territory was too close to our old homes. Even though we had sworn to never fight the White Eyes again, Miles said that he was certain we would escape from Indian Territory and go back to Arizona as hostiles. Important White Eyes took one man's side or the other as they fought their battles with words in newspapers and in talks to the War Department. They went from one city to another, each stating their case and making it seem foolish for us to be sent one place or the other. Captain Pratt also weighed in, saying that the plan to send Chiricahuas to North Carolina made no sense. The best plan was that all the Apache children be sent to his school immediately.

Mr. Wratten told me about those battles between the two warring generals. Each of their arguments about why we should not go to the place the other favored was making it sound as if the wisest thing to do would be to leave us where we were. Wratten was disgusted. "I am glad that I am no longer a white man," he said.

But the fighting about us between the two generals did not go on long. At the time we call When the Flowers Start, which is called

March by the White Eyes, General Crook's heart failed him while he was talking to newspaper men in Chicago.

Word of Nantan Lupan's passing was brought to us. The flags flew at half-mast at the army post, and guns were fired. Many Chiricahuas wept as openly at the death of the general as if he had been someone from our own families.

Kayahtenny came to my grandfather's cabin to bring him the news of Crook's passing. There were tears in Kayahtenny's eyes.

"The Gray Fox never deceived us," he said.

My grandfather nodded. But he did not weep for Nantan Lupan.

And we remained at Mount Vernon.

INDIAN SOLDIERS

1892

In his home the Indian is a good and faithful husband, a tender and affectionate father, full of cheerfulness, and, contrary to the general idea, a willing and industrious worker. He has an infinite fund of patience, and as clear and bright a mind as anyone would want in a pupil. He is, until ruined by contact with the whites, a man of absolute truthfulness, and as honest as the day is long.

LIEUTENANT WILLIAM WALLACE WOTHERSPOON

THE APACHE ROCK CRUMBLES

"HUT, TWO, THREE, FOUR," the White Eyes sergeant barked.

Our feet moved in perfect unision as we followed his commands.

"Halt. Ten-shun! Forward arms."

I swung my rifle smartly off my shoulder and held it out.

"Corporal Martine, front and center!"

"Yes, sir."

The man in uniform who walked down our line to inspect our

weapons was the perfect image of a proper corporal. His uniform was correct, his back straight, his mind intent on his task. Only the darkness of his skin and the Apache features that all of us in Company I of the United States Twelfth Army Regiment shared indicated that he was an Indian. Yes, it was none other than Martine, the same Chiricahua scout who had played at being a soldier that day at Fort Marion and made us all laugh so hard. But he was not playing today.

None of the eighty-five Apaches in our company was anything but serious. We were soldiers, real soldiers in the service of Uncle Sam. The men who stood at attention around me were both former scouts and men who had once been called hostiles. In fact, the other corporal for our company was none other than my grandfather's brother Fun.

Our ranks included not just Apaches who had been sent east as prisoners, but thirty men who had come this year from San Carlos. They were free Apaches who had volunteered to join the army and been sent from Arizona to our company. Fifty-five prisoners of war. Thirty free men. All of us soldiers. At the age of eighteen I was not only one of the youngest, but also the tallest. Not only that, I was an alternate company bugler behind Sam Hazaous and James Nicholas.

How had this come to be?

As had happened so often before, we had kept our promises to the White Eyes, but the promises made to us by the White Eyes had not been kept. A year passed, a year in which I grew like a young pine.

Despite the visits of Nantan Short Arm and Captain Bourke, General Howard's son and the Gray Fox himself, Nantan Crook, we remained at Mount Vernon. Despite the fact that the Cherokees were willing to sell land and have us live next to them like cousins, no land was bought for us.

Despite the fact that thirty of our young people sent off to Carlisle had now died, Captain Pratt still held young Apaches in his iron hand in faraway Pennsylvania.

The War Department, which seemed to own us the way we once owned livestock, had given us little that we really needed, almost nothing that we asked for. But they did give us a new commander at Mount Vernon. His name was Lieutenant William Wallace Wotherspoon. Lieutenant Wotherspoon had never met any Indians before. Maybe that is why he saw us as human beings.

He also saw how the war between General Miles and General Crook and their supporters had stopped all progress toward moving us to a new place. So he decided to do whatever he could to make our lives better where we were. He moved Apache Village to a new place, higher up on the plateau where the wind blew and the air was cooler, the mosquitoes not so bad. There we built new houses, much better than the log cabins we had been in before. He saw how much we all wanted to work, and so he allowed men to take jobs on the local farms to earn money, sometimes as much as fifty cents a day.

He also saw the whiskey sellers. I have not mentioned them before. I do not like mentioning bad people. They were like buzzards drawn by rotting flesh. They saw how we were weakened and sad. They saw that we made money from selling our souvenirs to visitors. Those whiskey sellers, some of whom were black White Eyes, set up saloons all around Mount Vernon. The soldiers themselves often visited such places, but these new saloons were especially for the Indians. The whiskey, which those of us who saw what it did called evil water, made us even sicker than we had been from the fevers and the coughing illness. The fevers and coughing sickness never made us fight each other or even fight ourselves the way that evil water did.

My grandfather had been weakened by whiskey in the past. He was now a justice of the peace for our village. He spoke up against those who were selling whiskey to our people. He ordered Apache men to be punished when they became drunk and abused others. But most did not listen to him when they had decided they were ready to get drunk. And Geronimo could do nothing about the whiskey sellers themselves.

But Lieutenant Wotherspoon could. He ordered those who sold whiskey to the Indians to be arrested and jailed. He even hired a private detective to help him identify and catch those whiskey sellers. Although Nantan Wotherspoon never got rid of all the whiskey, he did manage to drive away most of those who were selling that evil water to the Chiricahuas.

I liked Nantan Wotherspoon for his fairness. He judged us by our actions, not the lies told about us. One of the biggest of those liars was none other than the Turkey Gobbler himself, John Clum, the Indian agent at San Carlos who had caused so much trouble for my grandfather. He was now a United States postal inspector and just as fond of puffing himself up as he had been in Arizona. When he discovered that my grandfather was now the justice of the peace for Apache Village, Clum made a special visit to Mount Vernon. He was outraged and wanted to see my grandfather's job taken from him. He demanded a special meeting with Nantan Wotherspoon.

"Tell Inspector Clum that I am not feeling well enough to see him," Nantan Wotherspoon said.

Clum left quaking with rage. As he departed he heard more than one Chiricahua whispering, "Look out, the Turkey Gobbler is dragging his wings."

Best of all, as far as I was concerned, Nantan Wotherspoon put into practice an idea that came from the secretary of war. Since Indians had been such great fighters, Secretary Proctor thought, they would be useful as U.S. soldiers. Secretary Proctor came to Mount Vernon to meet with Wotherspoon. As they walked about our camp, they talked about the secretary's idea. I tailed along behind them, listening closely. I was no longer a little boy, but even though I was now taller than any other man in Apache Village, I still had my old talent of making myself inconspicuous.

"Your Chiricahuas here at Mount Vernon will be the base of the first such company," Secretary Proctor said. "The solution to the Indian problem here in the United States is to integrate the Indian fully into society. What better way than to have them serve their country as soldiers."

I couldn't believe what I was hearing. *Yes*, I thought. I *would like to be a soldier!* That may sound strange to you, since soldiers had been the ones who kept us Chiricahuas prisoners. But I liked the idea of wearing the uniform, marching, and having my own rifle. We could no longer prove our manhood in the old way, but going out as a soldier could be a substitute. I liked the idea of being one whose job it was to fight the enemies of the United States. If Apaches did well as soldiers, then perhaps we would be respected as a people and even be given full freedom.

Lieutenant Wotherspoon was not sure about the idea at first.

"The men might turn out to be desirable soldiers," he said. "But what about the Chiricahua women and children? They will be left to languish."

My heart sank as I listened. Would we be denied this chance? But I had nothing to worry about. Secretary Proctor was firm about his idea. So Lieutenant Wotherspoon obeyed.

The next day, after the secretary of war left, Nantan Wotherspoon asked for volunteers. To his surprise (but not mine, since I had already spread the word) every able-bodied man, including our head men, wanted to join up. Those who were too old, like Nana and my grandfather, were not allowed to enlist. But those who did were given new first names — which no one ever used except our three White Eyes sergeants, who had been detached from Company K, 12th Infantry. We were all also given the rank of private.

Because they knew how good we had always been in the field, our training included scouting and skirmishing. Soon they were taking us on long marches, going as much as fifty miles and camping in the forests along the way.

Being a U.S. soldier was like being a boy again and taking part in our war games with rocks and bows and arrows. But we now had guns, real guns with live ammunition. We all spent much time on the post firing range, shooting at targets. Our sergeants, who did not know that shooting straight had been the difference between life and death for us since childhood, were very impressed with our marksmanship.

"I sure do pity any enemy force that comes up against our boys," I heard one of our sergeants say to Lieutenant Wotherspoon. It made me feel proud.

This is the first case of suicide amongst these people and but for the
military discipline which has been severe and constant since the
organization of the company much trouble might have followed.

LIEUTENANT WILLIAM WALLACE WOTHERSPOON

THE APACHE ROCK CRUMBLES

"I AM WORRIED ABOUT YOUR BROTHER," Mr. Wratten said.

My grandfather nodded his head. We had all noticed how depressed Fun had become over the past month. Here at Mount Vernon and in Apache Village, small things had a way of becoming large. When there are no mountains, even the mound of dirt raised up by a mole can seem tall. Only a short time ago Geronimo — because of some small disagreement that neither one of them could now remember — had stopped talking entirely to Wratten for a period of several days and even gone so far as to ask Lieutenant Wotherspoon to fire him as interpreter. The lieutenant had made it clear that he intended to do no such thing, even though he did so in a respectful way. After all, my grandfather was the justice of the peace. Eventually, my grandfather's anger melted away, and now he and Wratten again were acting like old friends.

Another year had passed. Once again it was When the Flowers Start. I thought again about how hard it was for us to be shoved together in one small place after another, like prairie dogs in a burrow. I longed for the wide skies of our homeland, the land stretching out far in all directions, the sounds of coyotes singing to the stars. Here it seemed as if one could never stretch out his arms without bumping someone else in the chest. No wonder we sometimes found ourselves tense or angry or, like Fun, suspicious for no good reason.

His suspicions were about his wife. He was sure that she was being unfaithful to him. Even though everyone assured him that was not true, he grew more and more depressed about it. It was a strange thing for Fun to worry about. Not only was his wife devoted to him, but no other man was interested in her. Everyone knew that. After all, there were far more Chiricahua women of marriageable age here at Mount Vernon than there were men. It had always been that way. In the days when we had been free, because of the dangers in warfare and hunting, fewer Apache men than women survived to the age of marriage. Now that no man could have more than one wife any longer, that imbalance was even greater. Most of the San Carlos Apache men who had come here as soldiers had already found wives among our young women or were in the process of arranging for someone to speak for them to the families of girls they hoped to marry. But there were still more unattached young women.

I myself had thoughts about a certain young woman. I felt as if, now that I was a soldier, I had passed the test of manhood and could rightly expect to be respected by her family. I had been saving my money to purchase proper gifts to give them when the time came for me to be presented to them. She and I had already come to our own agreement about it. Before I had become a private first class, we had both been students in Miss Shepard's class, and there had been many times when we had talked with each other. But we had done so very discreetly, without putting our heads close together or holding hands as White Eyes young people loved to do in the books I was still reading about them. Although I had no parents of my own to shame by being rude in that way, I did not want to harm her reputation.

As soon as we came back from our big march on Mobile, which was planned for the following week, my grandfather would go to her mother and father to speak for me. I had been in Geronimo's cabin that day asking him to do that for me when Wratten came to express his concern about my fellow soldier.

"I hope that you will be able to help him," Wratten said. The urgency in his voice as he spoke those words to my grandfather brought my thoughts back from my own future happiness to the worry we all felt for Fun. He had always been so kind to me when I was a small child. Whenever I thought of what it meant to be a grown-up, a brave man who thought of others before himself, Fun had always been one of those I patterned myself after. I called him my uncle, and he had taken, in the last two years, to calling me his Taller Than a Pine Nephew. He had always been one to make others laugh at his jokes. But lately, all the laughter had gone out of him. His face had become a mask of pain and confusion. He behaved strangely, acting as if he heard voices that were not there.

I understood what Wratten hoped. My grandfather was not just the justice of the peace, he was a healer who could use our traditional ways to help someone who was suffering.

"I will go and talk to him," Geronimo said.

That evening, when he spoke again to Wratten, my grandfather was not hopeful.

"It is no good," Geronimo said. "He will not let me help him. There is nothing wrong with his wife, but he cannot see that. His thoughts are too confused."

The next day, though, Fun began acting like his old self. He was corporal of the guard in Apache Village that day, and so his job was to keep an eye on all that was going on. He smiled at me as we attended the morning lecture sessions. He stood watching, nodding his head, as we engaged in target practice. Then he returned to his final post for the day, which was to keep watch at the company guardhouse, where men who had been caught drinking or committing some other infraction were kept in confinement. Fun had always been strict about drinking. He never drank himself and had been one of those who helped catch the whiskey traders and then testified in their trials.

That day, no one was confined in the guardhouse. As I passed by, I saw Fun sitting there, cleaning his rifle. It troubled me, for he was no longer smiling. His eyes were on his own house that was only a short distance away. I did not say anything to him. I wonder if it would have made a difference if we had spoken, but I will never know.

Darkness fell. Suddenly the silence of the night was split by the crack of a rifle shot. I leaped from my bed, somehow knowing what it was. I began to run toward Fun's house. I could hear the voice of an older woman shouting in Apache.

"Do not harm us. Do not harm yourself."

Then two more shots came, close together.

For a time there was so much confusion in the darkness that no one knew what was happening. People had begun to arm themselves with knives and axes, even shovels, fearing that an enemy was attacking. There was a danger that they might hurt themselves or someone else. Those of us who were soldiers quickly took charge. We took their weapons away from them, made them go back into their houses. Gradually, it became calm again except for the wailing of the relatives of Fun's wife.

Fun had shot her. He had come home and found her sitting alone, waiting for him. Perhaps the craziness in his brain made him think he saw a man with her, even though there was none. He raised his gun and fired. He must have thought that his shot, which passed through her shoulder, had killed her. Nana's wife, Nahdoste, who was my grandfather's sister, came running from their nearby house. She tried to talk him into putting down his gun. My beloved uncle did not listen. He rested the barrel of his gun on the ground and slipped off his boot so that he could use his toe to pull the trigger to shoot himself twice in the head.

Fun's wife recovered. No one blamed her for what had happened. It was agreed that Fun's mind had become confused and that he had acted for no good reason.

Yet it seemed to me that there was at least one reason. This would never have happened if we had not been kept here as prisoners.

Our march to Mobile was not canceled. There were seventy-seven men in our column, which turned southward at 8:00 A.M. from Apache Village. Three white officers, four Apache corporals, sixty-five Apache privates, and two Apache musicians marched together. We carried our own bedding, haversacks, canteens, entrenching tools, field belts, rifles, and ammunition. A wagon drawn by four mules carried the tents and rations. It was a warm, pleasant March day, the weather perfect for a long march. We zigzagged through the woods and swamps and made over seventeen miles that first day before we pitched our tents by Gunnison's Creek.

At five the next morning our buglers blew reveille. Mobile was not far away, and we had marched much faster than any of our White Eyes officers had expected. At the rate we were going, we would enter Mobile too early in the morning. So we did not march straight into the city. We were routed through swamps, where we had to go one at a time over logs, and back and forth over the rail tracks.

By the time we entered Mobile, at the head of St. Joseph Street, it was mid-morning, and a good crowd was lining the streets. We marched smartly, our rifles over our shoulders. People were surprised to see men they had been told were fierce savages walking in perfect step, dressed in uniforms and bearing themselves with such dignity, as real United States soldiers. Those citizens of Mobile welcomed us. When we stood at attention and snapped to the commands of our sergeants, they applauded us. That made us all stand even straighter.

It was a good day, one that took our thoughts away from the sorrows we all felt at the loss of Fun. It was a day that helped us Indian soldiers all forget for a while that even though we were loyal recruits in the army of the United States, we were still officially Apache prisoners of war.

GOING HOME

"(These discharged Apaches) can no longer be held, but must be sent away from the presence of other prisoners. Each has a family at the post from which they are being separated, probably for all time."

LIEUTENANT ALLYN CAPRON

MOBILE REGISTER, AUGUST 23, 1894

ONE NEW MOON turned into another. The Ghost Face time of winter passed, and the time of leaves returned. That is how I had always measured time, but now, after eight years of captivity away from the seasons of our beloved homeland, I found myself thinking more and more in terms of the White Eyes calendar. It was 1894. It was August.

I was waiting in the office of Lieutenant Capron. Nantan Wotherspoon was no longer here at Mount Vernon. Just as happened to so many Apaches, the climate had made him sick. But because he was not an Apache, when his coughing grew bad, the army had transferred him to a new post in the north and promoted him to captain. The two officers in charge now were Lieutenant Allyn Capron and his superior, Lieutenant Charles G. Ballou.

As I stood waiting for my lieutenant to come back into the room, I glanced down at the paper that was turned toward me on the desk in front of me. It was nothing secret, just the monthly report to the War Department. A few simple numbers on that paper told an eloquent story about our eight years as prisoners.

Number of infants born prisoners of war: 165
Death rate of prisoners in 8 years: 246

Of the seventeen men who had been held at Fort Pickens, only ten still lived, my grandfather and Nana and Chief Naiche among them. Among those whose spirits had now passed on was Lozen, the sister of Victorio, whose ability to see into the future had not been able to save any of us from captivity. Thirteen of those who had died were Apache soldiers. Stones marked their resting places in the national cemetery in Mobile. At faraway Carlisle, there were also too many Apache graves, more than forty of them. Yet there were far more Chiricahuas who lay in secret graves in Florida and Alabama, many whose names would never be mentioned in any history.

I felt a tightness in my chest. Then it was as if a fist was caught in my throat, and it was hard to swallow. Somehow, I managed to take a breath and not stagger. The thought had come to me of one whose name I will not mention, that young woman I had hoped to spend my life with. The day never arrived when my grandfather spoke for me to her parents. The coughing sickness took her from us. The day after her passing, before dawn, I walked deep into the woods. I carried the blankets and other presents I had purchased to give to her family before our wedding. I made a fire and burned them all as the sun rose.

"Corporal?"

Lieutenant Capron's crisp voice brought me back to myself. I snapped to attention and saluted.

"Sir!"

Lieutenant Capron looked up at me. As always, his uniform was spotless, his round young face so clean-shaven that he might have been an Apache, his boots shiny enough to reflect your face. He had graduated from West Point shortly before his posting at Mount Vernon on detached duty from the 5th Infantry. Everyone knew his time here would be short. The army was trying to economize, and bases such as ours were on the list to be closed. Mount Vernon was far from essential in the defense of the United States. Our Indian Company had shrunk in size. There were now only forty-nine Indians in Company I, and six of them were not even Chiricahuas. Those six were an Oneida, a Chippewa, a Sioux, a Crow, and two remaining San Carlos Apaches. All of the other San Carlos men had been given the choice of going back to Arizona when their enlistments ran out. And that was what they did, leaving their Chiricahua spouses and children behind them when their wives all refused to leave their own families.

The War Department needed to save money. That was why it was not making much of an effort to encourage soldiers eligible for honorable discharges to reenlist. It was also one of the reasons why it seemed our people were finally going to be allowed to leave Alabama. Fort Sill in Indian Territory was again being seriously considered as the place to send the surviving 366 Chiricahuas.

"You've been a good soldier, Corporal," Lieutenant Capron said. He looked at the papers he held in his hand. "No, allow me to amend that statement. You have been an *excellent* soldier, superb, in fact. Not a single infraction."

"Thank you, sir," I said, looking straight ahead. It was hard to keep the emotion out of my voice.

Lieutenant Capron smiled. "At ease, Corporal."

"Yes, sir."

"Willie," Lieutenant Capron said, "I guess this is the time to thank you, not as a superior officer, but man to man, for the help you gave me in seeing . . . well, just where I've been this last year." He paused and looked out the door. "Ah, I cannot adequately express in words how much I admire you and your people. Nor can I say how damn sorry I am for everything that's been done to all of you, for all you've lost, and for . . ."

Lieutenant Capron stopped talking. I looked directly at him and saw that his hand was held out and his eyes were moist. I took his hand and shook it.

Lieutenant Capron bit his lip, trying to master his emotions. We were about the same age, he and I, but his world had been so different from mine, and would always be so different, that I found myself once again wondering how we became friends. I, too, would miss our conversations, those times when he had asked me — with an open and sincere interest — to help him understand our ways.

"Sure you won't reconsider, Willie? You could make a career of this, go to the Point. I'd recommend you. You could become our first Indian general." He smiled as he said it, but I knew he was not teasing me. His words were sincere.

I shook my head. "No, Al," I said, using his first name as I always did when we were talking as two friends.

Lieutenant Capron sighed. "Ah, I should know by now that when an Apache decides something, that is it." He put his arm around my shoulder as he walked me through the door. "I'm going to miss you dreadfully on our baseball team, you know. Where am I going to get another fielder who can run the way you do?"

We looked out together over the parade ground. "I told the paymaster to have your accumulated pay ready for you. $154.16. Quite a tidy little sum. You know, now that you have this honorable discharge you are also no longer a prisoner of war. You're a free man. Do you know where you are going?"

"Yes," I said. "Home."

Sam Hazaous and James Nicholas fell in beside me as I left the officers' quarters. They both had their bugles in their hands. Sam held his up. "Once my time is up," he said, "I am never going to play this thing again. No more taps. No more funerals."

I understood what Sam meant. As the head bugler it had been his job to board the morning train for Mobile and accompany the body of every Chiricahua soldier who died to the national cemetery.

"Not me," James said. "This music is good. I will make it my profession."

"Kiss the coyotes for me," Sam said, poking me in the ribs with his bugle. Then the two of them turned and walked away. There's no word for good-bye in Chiricahua.

My rucksack was packed, but I had one more stop to make before going down to the depot. I looked across Apache Village. Perhaps it was because of where I was headed now, to places that the eyes of my mind saw as clearly as they had when I was a small child, but everything around me in this little community where I had lived through the last five harvests looked new and strange. Instead of the bush and skin-covered wickiups that danced in my memory, I saw seventy-four neat, two-room framed houses with windows and doors. They were better built and better kept than the houses of many of the White Eyes families in the nearby towns.

Inside these new houses of Apache Village, wives and mothers cooked on stoves. Instead of walking to the stream, they got their water from the outside faucet connected by pipes to the big water tower. The school now had two rooms, where not only Miss Sophie Shepard, but also her sister, Margaret Shepard, taught about reading and writing and arithmetic and Jesus Christ. They were lovingly planting seeds of Christianity in the fields of the Lord.

There were real gardens here, too. Unlike Florida, or the first site of our village at Mount Vernon, the sandy soil here was fertile, and all kinds of vegetables grew, including the big watermelons that were my grandfather's favorites. I would often find him with his hoe in those gardens, painstakingly working the soil in his melon patch.

But I knew that my grandfather would not be in his garden today. He would be home with his wife Zi-yeh and his children. He would be helping care for Chapo.

Chapo had come home only a week ago from Carlisle. Just as so many of our young people did, he had staggered from the train, his body racked by that killing cough. Geronimo and the other older men who knew medicine had already put up a dance for him. The post doctor had offered him a bed in the hospital. I knew that none of it would do any good.

Talbot Gooday stood by the door. He was one of the few young men who came back from Carlisle still whole in body, and he was second only to Mr. Wratten as official interpreter here at Mount Vernon. Whenever my grandfather was angry at Wratten, he would ask that Talbot be appointed as his interpreter. Talbot had not left

Carlisle without his own wounds, though. He left behind his wife and their infant son in the Carlisle graveyard.

Talbot looked at me, shook his head, and then bit his lip. I went inside and just stood there, slowly breathing in and out. No one spoke to me, neither Geronimo, nor Zi-yeh, nor their two children, Eva, who was now four, and Fenton, who was twelve. Chapo's eyes were closed, and he was sleeping. We all knew how hard it was to sleep with the coughing sickness. No one wanted to say anything that might wake him.

I did not like the thought that came into my mind then, but I could not deny it. *Soon he will ride the ghost pony.*

My grandfather and Zi-yeh reached out to me and took my hands. Little Eva wrapped her arms around my right leg. Fenton sat by the bed, looking at the older brother he had never gotten to know. Then Geronimo and Zi-yeh let go of my hands. Eva unwrapped her arms, and I turned and went out the door. I had a long way to travel.

It took me four days to get to Arizona. I went first to Fort Bowie, then on to Fort Apache. Each place that I stopped had been part of our journey. Each place that I stopped, I picked up a small stone and placed it in my bag. People did not seem to notice me. Perhaps it was my power protecting me, for there were still many in Arizona who hated even the names of the Chiricahuas.

"If I were to go back to Arizona," my grandfather had said to me, a week before my departure, "I am sure that someone would kill me." Then he had chuckled. "But I still want to go there. I would like to die there."

There were still plenty of other Indians in Arizona. That may have been another reason no one paid attention to me. I had learned that we all look alike to most White Eyes. For all any White Eyes knew, I might have been Tohono O'odham or a tame person from some other harmless nation. I was not recognized as a Chiricahua.

I did not stay in houses. Throughout my journey, I slept first inside the trains as I traveled and on benches in railway stations. Then when I was at last in the Southwest, I slept under the sky, wrapped in my blankets. I bathed in the light of the moon and the stars, that wide sky embracing me like my mother's arms. I watched the shapes of the clouds during the day and listened to my dreams at night and that told me which way to go. I smelled the sage and heard the chirping of the quail and the long, sweet song of the coyotes.

Sometimes I went into trading posts, where I bought a few supplies, some coffee, some flour, a few pieces of candy. But I also accepted whatever the land was ready to give me in the way of food and cooked over a campfire using the one small pot I carried with me. I walked slowly, and I never felt alone. I could feel the presence of all those of our people who had been there before me. I could close my eyes and see the faces of those I loved and those who truly loved me. Some days, when I saw no other living human, each step I took made me feel as if I were dancing. The sun rose and set many times, and it became When the Wind Blows, then When It Snows on the Mountains. I saw that snow on the sacred mountains, and my vision blurred with tears.

The last place I went was Ojo Caliente. It was now When the Flowers Start, the month the White Eyes call February. People had built homes and ranches on the land that had once been the Warm Springs Reservation. I avoided them all. The place where I had to go was a spot where no cattle grazed, no ranches had been built. I found the valley of my birth. I found the fruit tree my parents had planted over my umbilical cord. It was tall and healthy. You know all this, for I spoke of it when I began my story. But it is good to say it again, for it was there and then that all the wounds of the years of my life truly began to heal. I took off my clothing and rolled upon the earth to each of the directions. Then, as I sat there, smiling and weeping, my face up to the sun, I began to hear someone singing. There was no other human person nearby, but I heard that song.

Hayaade-go. From the south.
O'i-ah'biyaahyu. From the west.
Hadaazhi. From the north.
Ch'igona'ai hanadahye. From the east.

I heard that song. I recognized Geronimo's voice. I knew what I had to do.

O, HA LE

1894

I very badly want to go to a place where I can farm, raise cattle and drink cool water. I have done everything I can to keep peace among my people. I have tried to keep my house clean. My people are poor and have nothing to look forward to. I want to see such plants as corn and flowers growing around my home... I consider that all white men are my brothers and all white women are my sisters. That is all I want to say.

GERONIMO

I RODE THE ROCK ISLAND TRAIN to the end of the line at Rush Springs. The morning I arrived, there were no army wagons waiting as there had been six months ago when 346 Apaches climbed down from the ten passenger cars of the special train they had boarded in Mobile.

"You got a walk ahead of you, son," the station agent at Rush Springs said. "It's twenty-nine miles to the military. You want, you can wait till a wagon shows up tomorrow."

I looked out at the land that stretched ahead of me, wide and dry with only a little green where a row of cottonwood trees followed the curves of a creek. Even though it was May, When Fruits Ripen, I could see that this land would never be humid and buried thickly in trees as it had been in Alabama. There was nothing ahead of me but the gentle roll of hills and plain and horizon as far as the eye could see. I saw not tall pine trees but mesquite bushes, whose beans could be gathered to make a meal that we Chiricahuas love.

"*Enjuh*," I whispered underneath my breath. "Good."

"What's that?" the agent said.

I smiled at him. "It's fine," I said, shouldering my pack. "That's not too far."

I took off my shoes, tied the laces together, and hung them around my neck. Then I started up the road at a walk that gradually turned into a loping jog as my feet found the rhythm of the land.

It was nearly dusk by the time I reached Fort Sill. That was good, for even though I could have kept running after dark, it would have been harder at night to see any snakes that came out onto the warmth of the dirt trail. There were many rattlesnakes here, some of them coiled right next to the road. But I had not been worried by them. I know that rattlesnakes, unlike the Whites Eyes, never strike for no reason and always give a warning first.

I was still smiling. I was pleased that my legs had not grown tired, but even more happy at what had begun to reach my ears as dusk gathered. From somewhere out on the wide prairie had come the howl of *shee-kizzen*, Coyote. The old trickster was here, too. I would learn later that his song had greeted the main body of our people when they neared Fort Sill. It had been so moving to hear that first song of a coyote since their exile that some of the older women had began to wail and cry. Then all the hills around had resounded with the calls of dozens of coyotes, answering and welcoming our people.

The first to greet me were not people, but a small pack of Indian dogs. They did not bark or growl, but trotted up to me as if they knew I was a friend and relative. It had been so long since our people had been able to have dogs. I learned that the neighboring tribes had helped us with that, giving puppies to any Chiricahua who wanted them. Of course, every family did.

As I was kneeling among the dogs, two men wearing the uniform of army scouts came up to me.

"Who is this I see, brother?" the first taller man said.

"Could it be someone with little feet?" said the second one.

It was Martine and Kayitah, as inseparable as ever.

I stood up and put my bare right foot next to Martine's boot. "Bigger than yours," I said.

Martine put his arms around me in a warm welcoming embrace. Then Kayitah did the same. Together we walked to the knoll that looked out over the new home of the Chiricahuas. They explained to me how things were here. No longer were they crowded together into one place. They had been allowed to break up into twelve rancheros, much like the old days when we were in family bands. Each of the twelve rancheros had its own headman.

Martine and Kayitah told me more good news.

"See any cows as you were going along?" Martine said.

I nodded. I had seen beef cows grazing as I approached the fort, not knowing whose they were.

"Ours," Kayitah said.

Eight hundred head of cattle had been entrusted to the Chiricahuas, who would finally be cattle ranchers. Over the next decade we would build up one of the biggest and best herds in the whole territory.

"Over there," Martine pointed with his chin, "is Chihuahua's village."

"And there, waaaaay over there," said Kayitah with a grin, pointing with his lips to our left, "is Chatto's."

"There is Naiche's."

"There is Loco's."

"Toclanny."

"Mangus."

"Kayahtenny."

"Perico."

"Noche."

"And there is the village with two headmen," Martine said, turning his head to the right.

"Because no one can decide which of the two is the best-looking," Kayitah added.

Both men chuckled and I chuckled with them. Some things never changed. Even when it came to leading a family band, these two friends had to do it together. But they were not done teasing yet. First they said nothing, waiting to see if I would be the first to ask.

Finally Martine spoke. "Is there anyone else you were hoping to find?" he said.

"Ha-ah," I said in a slow voice. "Yes."

Katiyah put his hand on my shoulder. "His village is there," he said, looking off to the right. "Along Cache Creek, by the biggest fields and as far from Chatto's village as possible. Where else would it be?"

It was fully dark by the time I reached the door of the small, two-room log house. A lantern had already been lit and glowed from the front window to the left. My eyes turned, though, not to the house but to the brush wickiup built next to it. Inside that wickiup, someone was singing in a voice that was deep and rich.

O, ha le
O, ha le
Through the air
I fly upon a cloud
Toward the sky, far, far, far

O, ha le

O, ha le

There to find the holy place

Ah, now the change comes over me

O, ha le

O, ha le

I bent to look within.

"Grandson," Geronimo said, "I have been waiting."

FORT SILL

1908

With earnest entreaties, and every prayer that an Indian can utter, they beg of you to do all in your power to have their children returned to them.

LETTER FROM GEORGE WRATTEN TO CAPTAIN SCOTT,

COMMANDER AT FORT SILL

THE APACHE ROCK CRUMBLES

YOU WILL REMEMBER IT ALL," my grandfather said.

Perhaps I have. I know that there are too many memories for me to tell them all. But I will share a few more good ones before I put down my final grain of corn.

At dawn on the morning after my arrival at Fort Sill, I went to the fort. One of the first people I saw there was Sergeant Martin Grab. He was a short, stocky white man who had been one of the most devoted soldiers at Mount Vernon. Sergeant Grab was a rough, straightforward fellow who never had a bad word to say about anyone.

"Corporal," he said, seizing my hand and squeezing it so hard that it hurt. Much as he liked Indians, he had never learned that our way of taking another man's hand is always gentle.

"Ex-corporal, sir," I replied. "Can you take me to whoever is in command of the company?"

In no time I was hustled into the office of my old friend Lieutenant Capron. He welcomed me first with a very military salute and then with a hug just as warm as those my Chiricahua friends had given me.

"I wish to reenlist in Company I," I told him.

A strange look came over his face. "Ah," he said, looking down at his desk. "You know there are two problems about your reenlisting."

My heart sank. "What are the problems?"

"First of all," he said, "you have to give up your status as a free man. It is crazy, I know, but the rules are clear. The only way a Chiricahua can be a soldier in the United States Army is as a prisoner of war."

"I understand," I said. "I know that." And I did. I was not the only Chiricahua who had been given an honorable discharge and his freedom before the move to Fort Sill. Harold Dick, Paul Geykelkon, and Waldo Tseedekizen had also chosen to go to Arizona after being freed in August. But being away from their families had been too hard for them. All three made their way to Fort Sill in November, accepted the status of prisoner of war once more, and reenlisted.

"Ah," Lieutenant Capron said, turning from me as he said so. "But there is one other problem that will prevent your rejoining Company I. It seems that our company will no longer be part of the 12th. As of July, our old Company I will be no more."

"What?" I said. I was shocked.

Then Lieutenant Capron spun around to show the grin that he had been hiding. "Got you, Willie!" he said. "Yes, the old Company I will be no more because I have succeeded in getting us transferred. No more foot soldiers, Willie. We'll be members of Troop L of the 7th Cavalry. Horses, my friend. Do you want to ride horses?"

I rode horses as a member of the 7th Cavalry for the next two years, although never into battle. When the war with the Spanish came in 1898, many of us Apache soldiers wanted to go and fight for the United States. We were denied that honor. My friend Lieutenant Capron shook my hand before he left to go to Cuba.

"I wish I could have you by my side, Willie," Al said. "Together we would give the Dons hell."

I nodded. But the voice that speaks at times within my mind told me I would not see him again. As always, that voice spoke true. Lieutenant Allyn Capron was the first American army officer killed in the Spanish-American War.

One of the important White Eyes who fought in that war was the man who had been secretary of the navy. His name was Theodore Roosevelt. He was a man who knew more about Indians than most white leaders. When he became president of the United States, he invited many Indians to come to Washington for his inauguration. My grandfather, Geronimo, rode close behind President Roosevelt in his inaugural parade.

"Roosevelt, Number One," the big crowds chanted. "Geronimo, Number Two."

But even President Roosevelt did not grant my grandfather his wish to go home and die in Arizona.

We had fine land at Fort Sill. The story of how we got that land is a very good one. It was not bought for us by the government or any of the groups that said they wanted to help the Indians. It was given to us by other Indians. Quanah Parker, the chief of the Comanches, decided that we needed help. Along with the leaders of the Kiowa and Kiowa-Apache tribes, he deeded to our people more than 25,000 acres.

Soon after our people were sent to Fort Sill, many mothers and fathers begged for their daughters and sons still at Carlisle to be returned to them. They were old and weak, and it was hard for them to farm and keep livestock without the help of their children. When they were asked if they wanted to leave the school, where some of them had been for almost ten years, every one of them said yes. You may ask why they were there so long, and the only answer I can think to give is that Captain Pratt thought he owned the Indian students at Carlisle. He never wanted to give them up. More than

10,000 Indians from many tribes went to Carlisle. No more than one in every ten ever graduated, no matter how long they stayed.

When that request came to Carlisle, Captain Pratt was away. Someone else at the school read the request and gave permission for fourteen boys and five girls to go to their families at Fort Sill. Among them was Chihuahua's daughter, Ramona. Captain Pratt was enraged when he returned and discovered those young Apaches had escaped his clutches. He demanded that they be returned, saying they would be happier with him. Strangely, all of them said they were happier with their own families. Pratt tried to get Mr. Wratten fired from his job as supervisor of the Chiricahuas at Fort Sill, but he did not succeed, even though he slandered Wratten badly and said he was well known for having abused the trust of his Apache charges.

"Wratten does not really love the Apaches," Pratt said.

Those words made me laugh. Anyone who ever saw Wratten with the two daughters who had been born to him and his Chiricahua wife, Annie, knew how wrong Pratt's cynical and jealous words were. Wratten had been born white, but his family was Apache.

Among the Carlisle students who joined us at Fort Sill was my old friend Daklugie. He was as tough and strong as ever.

"Is your name Asa now?" I asked him, trying to tease him just a little.

"I hate that name," he answered with a scowl. "If you wish to stay my friend, never speak it to me again."

The years at Carlisle had not broken Daklugie or turned him into one of those who looked for nothing but another drink of whiskey. He had come home to work and work hard. One of the things they did at Carlisle was to send out the Indian students to farmers, sometimes for a year at a time. Daklugie liked those times away from Carlisle. He used what he had learned at those farms about raising livestock to help build our beautiful Chiricahua cattle herd. He also quickly became my grandfather's most trusted interpreter.

I have already mentioned that when S. M. Barrett, that schoolteacher from Lawton, wrote down my grandfather's story in his book, Daklugie was the one who acted as the interpreter, carefully giving the man my grandfather's words in English. But both Daklugie and my grandfather were even more careful about what was not said. They knew that book would be read by many people. Some might want to use my grandfather's words to accuse him of old crimes and punish him. So there is some in that book that is good, some that was changed by Barrett himself, and even more that is left out. And there are many mistakes. If you know our story, you can see some of the mistakes. For example, that book says that we were held in Vermont, Alabama, not Mount Vernon. In its telling of the story of Child of Water, it calls Hungry Giant a "dragon." Those are only two of the things that were not right.

And there is one more thing that I think was not right. I know that when books are published, they are sold for money. People are paid money for their stories. That is just good business. But Barrett did not do good business with Geronimo. I do not know of any money that was given to any Apache for that book.

There is one story I must tell you about my friend Daklugie. It is my favorite. While he was at Carlisle, one of his teachers decided to punish him. He did not deserve to be punished, and Daklugie knew this. Daklugie was sent to Captain Pratt's office.

"You have behaved badly," Captain Pratt said. Then he took out a long black whip from his desk. He was going to beat Daklugie as you beat a horse.

Daklugie, though, was bigger than Captain Pratt. He grabbed the whip out of Pratt's hands and threw it away. Captain Pratt took Daklugie by the collar. Daklugie, though, grabbed Captain Pratt by his collar, picked him up off the ground, shook him a few times, and dropped him.

"If you think you can whip me," Daklugie said, "you are *muy loco*. Nobody has ever struck me in all my life, and nobody ever will. I could break your neck with my bare hands."

Captain Pratt became very calm. He begged Daklugie to sit down and asked him if he would please try to be courteous to his teachers in the future.

Daklugie left Pratt's office shaking his head about the craziness of the White Eyes. When he left Carlisle, Daklugie was one Chiricahua student that Captain Pratt did not want to get back.

Daklugie married Ramona Chihuahua here at Fort Sill, not long after they returned from Carlisle. I do not know of any married couple that is happier than they are . . . except perhaps for one.

At Fort Sill, my grandfather did many things over the years that followed. He, too, joined the army as a scout. He conducted ceremonies for many of our people when they needed help. He became a member of the Dutch Reformed Church. He tried to lead a good life, even though at times he became depressed and drank too much. As always, people came to see him and write stories about him. Far too many of those stories are mostly lies.

He is happy with our family. Zi-yeh passed on in 1904, but he has married twice since then, once to a widow who decided after a few months their marriage was not good and divorced him, and now to Azul, another widow who has been his wife since 1906. Although he has lost so many children and grandchildren, there is always family around him. Dohn-say and her husband have both passed, but Geronimo took in their children and has been raising them as his own. He cannot help being a good grandfather. After I married — and that is another story to tell at another time — my wife and I also added to Geronimo's family.

Our own five children call him grandfather. Our two oldest boys tag along with him down to the station several times a week, helping him carry his bundles. We now have train service here at Fort Sill, with two or three trains stopping every day. The conductors always announce to the passengers that they are arriving at Fort Sill, home of Geronimo. My grandfather gives those conductors good tips to make such announcements. They ensure better sales from the curious White Eyes who climb out onto the new pine boards of the platform to look at his stock of canes and bows and purchase souvenirs and autographs from him. Our two boys help out. In fact, they stay so close to him that my grandfather sometimes jokes about them when they are not around.

"The sun must not be shining," he says. "I do not see my Twin Shadows."

When no one is buying anything from him, though, my grandfather's eyes often turn down the tracks to the southwest. That way is Arizona.

"I want to go there," he sometimes says to me. "The mountains and the piñon trees, the wild turkeys and the coyotes miss this old man."

AUTHOR'S AFTERWORD

Geronimo never got his wish to go home. Accounts of his death vary, but everyone agrees that it happened because he was drinking and fell from his horse and spent the night out in a rainstorm. He developed pneumonia and was taken to the military hospital where friends and family came to his side. "I will soon escape from this earth," Geronimo said to Eugene Chihuahua, a Carlisle student who was one of the sons of Chief Chihuahua. "I should never have surrendered. I should have died fighting for my freedom."

On February 17, 1909, Geronimo rode the ghost pony.

His wish had been to be buried in Arizona, in a secret place. He feared his bones would be stolen. Instead, his grave is at Fort Sill — not in the military cemetery, but off on its own on what was the military firing range. His services were conducted by the Reformed Church which he had belonged to for the previous six years. His riding whip and blanket were placed in his grave with him, but his widow did not heed his last wish to have his horse tied to a nearby tree to wait for his return and his favorite possessions hung in a bag on the east side of the grave. As to his material worth on his death, there was more than ten thousand dollars in his Lawton bank, a small fortune at that time. He had done much good business.

A stone eagle spreads its wings atop the tall rock monument that marks what was meant to be his resting place. Geronimo had feared he would not be allowed to rest in peace. His worries about his grave being disturbed turned out to be well-founded. Although his grave was guarded by men who had loved him, within a decade of his death a group of men said to be college students from an Ivy League school succeeded in digging up his grave. His skull was stolen and is rumored to be prominently displayed in the crypt of Skull and Bones, a private fraternity at Yale.

In 1911, the Apaches at Fort Sill were asked what they wanted. Chief Naiche was their spokesman.

"All we want is to be freed and be released as prisoners and given land and given homes that we can call our own," Naiche said. "You have held us long enough. We want something else now."

On August 24, 1912, a law was passed by Congress releasing the remaining Apaches held as prisoners, many of whom were the children and grand-children of the men who had fought against the United States and had been born into captivity. They were not allowed to go home to Arizona, but told that they could, if they chose, go to New Mexico where they would have land on the Mescalero Apache Reservation on equal terms. By now, the number of Chiricahuas had shrunk to a census of 261. Seventy-eight decided to remain in Oklahoma, 183 chose to go to New Mexico.

The U.S. government, however, would not appropriate money for their removal. The Apaches had to pay for it themselves. The great Apache cattle herd of more than 6,000 head was sold and its proceeds put toward Apache resettlement. On April 4, 1913, a special train containing the Chiricahuas arrived in Tularosa, New Mexico. They had been told they could have their horses, which were in a special car, but they were strictly forbidden to bring any other animals, especially their pet dogs. However, as observers on the scene attested, when the train stopped, dogs "boiled out" from every door. One Apache was observed to also have three parrots with him.

Two of those who went to Mescalero were surviving members of "Geronimo's Band" at Fort Pickens — Naiche and Perico. Nana, Loco, and Mangus had been buried at Fort Sill, along with Chihuahua. Of the surviving scouts, Martine, Kayitah, Kayahtenny, Noche, Toclanny . . . and Chatto were among those who went to Mescalero. George Wratten, the interpreter who chose to live his life among those whose surrender he had helped negotiate, had been terminally ill when the decision was made to finally free the Chiricahuas. Although in great pain, he continued to work on the terms of their removal and establishment until he could do no more. On June 23, 1912, lying on a cot in a tent outside his home, Wratten took his last breath.

Today, the Chiricahuas still survive, both in Oklahoma and in New Mexico. In many ways they have thrived. They remember the stories of their long exile. They still speak of those men and women who showed such courage and endurance against such great odds.

And, in Arizona, the mountains and the piñon trees, the wild turkeys and coyotes still wait for Geronimo's return.

GERONIMO CHRONOLOGY

Circa 1823, June: Probable birth date of Geronimo (1829 is also given as a birth date) in No-Doyon Canyon. Some locate this in Arizona at the headwaters of the Gila River in southeastern Arizona, probably near Clifton, Arizona. Others place it in New Mexico, along the Gila River north of Pinos Altos. He is given the name of Goyathlay, which might be translated at "the Yawner" or "the Clever One," and grows up during a time of relative peace with the Mexicans.

Circa 1846: Geronimo marries his first wife, Alope.

1846–1848: War Between Mexico and United States.

1848: Treaty of Guadelupe-Hidalgo conveys the southwest to the United States.

1850: Territory of New Mexico established (incorporating present states of New Mexico, Arizona, and southern Colorado).

March 5, 1851: (Barrett in *Geronimo's Story of His Life* says that Geronimo told him this occurred in 1858, but this date, like many others in the Barrett book, is clearly wrong.) Geronimo's wife, children, and mother are slaughtered by Mexican soldiers, led by Colonel Jose Maria Carrasco, who attack the Apache camp while the men, who have been assured they are in a state of peace, are trading at Janos in Chihuahua, Mexico. A truce had been signed between the Apaches and the state of Chihuahua in June of 1850. Shortly after this, Geronimo receives his gift of power— he cannot be killed in battle.

1852: Led by Cochise, Mangas Coloradas, and Juh, an Apache coalition of several different tribes including Chiricahuas, Nednais, Mimbrenos, and Bedonkohes takes revenge in a battle at Kaskiyeh (probably the Sonoran town of Arispe), wiping out most of the military force of cavalry and infantry that had perpetrated the massacre. Geronimo is in the forefront of the attack. Geronimo obtains his well-known name during this battle, apparently because that is the name the Mexican soldiers call out whenever they see him.

(1858–1877: DURATION OF WARM SPRINGS RESERVATION)

Summer of 1860: Mangas Coloradus is beaten by miners, goes to war against the miners and Mexicans as a result, enlisting Cochise to help him. Geronimo fights in this campaign.

January 1861: Chiricahuas wrongly accused of kidnapping Felix Ward, a half-Apache, half-Mexican boy whose stepfather was John Ward. The boy was actually taken by Western Apaches, ended up among the White Mountain Apaches where he was raised and grew up to be the notoriously unreliable scout and interpreter, Mickey Free. This leads to the "Cut the Tent" episode and Cochise making war.

Sometime around 1861: Geronimo marries his second wife, She-gah, who is the sister of Yahnozhe and is Chiricahua/Nednai. She-gah is with him in Florida and dies at Fort Pickens on 9/8/1887.

WIVES OF GERONIMO:

ALOPE (Becomes Geronimo's wife around 1846. Bedonkohe. Killed with their 3 children by Mexican soldiers near Janos in 1851.)

CHEE-HASH-KISH (Becomes Geronimo's second wife around 1851.) Bedonkohe. Captured by Mexicans in 1882 and never seen again, even though Geronimo tries in vain to find her. Mother of Chappo and Dohn-say.

NANA-THA-THTITH (Becomes Geronimo's third wife around 1851.

Bedonkohe. Only a highly successful hunter and warrior could support two households at once. Killed with their small child by Mexican soldiers around 1853.)

SHE-GAH (Becomes Geronimo's wife around 1861. Chokonen, sister of Yahnozhe. Taken to Florida, reunited with Geronimo at Fort Pickens, dies there 9/28/87, the only Apache to die at Fort Pickens.)

ZI-YEH (Becomes Geronimo's wife around 1882, after the loss of Chee-hash-kish. Daughter of a Nednai woman and Dji-li-kinne, a white man captured as a child and raised as an Apache. Taken to Fort Marion. Reunited with Geronimo in Alabama. Dies in 1904 in Oklahoma.)

IH-TEDDA (Becomes Geronimo's wife around September 1885. Mescalero, captured by Geronimo during his break-out from Fort Apache.)

SOUSCHE, also known as Mrs. Mary Loto (Becomes Geronimo's wife on December 25, 1905. Marriage only lasts about 5 months and they divorce in spring of 1906.)

AZUL, also known as Sunseto, a widow (Becomes Geronimo's wife in 1906. Geronimo's last wife, is with him at his death on 2/17/09.)

January 18, 1863: Mangas Coloradas murdered while held as a prisoner.

February 24, 1863: Western New Mexico becomes the new territory of Arizona.

June 8, 1874: Cochise dies.

August 4, 1874: John Clum "Turkey Gobbler" becomes Indian Agent at San Carlos.

1877: Warm Springs Apaches removed to San Carlos.

April 21, 1877: Agent John Clum seizes Geronimo under pretense of a parlay at Ojo Caliente, Warm Springs Agency. Along with all his Chiricahuas, he is taken in shackles to San Carlos. Held as prisoner for 2 months.

July 1, 1877: John Clum resigns as Indian Agent at San Carlos, later becomes mayor of Tombstone. Geronimo is released by the new agent, Henry Lyman Hart.

September 2, 1877: Victorio and Loco break out from San Carlos with 323 of their followers.

April 4, 1878: Geronimo, Juh, Ponce, and others leave for Mexico but eventually return to San Carlos without joining Victorio.

October 14, 1880: Victorio and most of his band are wiped out by a Mexican and Tarahumara Indian force led by Colonel Joaquin Terrazas at Tres Castillos on the plains of Chihuahua.

Spring of 1881: White Mountain Apache prophet Noch-del-Klinne, a slender, gentle and peaceful young man who was a former Apache scout, gains many followers. They do not believe in violence, but they dance to bring back such dead Apache chiefs as Mangus Coloradas and Cochise and to make the white men disappear.

July 1881: Nana's Raid.

August 29, 1881: Commander at Fort Apache, Colonel Eugene Asa Carr, issues orders about prophet: "I want him arrested or killed or both." One-hundred-seventeen men, including 23 Apache scouts, are sent out to do this. Noch-del-Klinne surrenders peacefully, but is killed. Battle ensues in which all Apache scouts but one desert.

September 1, 1881: Apaches, including Apache scouts, attack Fort Apache.

September 30, 1881: Geronimo and Juh flee the reservation.

April 19, 1882: Geronimo and Juh raid the San Carlos Reservation to force Loco and his Warm Springs Apaches to go with them to Mexico.

1883: Geronimo and Juh separate, Juh dies soon after, probably of a stroke.

March 1883: Chatto's raid.

May 1883: Crook meets with Geronimo.

February 1884: Chatto comes in with his band. Medicine man with Davis sees a vision of Geronomo coming in on a white mule with many horses. A few days later Geronimo arrives on a white horse, driving 350 head of cattle, surrenders to Britton Davis.

June 1884: The 512 Chiricahuas are settled at Turkey Creek on the Black River, on the Fort Apache reservation, 40 miles northeast of San Carlos.

May 17, 1885: Geronimo, Chihuahua, Nana, Naiche, and Mangus lead breakout of 35 men, 8 boys old enough to bear arms, and 92 women and children. Three Apache scouts, including Perico and Chappo (Geronimo's son), slip away and join them.

August 7, 1885: Seventy-eight of Davis's Apache scouts engage with the breakout group and manage to capture most of the women and children, including Geronimo's wives She-gah and Zi-yeh.

November 1885: Jolsanny (also known as Ulzana) makes a spectacular raid from Mexico into New Mexico and Arizona, including a November 23rd attack at Fort Apache.

January 11, 1886: Captain Crawford and his scouts, while waiting to meet with Geronimo, are attacked by Mexican soldiers. Crawford is killed.

January 15: Geronimo meets with Lieutenant Maus, pledges to meet later, and surrenders 9 band members (including his wife, Ih-Tedda) as hostages.

March 25: Geronimo meets with Crook to surrender. (Famous photos by C.S. Fly are taken at this time.)

March 28: Bootlegger named Tribolett sells liquor to the Apaches and tells them that Crook is treacherous and they shouldn't trust him. Geronimo and others become fearful they will be hung or sent to prison. Geronimo and Naiche, with 20 men, 14 women, and 6 children escape into the night.

April 12, 1886: General Miles comes to relieve General Crook. Gets rid of the Apache scouts, increases number of troops, begins to use heliograph system. All of these actions fail to help him find Geronimo and Naiche and their band of 40 to 50 Chiricahuas in Mexico.

August 23, 1886: Lieutenant Gatewood and Apache scouts find Geronimo. Two scouts (Martine and Kayihtah) are sent in to ask him to meet with Gatewood, which he does the following day when he agrees to surrender. George Wratten, Chief of Scouts and then 21 years old, is interpreter

September 5, 1886: Geronimo's final formal surrender to General Miles is taken to Fort Bowie.

FLORIDA April 1886–May 1888

April 7, 1886: First Chiricahuas, Chihuahua's group of 73, depart from Fort Bowie, arrive at Fort Marion on April 13th and are lodged in the old Spanish moated fort, the Castillo de San Maros.

July 26, 1886: Chatto and his delegation meet with Secretary of War William C. Endicott in Washington, D.C. Translators with them are Mickey Free, Sam Bowman (part Choctaw), and Concepcion (Mexican who speaks Chiricahua and Spanish). Chatto given a medal and meets President Cleveland. However, the president and General Sheridan have agreed that all the Chiricahuas (including Chatto) must be sent to Florida as prisoners of war. In August, Chatto's train is stopped in Kansas and he is sent to Fort Leavenworth, then to Fort Marion in Florida.

September 6, 1886: Largest group of 434 Apache POWs (who are mostly Chiricahuas, but also number a few Mescaleros) leave Fort Bowie. Includes Jason Betzinez (*I Fought With Geronimo*). Train goes by way of Gallup, Albuquerque, Kansas City, St. Louis, through Kentucky to

Chattanooga, to Jacksonville. Taken by wagon that night to Fort Marion in St. Augustine.

September 8, 1886: At 2 P.M., Geronimo's group of 34 prisoners leaves the rail station. Taken by way of San Antonio where they are stopped and held in Fort Sam Houston for 6 weeks. Then to Pensacola, Florida, on October 25th, where Geronimo and all the men are taken to Fort Pickens. The women (11) and children (6) and 2 scouts are taken on the train to Jacksonville and Fort Marion, 350 miles away.

November 1886: Final group of Chiricahuas, Mangus's band, including Daklugie, arrives at Pensacola where men are taken to Fort Pickens and then woman taken on to Jacksonville and Fort Marion.

Fort Marion (April 1886–April 1887): Apache POWs held at Fort Marion include 82 adult males (65 are scouts), 365 women and children.

Fort Pickens (October 1886–May 1888): Seventeen POWs held in Fort Pickens include the 15 members of Geronimo's group plus Mangus and Goso. The interpreter, George Wratten, is also with them.

October 1886: Forty-one older (ages 12–21) Apache children (25 boys, 15 girls) selected to be sent to Carlisle Indian School in Pennsylvania. Children from Mangus group, including Daklugie, Ramona Chihuahua, and Dorothy Naiche, are sent in December. Forty-four Chiricahua children now at Carlisle.

April 1887: Captain Pratt comes to Fort Marion, selects 62 more Apache students and takes them to Carlisle. At least 30 of the 112 Apache children sent to Carlisle die there, mostly from tuberculosis, which is endemic at the school. Some are sent home while ill and die at Fort Marion or Mount Vernon.

April 27, 1887: All Apaches remaining at Fort Marion are removed from the fort. Train stops at Pensacola where the immediate families of the 17 Apache men are allowed to reunite at Fort Pickens (20 women and 11 children, making the number of Apaches held at Fort Pickens a total of 48 people).

ALABAMA (April 1887–October 1894)

April 28, 1887: First Apaches POWs arrive at Mount Vernon Barracks in Alabama. Commander of the small garrison of infantry there is Captain William Sinclair.

May 13, 1888: Geronimo and others from Fort Pickens are sent to Mount Vernon, Alabama. George Wratten comes with them.

July 1888: Geronimo's 24-year-old son Chappo and 4 other Apache young men go to Carlisle. All but one contract tuberculosis and die. (Chappo is sent home ill to Alabama in 1889 and dies there.)

Apaches held at Mount Vernon continue to die of tuberculosis. On December 23, 1889, Lieutenant Guy Howard (General Howard's son) visits to investigate conditions and reports that almost one-fourth of the Apaches have died over the 3 ½ years of captivity (89 adults, 30 children at Carlisle).

Early 1889: Twelve Mescaleros who were swept up with the Chiricahuas are allowed by the War Department to return to their relatives on the Mescalero reservation in New Mexico. Among them is Geronimo's wife Ih-tedda. Geronimo urges her to go to escape captivity and the deadly climate of Alabama. She gives birth a few months after arriving in New Mexico to the boy who would end up being Geronimo's only surviving son, Robert Geronimo.

Lozen dies of tuberculosis.

January 1890: General Crook visits Mount Vernon Barracks.

1891: War Department allows Apache men at Mount Vernon to enlist as soldiers. Forty-six enlist in May 1891, become Company I of the 12th infantry (31 young Apache men from San Carlos also enlist and are brought to Mount Vernon from Arizona). Geronimo is among the POWs who enlist.

October 2, 1894: Surviving Apaches in Alabama (45 Apache youths are still at Carlisle) are moved with their consent to Oklahoma.

Three-hundred-forty-six Apaches, including Geronimo and his one surviving wife Zi-yeh, board a special train in Mobile. Ten passenger cars and two baggage cars containing furntiture, Apache baskets, windows and doors for their new homes arrive at the New Orleans Esplanade Depot at 8 P.M. They then take the Southern Pacific Railroad to Houston, the Texas Central to Fort Worth, and the Rock Island to the end of the line at Rush Springs, Oklahoma. Wagons then take them the remaining 29 miles to Fort Sill.

BIBLIOGRAPHY

Adams, Alexander B. *Geronimo, a Biography.* New York: Putnam, 1971.

Aleshire, Peter. *The Fox and the Whirlwind.* New York: John Wiley & Sons, 2000.

———. *Reaping the Whirlwind.* New York: Facts on File, 1998.

Ball, Eve. *Indeh: An Apache Odyssey.* Norman, OK: University of Oklahoma Press, 1988.

———. *In the Days of Victorio.* Tucson, AZ: University of Arizona Press, 1970.

Barrett, S. M. *Geronimo's Story of His Life.* Lafayette, LA: Alexander Books, 1999.

Basso, Keith H. *Wisdom Sits in Places.* Albuquerque, NM: University of New Mexico Press, 1996.

———. *Portraits of "the Whiteman."* Cambridge: Cambridge University Press, 1979.

Betzinez, Jason, with Wilbur Sturtevant Nye. *I Fought With Geronimo.* Lincoln, NE: University of Nebraska Press, 1987.

Bourke, John G. *An Apache Campaign in the Sierra Madres.* New York: Charles Scribner's Sons, 1958.

———. *On the Border with Crook.* Lincoln, NE: University of Nebraska Press, 1971.

Bray, Dorothy (ed.). *Western Apache-English Dictionary.* Tempe, AZ: Bilingual Press, 1998.

Clarke, LaVerne Harrell. *They Sang for Horses.* Tucson, AZ: University of Arizona Press, 1966.

Clum, Woodward. *Apache Agent: The Story of John P. Clum*. Lincoln, NE: University of Nebraska Press, 1978.

Cremony, John. *Life Among the Apaches*. Lincoln, NE: University of Nebraska Press, 1983.

Cuevas, Lou. *Apache Legends: Songs of the Wind Dancer*. Happy Camp, CA: Naturegraph Publishers: 1991

Davis, Britton. *The Truth About Geronimo*. Lincoln, NE: University of Nebraska Press, 1971.

Debo, Angie. *Geronimo: the Man, His Time, His Place*. Norman, OK: University of Oklahoma Press, 1976.

Farrer, Claire R. *Living Life's Circle: Mescalero Apache Cosmovision*. Albuquerque, NM: University of New Mexico Press, 1991.

Forbes, Jack D. *Apache, Navajo and Spaniard*. Norman, OK: University of Oklahoma Press, 1960.

Goddard, Pliny Earle. *Myths and Tales from the San Carlos Apache*. New York: 1918.

Golston, Sydele E. *Changing Woman of the Apache*. New York: Franklin Watts, 1996.

Goodman, David Michael. *Apaches as Prisoners of War: 1886–1894*. Ph.D. diss., Fort Worth: Texas Christian University, 1968.

Goodwin, Grenville. *Myths and Tale of the White Mountain Apache*. Tucson, AZ: University of Arizona Press, 1994.

————. *The Social Organization of the Western Apaches*. Tucson, AZ: University of Arizona Press, 1969.

————(ed.). *Western Apache Raiding and Warfare*. Tucson, AZ: University of Arizona Press, 1971.

Goodwin, Neil, and Grenville Goodwin. *The Apache Diaries, a Father-Son Journey*. Lincoln, NE: University of Nebraska Press, 2000.

Howard, Oliver Otis. *Famous Indian Chiefs I Have Known*. New York: 1907.

———. *My Life and Experience Among Our Hostile Indians*. Hartford, CT: 1907.

Kraft, Louis. *Gatewood and Geronimo*. Albuquerque, NM: University of New Mexico Press, 2000.

Melody, Michael E. *The Apache*. New York: Chelsea House, 1989.

Opler, Morris Edward. *An Apache Life-Way*. Lincoln, NE: University of Nebraska Press, 1966.

———. *Myths and Tales of the Chiricahua Apache Indians*. Lincoln, NE: University of Nebraska Press, 1994.

———. *Myths and Tales of the Jicarilla Apache Indians*. Mineola, NY: Dover, 1994.

Roberts, David. *Once They Moved like the Wind*. New York: Touchstone Press, 1994.

Schmidt, Martin F. (ed.), *General Crook: His Autobiography*. Norman, OK: University of Oklahoma Press, 1986.

Schwartz, Melissa. *Geronimo: Apache Warrior*. New York: Chelsea House, 1992.

Skinner, Woodward B. *The Apache Rock Crumbles: The Captivity of Geronimo's People*. Pensacola, FL: Skinner Publications, 1987.

Ortiz, Alfonso (ed.). *Handbook of North American Indians: Southwest*. Washington, DC: Smithsonian Institution, 1983.

Sweeney, Edwin R. *Cochise*. Norman, OK: University of Oklahoma Press, 1991.

———(ed.). *Making Peace with Cochise: The 1872 Journal of Captain Joseph Alden Sladen*. Norman, OK: University of Oklahoma Press, 1997.

Thrapp, Dan. L. *Al Sieber, Chief of Scouts*. Norman, OK: University of Oklahoma Press, 1964.

———. *The Conquest of Apacheria*. Norman, OK: University of Oklahoma Press, 1967.

———. *Juh, an Incredible Indian*. El Paso, TX: 1973.

———. *Victorio and the Mimbres Apaches*. Norman, OK: University of Oklahoma Press, 1974.

Note: This is not an exhaustive bibliography. I have not listed the innumerable newspaper accounts and essays published about Geronimo.